ELEMENTAL UPRISING

BOOK 2 ELEMENTAL GAMES

TAMAR SLOAN

HEIDI CATHERINE

SEQUEL HOUSE

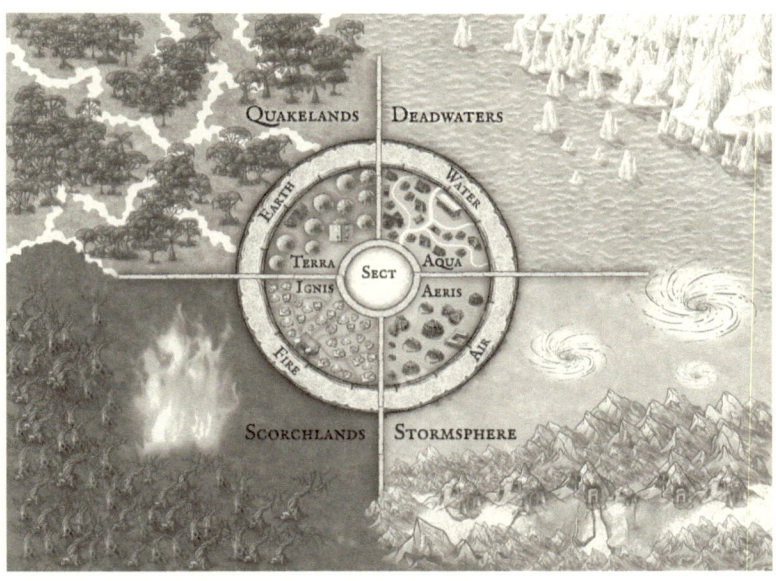

CHAPTER
ONE
AURA

Aura sits up and looks around.

White.

Everything is white.

White walls. White floor. White ceiling. White...bodysuits? What the damnatus is happening? No Quadrant wears white. No place in the world is this devoid of color, not even the Deadwaters.

Jewel is asleep, tucked into Aura's side in one of the corners of this sterile, cube-shaped room that doesn't seem to have a door. Tempo and Pace are curled into each other in the corner a few feet to Aura's left. And Skylus is using Atmos's chest as a pillow in the one to the right.

The corner directly ahead is empty. It's a stark reminder that something isn't right.

Four corners. Four Quadrants. Two teens to represent each.

That's how it's supposed to be. Except, it's not.

Geo only got one chance.

And now, so did Hayze.

Leaving Aura and Jewel to partner with each other, despite

1

Water and Earth never being a successful mix. They tend to make mud more than magic.

Agony spears Aura in the chest at the memory of Hayze being consumed by lava. The look of shock on his face as he was sucked back down into the mine has haunted her ever since.

It always will.

How ironic that a boy from Water should die in a sea of angry fire. It doesn't seem right. Then again, neither has any of the rest of this. The only thing that ever made sense out here was the person who died saving her. And she misses him like her heart has been torn from her chest.

She's not sure she can go on.

Jewel stirs, draping her arm across Aura's legs, then opening her eyes. She blinks. Focuses. Then immediately sits up.

"What is this place?" she asks, shuffling closer.

Aura shakes her head, knowing this is the reason she has to go on. Jewel needs her. Her parents need her. Not Brando and Vesta and their muddled heads, but her real parents back in the Deadwaters. But most of all, she needs to do this for Hayze. She can't give up, no matter how impossible it feels to take a single step without him by her side.

"I don't know," she tells Jewel. "I only just woke up."

Jewel frowns. "Where are the others?"

At first, Aura's confused. Surely, Jewel can see the other four teens, even if their suits are blending with the stark, white walls. Then she realizes what Jewel means.

After Hayze had...been taken from her, she ran through the Scorchlands with the people of the Fire Quadrant. Pace had gripped Aura's hand and forced her feet into motion, with Brando and Vesta staying close behind, insisting on calling her their daughter.

They ran until their feet were covered in ash and their lungs heaved for clean air. Eventually, they collapsed beside a trickle of a stream and darkness blanketed them. Aura thought they fell asleep, but now she's not so sure.

Because they woke up here, with nobody from Fire in sight. Apart from Tempo and Pace, of course. Which means they're still trapped in this strange world.

"It's just us," says Jewel, answering her own question. "Everyone else has gone."

"Right," says Aura, even though she's not sure that's accurate. They're the ones who've gone. But where?

Their voices must wake the others as they sit up with wide eyes. Pace and Tempo get immediately to their feet, while Skylus and Atmos remain frozen.

"Not this again," Tempo groans.

"What do you mean, again?" Pace raises a brow. "We've never been here before."

"That's not what I meant." Tempo shoots Pace an irritated glare. "I was hoping we might stay in Fire a little longer."

Tempo must've been hoping that in time Brando and Vesta might remember the truth—that Tempo's their daughter, not Aura. But now they'll never get the chance.

Pace walks away from Tempo and starts tapping on the walls. "There must be an opening somewhere. How else did we get in here?"

"Good point," says Tempo, seeming to have dropped her annoyance as she joins him.

Aura contemplates standing, but finding the energy is too hard. What's the point in working her way out of here when there's no chance of finding Hayze? Then she remembers her promise to herself, and she stands, stretching out her hand to help Jewel up.

Her white suit feels both familiar and foreign. It's a lot like the blue suit she grew up wearing in the Water Quadrant, except this fabric is thinner. It lacks the warmth of her regular suit, which admittedly isn't needed in this stifling room. And her feet are bare.

"Let's think about this," says Atmos, dragging himself upright. "We have no food. No water. And who knows how long the oxygen will last."

"Well, aren't you Mr. Cheerful." Tempo rolls her eyes.

"He's being realistic," says Skylus, the last to stand. She looks down disapprovingly at her white suit, so different to her usual flowing purple robes. "There's barely any oxygen in here as it is."

Aura draws in a deep breath, aware of the way her body betrays her when she feels trapped. Except, the whiteness of this room is helping. It's hard to see where the walls start and where they end. Which is fortunate. It's not like she can ask Pace to draw her one of his landscapes.

Then another thought occurs to her. If Pace drew those pictures on Tempo's walls, why is it Aura who's afraid of enclosed spaces? She never had this fear growing up in Water. Which means, Tempo should have had the panic attack in the tunnels, not Aura.

"Actually." Skylus holds a hand to her forehead dramatically, drawing Aura's attention back to her. "I'm feeling *very* faint already."

"Perhaps you could make some more air for us?" Jewel suggests quietly.

Skylus and Atmos look at each other as they consider this, even though Aura's not certain Jewel was being serious.

"We could try," says Skylus. "If we can't find our way out of here first. Remember what Cyclonis told us. We need to harness our Element. Which one would be most useful in this situation?"

"Aura could fill the room with water," says Jewel, a little more animated now. "We could float to the top and see if there's a panel in the ceiling."

"No." Aura feels ill at the thought, remembering all the rain she caused in the Stormsphere when Tempo and Pace were trying desperately to burn down the door. "I might not be able to make the water stop, and we'll drown."

"Then we'll burn a hole in the wall." Pace runs his hand down the smooth surface.

"The whole thing could catch on fire," Atmos points out. "We'll suffocate or burn to death."

"Jewel could make an earthquake," Tempo suggests. "If the walls shake hard enough, surely, they'll fall down."

"Yeah," says Atmos. "Right on top of our heads."

"Maybe this isn't about using one Element," says Aura, chewing on her lip. "Maybe this is about using *all* the Elements."

"What do you mean?" Jewel tilts her head as she listens intently.

"Tempo and Pace start a fire." Aura looks at them pointedly. "I'll make water so the fire doesn't get out of control. Jewel causes a tremor to bring down the walls. And Skylus and Atmos make wind to sweep the rubble away before it can harm us."

Jewel's eyes widen. "Aura," she breathes. "You're amazing."

"It's a risky plan." Aura waves a hand, brushing away the compliment. "Can anyone think of anything else?"

Five blank faces stare back at her.

"I think we should try it." Jewel steps closer to Aura. "Because it really is a very clever idea."

Aura isn't sure if Jewel is being so nice to her because she's just lost Hayze or if she's genuine. Then again, Jewel has always been sweet to her. And right now, she's the best friend Aura has.

"Okay," Tempo and Pace say in unison as they link hands. As annoying as their displays of affection can be, Aura far prefers it when these two run hot than cold. It must be difficult to be from Fire and have feelings that are so intense. It's hard enough for Aura with the sharp pain in her aching heart of Water. Maybe it would feel better if she could turn it into ice...

"Do we all agree?" Aura asks, directing her question at Skylus and Atmos. "We all need to have our say."

"Fine," Skylus huffs. "Because like I said...I'm feeling quite faint in here."

"And it's what Cyclonis asked us to do," Atmos adds.

Skylus straightens her back. "Yes. That too, of course."

"Let's take one wall each," says Tempo, marching to the one behind her.

For a moment, Aura's confused. There are six of them and only four walls. Then she remembers she's on her own and the pain in her heart stabs at her once more.

"Good idea," she says, grimacing.

Each Element selects a wall and stands in front of it as they press their palms to the smooth surface and prepare to call on their powers.

"What do you think's behind it?" asks Skylus.

"Shh!" Pace hushes.

"I was just asking!" Skylus huffs. "I thought we might be back in Air."

"Let's find out," says Aura, wishing more than ever Hayze was standing beside her. This feels like too much pressure for one person. This strange world was so much easier to navigate when the other half to her whole was here. She feels like she's trying to row a boat using only one arm.

"I am Fire!" Pace and Tempo call out.

"I am Air!" Skylus and Atmos follow.

Jewel clears her throat. "I am Earth!"

"I am Water!" Aura shouts, swelling with pride for her Quadrant.

So many things happen at once, it's hard to figure out what's going on.

The walls tremble, then begin to shake as the scent of smoke fills the room. Water pools at Aura's feet and a breeze brushes her hair in front of her eyes.

"Focus!" Pace calls. "Keep it going!"

"Hayze," whispers Aura, a shiver running down her spine. "It's working. It's actually working."

Nobody hears her over the growing sounds that swirl in the room.

Cracking.

Roaring.

Whistling.

Trickling.

The Elements are amplifying as they feed off each other. So, Aura talks to Hayze again, wanting to pretend just for one moment that he's actually here.

"I miss you," she gasps, the pain in her heart leaping into her throat. "You should have left me in the mine. I told you to save yourself. Why, Hayze? Why? You knew you only had one chance."

"I can't hold the fire!" Tempo pants. "It's dwindling."

"Try harder!" Pace shouts at her.

"I am!" she bites back. "You try harder."

"There's too much water," calls Atmos. "Slow it down, Aura!"

Aura snaps back to attention, realizing they're knee-deep in freezing water. She can't afford to lose her concentration like that again or they'll all drown.

"Sorry!" She focuses on the floor as the wind whips at her hair, trying to stop the water level from rising, but only a few seconds pass and it's already up to her thighs. It seems these powers are easier to turn on than they are to turn off.

"Now the fire's gone out altogether!" Pace groans loudly. "It's too wet in here."

As the Fire couple work hard to start their fire again, Aura continues to try to extinguish her Element. But they seem to be working against each other. The more Aura tries to stop the water, the more liquid fills the space. And the more Tempo and Pace try to spark a flame, the less successful they are.

The room shakes so violently that Aura's bare feet slip on the floor and she's sent plunging into the freezing water. She fights her way to the surface and struggles to her feet, only to find the level's now past her waist. The wind whips at her wet hair, prickling her entire body with cold.

"I am Earth!" Jewel shouts again, the passion in her voice unmistakable. "I. Am. Earth!"

The walls crack and groan, breaking apart at the corners as the ceiling peels back at one edge. It reminds Aura of the jack-in-the-box Hayze owned as a child. No, it couldn't have been Hayze. She didn't know him as a child. She can't think straight with everything that's going on!

"I am Air!" Atmos cries as Skylus waves her arms at the ceiling. It tears away, lifting up, out of harm's way as it disappears into oblivion. With no support, the walls crash outward, sending water gushing as it drains away. The wind dies away like someone shut off a switch and an eerie silence fills Aura's ears.

The six teens let their arms fall to their sides as they turn in a circle, unable to believe where they've found themselves.

"It can't be," Aura breathes, shaking her head, her eyes wide. "Please tell me this isn't happening."

"No!" Jewel sobs. "No."

Aura clenches her fists as she prepares herself for what's to come.

Someone's playing games with them.

And she's *not* having fun.

CHAPTER
TWO

HAYZE

Hayze thought being in the Quadrants was a nightmare. Except they were nothing but a simulation. A *game*.

Turns out, watching it is the true torture.

Aura and the others stand in the white room, open-mouthed and blinking. She executes a slow spin, confirming what she's seeing. They escaped the blank box they were in. Used Elemental powers to do it.

Only to discover they're in a bigger white box.

"What's going on?" Tempo cries out.

Finding he can hear what's happening was a surprise for Hayze, one he quickly learned is a bittersweet blessing. Or a curse he'd willingly live under. He could hear Aura make their plans to use the Elements to break out of the room. He heard her say his name with such heartbreak it made his eyes sting.

Then he could hear the panic as Water and Fire couldn't be controlled.

The whole time, all he could do was lie on this bed and watch. In the beginning, he screamed and shouted. He tried to tell Aura she's not Water. She never was.

That any attempt to wield the Element she was never born into will only fuel Fire.

But no one can hear him. Aura and the others continued on. The water level rose. Fire went out.

If it wasn't for Jewel and the Air teens...

Hayze flops back onto the bed, breathing hard as if he's in there with them. His throat hurts from screaming. His wrists are raw from fighting the bonds. His body is covered in a fine sheen of sweat.

And none of it made a difference.

Aura and the others managed to destroy the white room, unscathed. Only to become trapped in a larger one. Like some sort of sick babushka doll.

"You're evil," Hayze shouts, this time hurling the words at the door. "This is nothing but cruel!"

The door remains shut, as heedless to his pain as the screens. Or Geo beside him.

Hayze glances at the Earth boy, and swallows hard. The longer he's spent in this room, the more he's realized this could've been his fate. Little more than a body being kept alive by machines.

All because Geo's mind believes he's dead.

"Cruel!" Hayze shouts again, yanking his gaze back to the door.

"We have to do it again," Aura says, snapping his attention to the screens. "Take down the walls like we just did a moment ago."

Pace lets out a long sigh, but then moves to the closest one. "It's not like we have a choice."

Skylus nods, settling her shoulders into determined lines. "Eterna's testing us."

"Someone is," Hayze growls.

The very leaders they've trusted all their lives to rule the

Quadrants.

Jewel moves to another wall, drawing in a deep breath. "Hopefully it won't be as hard as the first time."

Hayze angles his head up as he squints at the screen. The white suit makes Jewel look even smaller and more child-like, but her temples are damp with sweat. Her hands tremble slightly before she presses them to the white surface. She's tiring.

"We know what we're doing this time," Aura assures her with a smile. "You've got this."

Jewel grows an inch under Aura's praise. The face that turns back to the wall is harder, has a little more color. Hayze's heart spasms in his chest. Aura did the same for him when he lost faith in Elemental powers. They spent hours and days and years training with his father, trying to summon Fire. There was never so much as a spark. Yet Aura always encouraged him.

"You've got this," she'd say, no matter how exhausted he looked.

And he believed her. Just like he does now.

Ultimately, she was right. Aura has harnessed her Element, just like Hayze.

Except she doesn't know it.

She braces herself against the expanse of white, clenching her jaw. "Like last time," she tells the others. "Tempo and Pace start a fire. I'll draw up water. Jewel, you destabilize the wall. And Skylus and Atmos, make sure we're not crushed."

There's a round of nods and the teens all push against their wall, teeth gritted and brows pulled low.

Hayze finds he's holding his breath as the same scenario unfolds. The walls tremble, a rumble carrying through the speakers and making his pulse shiver. Then there's the smoke, the water puddling on the floor.

Just like last time, the fire flares but then dies out because Aura has no idea she's the one suppressing it.

The water keeps coming up, because Pace and Tempo are working double time, clueless they're the ones progressively filling the room.

Hayze groans. "Jewel, hurry," he whispers.

If the walls don't crumble, the scene he's forced to watch is going to turn into a horror show.

Jewel's skin pales as the water climbs up her legs. She splays her fingers out wide, scrunching her eyes tightly closed. "I am Earth," she chokes out.

"Aura, the water!" Skylus cries out. "You're doing it again!"

"I know. I'm sorry," Aura gasps, guilt twisting her features.

"It's not your fault!" Hayze cries out. "None if it is!"

But Aura can't hear him. She presses her cheek to the wall, murmuring the same words over and over. "I am Water."

The rumbling continues, but nothing happens. Except for the water. It continues to rise.

Jewel pants as her arms tremble. "This time is harder."

Hayze groans again. He has no doubt the leaders have upped the ante. These walls are thicker. Stronger.

It's going to take more effort, more *power*, to bring them down.

Pace grunts as he pushes harder. "We need more Fire. It's time to burn these walls down."

If Hayze wasn't watching the screens so intently, he'd slam his head back against the mattress. It's not going to hurt, but it's the only way to let out the desperate frustration that's exploding through him.

Watching this is the worst thing he's been through so far.

The water is now at their waists, and with the way Tempo and Pace are concentrating, that's only going to increase. Panic flickers across Aura's face, and she presses her entire torso to the wall. Except she's working hard to suppress her Element. Fire.

Skylus and Atmos's voices fill the room. "We are Air!" they cry over and over.

The water level's rising faster this time. Each time the walls shudder, they send ripples across its surface. It laps Aura's waist, then chest, then torso.

"Jewel, the walls!" Tempo cries.

"Get the ceiling off," Pace roars.

Aura whimpers. "Hayze, I need you."

"I'm here," he whispers back. His heart feels like it's being crushed by a vise. He may be watching this, but he's powerless to help. "Stay alive, Aura. Please."

The water's now at everyone's chins. Jewel's paddling as the rising level sweeps her off her feet, no longer able to keep her hands on the wall.

"I am Air!" Skylus screams, throwing her head back as she glares at the ceiling.

It rips off with a thundering crack and rumble, disappearing into the endless beyond. Just like last time, the walls crumble and fall away, no longer able to support the weight of the water as the wind takes them too. Aura and the others are swept in every direction as the water dissipates, leaving them sprawled over white floor.

The water drains away like it never existed. Because it didn't.

None of it is real.

It's all a *game*.

Hayze falls back, letting out the breath that's been trapped in his lungs for what feels like a lifetime. They made it.

"No!" Tempo cries.

He raises his head to look again, already suspecting he knows what he'll see and dreading it.

Aura and the others are in an even larger white room.

They have to do it again.

"Stop!" Hayze cries out, staring at the walls, the ceiling, the door. "Please! You need to stop this!"

Faint beeping and his own thundering pulse are his only response.

Aura drags herself to her feet, breathing hard. "We have to do it again," she chokes out.

"Eterna's testing us," Skylus says, bending over at the waist as she pants. "We can't stop."

Pace and Tempo stagger to their feet, supporting and helping each other. For the first time, Hayze realizes it was Pace's memories that he carried in the Elemental Games. And Aura has Tempo's. No wonder Pace and Tempo are so confused. They remember being childhood sweethearts, but the truth is, they've grown up childhood enemies. Their hearts and minds are at war.

Hayze knows exactly how that feels.

Jewel's the only one who remains collapsed on the floor. She tries to get up, but her arms give out. "What's the point?" she whispers, curling up. "There'll be just another room on the other side."

Atmos frowns. "What do you think testing means?"

Aura glares at him as she moves to kneel beside Jewel. She draws her up against her chest and Hayze realizes Jewel's teeth are chattering. The two dunks in cold water are taking their toll on the fragile Earth girl.

"We have to try," Aura tells Jewel as she brushes her wet hair back from her face. "It's the only way out."

Jewel blinks up at her. "To go where?"

Aura stills. No one in the world Hayze is currently watching knows the point of what they're going through. They have no idea they're supposed to make their way to the Sect.

But then Aura smiles, even as her eyes mist. "Home," she whispers.

Hayze hears the layers in that one word. Aura wants to go home. Except the home she's yearning for isn't her home at all. If only he could tell her the truth. The truth her heart knows.

Her parents are Fire.

Her home is Fire.

Her home is a bunker, covered in the landscapes he painted for her.

And he'll be there waiting for her—he'll make sure of it.

"I'm certain your mom misses you," Aura continues. "She'll want to see you again more than anything."

Jewel's face twists with anguish. "She loves me so much."

"I have no doubt she does," Aura assures her. She gets to her feet and extends her hand. "Let's get you back to her."

Jewel takes Aura's hand and rises to her feet. "I like the sound of that."

Hayze's hands twitch as the need to hold Aura overcomes him. Yet they remain bound by his side, just like he remains on the bed while she's in a simulation that could kill her.

It starts all over again. The determination. The impressive harnessing of Elemental powers.

The horror.

The walls shudder as Jewel calls on the power of Earth. The ceiling groans as Skylus and Atmos wield Air.

Fire dies and Water rises as Aura, Pace, and Tempo have no idea they're not who they believe themselves to be.

"It's harder again," Jewel gasps. "I can feel the walls are thicker."

"More fire!" Pace shouts.

It's inevitable the water will rise at an alarming rate. It's at the teens' hips in less than a minute.

"Aura!" Atmos shouts, angry and scared. "Make it stop!"

"I'm trying!" she cries back.

"It's not you, Aura," Hayze moans, hating that she feels responsible for what's happening. "Cyclonis! Infernos! Oceania! Avalan!" he screams, wanting those who are doing this to be here. For them to stop this torture.

No one comes.

The nightmare continues.

The water keeps rising, filling the room even though it's the biggest so far. In a repeat of a few minutes ago, Jewel's the first to be unable to touch the floor. She gasps as she can't remain by the wall, her head disappearing beneath the surface. Her hands thrash as she focuses on keeping herself afloat.

Meaning the walls stop rumbling and trembling.

"Aura!" Tempo screams. "You're going to drown us!"

Pace leaps toward her, water splashing his half-submerged face. "We can't swim!"

Hayze groans. They can. They grew up in Water.

But they don't remember.

Aura's paddling, her face dipping under the surface as she struggles. "I'm...trying."

Except she won't succeed.

They're all drawn upward by the water toward the ceiling. Jewel swims back to the wall, clinging to it as she tries to keep her head above the surface. Aura quickly swims to her, clearly determined to help although she actually has no experience staying afloat in deep water.

Tempo disappears under the surface and Pace screams her name. He dives down and surfaces again, holding her. "Someone do something!" he shouts.

Except Jewel's a shivering, sodden mess now being held by Aura. She doesn't have the strength to break the walls.

"Aur—" Pace's desperate cry is cut off as he's pulled under by Tempo's weight.

Hayze is also choking, although on helplessness rather than water as he watches Aura try to keep Jewel from sinking as she looks around frantically. The devastation that she's causing this is etched across her face.

Skylus swims to the center of the room. "You push the ceiling," she pants, looking at Atmos. "I'll push the walls."

He nods, quickly joining her.

Throughout it all, the water level keeps rising. Even if Tempo and Pace knew they're Water, Tempo's now unconscious and Pace is completely focused on keeping her from drowning.

Skylus reaches up and touches the ceiling. "I...am Air," she gasps.

Atmos draws in a choked breath. "I am—"

His cry is cut off as water splashes into his mouth.

"Aura," Hayze whispers, her name little more than a pained plea.

He can't watch her die.

He just can't.

Except looking away isn't an option.

It means he sees it before the others realize it. The edge of the ceiling cracking, crumbling. Then shearing away.

"Yes!" he hisses. "Yes!"

The walls bow, then tear from the ceiling. Hayze sits up as much as he can, now wanting to see this. Wanting to see Aura survive.

Except Atmos disappears under the water.

The walls fall away. The ceiling fractures into jagged pieces, then crashes into the water.

"No!" Hayze screams. "Please, no!"

The water recedes just like the first two times. Except this time, there aren't just drenched teens sprawled on the floor.

Chunks of white stone are scattered everywhere, small and large, in piles or in slabs.

Hayze's eyes desperately scan the screen. His breath explodes out of his chest when he sees Aura curled around Jewel, both alive and safe. Skylus and Atmos aren't far away, staring in shock as Atmos jerks his sleeve out from under a large piece of ceiling. A slight twist of fate and he would've been crushed.

"Tempo!" Pace screams, drawing Hayze's attention.

He runs toward a pile of stone, one that's higher and wider than any of the others. Another quick scan reveals Tempo's nowhere to be seen.

"Tempo," Pace wails. "We only get one chance!" He claws at the pieces, sobbing as he tries to pull the chunks away.

Bile stings Hayze's throat. His stomach revolts against everything he saw just as much as his mind. He already knows there won't be a body to be found under the rubble. That it'll be wheeled into this room to be hooked up to machines, just like Geo.

Tempo just lost the game.

Never knowing she was a part of it.

CHAPTER
THREE
AURA

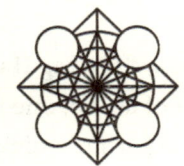

Aura uncurls herself from around Jewel, aware there's someone who needs her even more than her friend from Earth.

Pace.

He stayed right by her side in the Scorchlands when Hayze was consumed by lava. She needs to be there for him now. There's no way Tempo could have survived that amount of rubble landing on top of her.

Pace claws at the stones that fell from the ceiling, but they're too heavy, making his efforts useless.

"Pace." Aura reaches for him, putting a gentle hand on his arm.

He spins to look at her, tears streaming down his face. "One chance," he whispers. "She already used up her chance."

Aura nods, knowing there are no words to make this better.

Geo left them. Then Hayze. And now Tempo.

Eight have become five. And not one of them wants to be here. But they all know the alternative is far worse. At least here they have a chance of getting back to their families.

Aura thinks of Tempo's parents, Vesta and Brando, and sadness stabs at her heart. They were so kind to Aura. It was obvious Tempo had been raised with love, even if something had happened to cause them not to remember their own daughter. And now they'll never get the chance. Because they'll never see her again.

"I need to get her out from under there," says Pace. "Please, help me."

At first, Aura thinks his eyes have lost their focus. Then she realizes he's looking over her shoulder at Jewel.

"The stones are too heavy." He goes to Jewel, imploring her with his eyes. "If you use your powers—"

"I can't," says Jewel, blinking back tears of her own. "I'll only make things worse."

"You have to." Pace returns to the stones and heaves at one of them, managing to shift it by about an inch. "Please. I need to see her."

Aura swallows. She understands. If she hadn't seen Hayze swallowed by lava, she might almost believe he's still alive. He still feels alive in her heart. Her mind. Her soul. The world should feel different without him in it.

But it doesn't.

Or maybe it does. It feels emptier. And Aura feels lost.

"Please help him," she says, turning to Jewel. "He needs this."

Jewel's face fills with uncertainty. It's clear she wants to please Aura, but she's also afraid of what might happen if things go wrong.

"Please?" says Aura, touching Jewel on the arm. "It's important."

Atmos joins them, brushing himself down and narrowing his eyes. "We need to use our powers to get out of here. It's too late for Tempo."

"We're not getting out of here," Pace growls. "Haven't you worked that out by now? If we break open this box, there'll be another one. Then another. Then another. You can't keep doing the same thing over and over and expect a different result."

Atmos rolls his eyes. "Finding Tempo isn't going to give us a different result either."

"It will for Pace," says Aura.

"Yeah, when a stone hits him on the head," Atmos grumbles.

"Like you did to Tempo." Pace glares at him. "If you had lifted the ceiling away, she'd still be here."

"I'll do it," says Jewel, stepping between the two males. "Stand aside, Atmos."

Atmos goes back to Skylus, shaking his head. They both raise their palms, ready to deflect any stray stones with a gust of wind.

Aura turns her back on them, tiring of their attitude, even though they seem to be the only ones here who are truly mastering their powers.

"Thank you, Jewel." She gives her friend a smile.

Jewel nods, lifts her arms, and focuses on the pile of stones.

Aura slips her hand into the crook of Pace's arm and urges him to stand back. He hasn't used up any of his chances yet, and she'd like to keep it that way. They all need to stay safe.

The stones start to vibrate, and very slowly the energy builds as if they're coming alive.

"It's working," breathes Pace, even though he really shouldn't be surprised by now.

The smaller stones tumble backward in the same way they had in the Stormsphere when Geo had first harnessed his powers, gathering at the rear of the room, and Aura's glad this time they're not peppering her shins.

Jewel winces, concentrating intently as the larger stone

22

slabs gather momentum, first moving back and then lifting off the floor until they're hovering in the air...

Revealing nothing but a bare, stone floor underneath.

Pace makes a move to dart forward, but Aura holds him back. If Jewel loses concentration, those stones will crash down and crush him.

"Let me go," he whimpers. "She has to be there."

"She's not there!" Aura says, struggling to keep hold of him. "She's gone."

"Gone where?" he cries.

Jewel's arms fall to her sides and the stones immediately plummet, breaking apart as they smash. The sound is deafening, and Aura lets go of Pace to cover her ears as a cloud of dust swirls in the stale air before settling on the damp floor.

"Gone where?" Pace repeats, tearing at his mess of dark hair. "There's nowhere else she could be. She can't have just vanished."

But it appears that's exactly what Tempo has done. Not only was her life taken by that pile of stones, but so was her body. How is that even possible?

"I don't know," says Aura quietly. "But she's not here."

"Maybe she blew out of the roof," says Skylus. "The wind was very strong."

Pace shakes his head, not accepting that. "She was right here. Then the ceiling fell in. Then she was...gone."

"Maybe she's in the next box," says Jewel. "Let's break this one open and see."

Aura nods, although it's hard to muster enough enthusiasm to reach her eyes. She doesn't believe Tempo will be in the next box. Why would she? She used up her chance, just like Hayze and Geo.

Tempo has gone. But if it makes Pace feel better, she's willing to try anything.

"No." Pace crosses his arms. "I refuse to play this sick game for one minute longer. Enough is enough."

"What game?" Jewel asks. "This isn't a game. Because I'm definitely not enjoying myself."

"Not all games are fun," says Aura, having had the same thought as Pace. "The leaders are behind this. Cyclonis said as much himself."

"He didn't say that," Atmos snaps. "He said we were chosen to harness our powers. He never said anything about a game."

"What did he say exactly?" Aura asks, deciding it's well past time to start piecing together what's happening.

"He said we were chosen," says Skylus, her eyes shining with pride. "That we have the ability to wield Elemental powers."

"But what else did he say?" Aura tries to remember the Air leader's exact words. "He said the elders have been watching us for a long time."

Jewel nods. "He said they all know we're here. That we're ready."

"Ready for what, though?" Aura asks. "Because so far all we seem to have proven is that we're far from ready. Otherwise, we wouldn't have lost our friends."

Pace lets out a whimper and Aura feels his pain echoing deep in her chest.

"He said he'd teach us," says Jewel. "But so far, he hasn't taught us anything."

"That's not true," says Atmos. "He taught us everything."

Jewel raises her brows. "By locking us out in a storm while he ran to safety?"

"No." Atmos lets out a long sigh. "By putting us in situations that have forced us to call on our powers. We'd never have succeeded otherwise."

"Cyclonis is wise." Skylus nods. "We must trust in him."

Aura grimaces, unwilling to trust in anyone responsible for putting them in a situation that ended Hayze's life, no matter what they were trying to achieve.

"He told us he got permission from our parents," Pace says. "Why would they give that permission?"

"Because they were paid for it." Aura clenches her fists at her sides as the pieces begin to fall together.

"They sold us?" Pace's eyes open wide.

"Not exactly," says Aura. "I'm guessing they were offered a large sum of edrian in exchange for promising our cooperation when we turned eighteen." She's also willing to bet she knows exactly how much—half the price of entry into each Quadrant's capital. That's why Hayze's family stole from hers. The leaders were testing the family's ethics, just as much as they're testing their powers now.

"Yeah, sounds like they sold us," says Pace, shaking his head.

"They were desperate." Jewel throws out her hands. "You know how hard life is in the Quadrants. They were probably led to believe they could change the outcome by saving enough edrian to get us out of the deal."

Pace nods. "Or by teaching us to harness our powers first. That's why my parents were so insistent on training me. They thought if I already had my powers, Infernos wouldn't need to take me."

"And how did that work out for you?" Skylus asks.

Pace shakes his head. "I could never do it. I couldn't make even as much as a spark."

Skylus rolls her eyes. "That's what I've been trying to tell you. You couldn't do it because your life wasn't in danger. You needed the situations we've been put in to bring your powers out. Our wise leaders know what they're doing."

Aura hates that this is starting to make sense. Why her parents had chased Hayze's all the way to Aqua. They hadn't just stolen their edrian, they'd stolen their daughter's future. And her parents only had until she turned eighteen to make it right. It explains why they'd been so devastated when they'd lost their haul the last time Aura went mining with them in the icefields. They knew they were out of time.

"Why do we have the same birthday?" Jewel sits down, leaning against a large slab of stone and yawning. "That's got to be important, doesn't it?"

Skylus sighs deeply. "Don't you people know anything? We were born on the day of the great conjunction."

"The what?" Pace tilts his head.

"Honestly, I don't know what your parents spent their time teaching you." Skylus looks at Atmos who gives her an amused smile. "The day we were born, six planets aligned in the morning sky, including Saturn and Jupiter, which were only six arcminutes apart."

"I think we're getting off track here," says Aura, unsure whether any of this is useful.

"It's a day of great spiritual significance." Atmos uses an irritated tone. "It was why we were chosen from amongst our peers."

"But it doesn't explain where Tempo went," says Pace, his eyes still searching the piles of stones. "Or how we keep waking up in new places."

Skylus opens her mouth then closes it when she realizes she doesn't have an answer for this.

"Right," says Aura, trying to add up everything they know. "So, we were chosen by the leaders because we were born on a significant day. And they paid our parents in exchange to gain access to us at age eighteen. And we've been put out here—

wherever here is—to harness the powers the leaders believe we have."

"And it's been very successful so far," says Atmos smugly.

Pace launches himself at Atmos and grips him by the throat. "Take that back!"

Atmos chokes, pulling at Pace's hands as he turns purple.

"Pace!" Aura cries, rushing to him and trying to prize his hands away. "Stop it! That's not the answer."

"Take it back!" Pace growls again, not loosening his grip.

"He can't talk." Aura feels panic surge up her spine. "Let him go."

A breeze picks up inside the room as Skylus tries to use her powers to blow Pace away. But it's for nothing as Pace lets go of Atmos, who crumples to the floor.

"People dying isn't a success," Pace spits out, his eyes full of hatred for the boy from Air as he stalks away.

"I take it back," Atmos says between huge gasping breaths. "I take it back."

Skylus sits beside him, rubbing his back and whispering soothing words.

As much as Aura hates what Pace just did, she goes to him, understanding what drove his anger. He lost the girl he's been in love with since he was a boy. Aura is struggling enough with losing Hayze and he only occupied a space in her heart for a blink in time.

She puts her arms around Pace's tense shoulders and hugs him. "It's okay," she tells him, even though it's not. "But please don't do that again."

His body relaxes, then he wraps his arms around Aura, burying his face in her shoulder and letting out heaving sobs. "She's gone, Aura. Gone."

"I know," she says, more honestly this time.

She holds the boy from Fire for long minutes, giving him

the only comfort she can. When she first met Pace, he was her opposite. But now, they have so much in common.

His sobs subside and she releases him, turning to see Jewel has fallen asleep. Moving those stones must have exhausted her.

"We could all use a rest," Aura says, feeling overwhelmingly tired herself. "Let's take a break, then we can try again."

"You stay over that side of the room." Atmos scowls at Pace.

Pace holds up his hands. "Keep your mouth shut and we have a deal."

Atmos goes to reply but Skylus puts a hand on his arm to silence him.

"Leave it," she says, sternly.

He nods, leaving Aura wondering about the nature of their relationship. They don't seem romantically entwined but they do seem closer than regular friends. Then again, this situation has been known to make even sworn enemies fall in love. It makes sense those two would become close.

Aura goes to Jewel and sits beside her. Sensing her presence, Jewel curls into Aura's side. Pace looks lost, so Aura pats the floor beside her and he joins them. They huddle together, and Aura leans back on a slab of cold stone and closes her eyes.

How can she feel so lonely when she has a friend on either side?

She knows the answer before her mind has even finished asking the question. It's because Hayze isn't here. She'll be lonely without him every day for the rest of her life.

Sleep begins to claim her, and she welcomes the temporary oblivion she knows it will provide. She imagines a life with Hayze if things had turned out differently. He told her if they got out of this nightmare, he'd come and find her. And while she hadn't believed him at the time he said it, she does now.

Because she loves him.

She always has.

No...that's not right. She only just met him.

An image of Hayze as a young boy fills her dreams. Big dark eyes, tousled blond hair, and hands and feet that seem too large for his lanky frame. He's smiling at her, stretching out his arm as he urges her to come and play.

She slips her hand into his, and together, they run into their forest built from ash.

Aura and Hayze.

Now, then, and always.

Nothing can tear them apart.

CHAPTER
FOUR

HAYZE

Hayze's cheeks are wet as he watches Aura and the others fall asleep. His throat is hoarse, his wrists are raw, his muscles ache. Yet he's still here. And she's still there.

Jewel hiccups in her sleep, curling closer to Aura. Pace moans as he tosses his head from side to side, and Aura instinctively reaches out to press a hand to his shoulder. Even in her sleep, she's comforting him. Pace relaxes, then extends his own hand to cover hers as he stills. Aura lets out a breath and sinks deeper into the hold sleep has on her.

The screen flickers, then goes black, making Hayze gasp. "What? No!" He yanks on his bonds, wincing at the pain.

But like everything else that's happened since he woke up, nothing changes. He has no impact on his surroundings. The screens flicker off, one after the other, until eight blank rectangles are staring back at him. Just when he thought it couldn't get more wretched...

Watching was torture.

Having that taken away from him, not being able to see Aura, is profoundly worse.

Hayze's head falls back. All he has is the last image—Aura with Jewel and Pace. Something hot flashes through his body. More specifically, Aura holding hands with Pace.

Hayze has never seen anything so...unsettling.

There were others their age in the village as Aura and Hayze grew up, but they were always in the periphery. Planets orbiting the sun that Hayze and Aura were. They didn't need anyone else. The other was their everything.

The bond was unshakable...until the night before their eighteenth birthday—

Hayze shakes his head, pushing away the one memory he hasn't welcomed since everything rushed back. The words they said are no longer important.

Not now, when they've been forced into the Games. When Aura's with Pace. They're bonding over the shared loss they believe they've suffered. The shared loss they *have* suffered because that's what the Games have them living.

Another flash of heat scorches Hayze's veins, putting his teeth on edge. Although the emotion is new, he recognizes it as jealousy. Pace is there to comfort Aura and he isn't.

Hayze glances down at the thick leather cuffs strapped around his wrists, the first barrier holding him from getting to her. The leather is wrapped tightly by a strip of metal, then some complicated clasp he can't even tell what's needed to undo. His gaze drifts to the symbol on the back of his right hand.

The symbol of Fire.

Not for the first time, the realization that he can wield it sinks into his awareness. Except this time, it does it with such swiftness, Hayze gasps. It's quickly followed by Skylus's words.

You couldn't do it because your life wasn't in danger. You needed the situations we've been put in to bring your powers out.

It was Hayze's memories that Pace was talking about when

he recollected training to harness Fire. It was Hayze's father who worked tirelessly to bring the latent ability to life.

All because Hayze's parents tried to buy some hope. The possibility they could give their child a chance at life beyond the Scorchlands.

Hayze finds he isn't angry. Not even disappointed. Although he'll never agree with what his parents did, he understands. Life in the Quadrants is hard. It's defined by struggle, poverty, and the ever-present promise that after everything, death will be the ultimate victor.

And he doubts they had any idea what the leaders had in store for the eight lives they bought by putting a price on a parent's desperation.

"I did it," Hayze whispers, wishing his father could hear him. "Even when I didn't realize what Element I was wielding, I did it."

It was probably Hayze who incinerated the feather Skylus and Atmos were levitating, because he was angry that it was happening at all. It was him who melted rock and soil as he tried to draw up water. It was him and Aura who inadvertently multiplied the lava that consumed their village.

In a world that wasn't real.

"But now I know," he grinds out. "Now, this is real."

Hayze glares down at the cuffs. Now, he has control of his fate in ways he didn't in the Games.

"I'm coming, Aura," he whispers fiercely. "And I'll bring the truth with me."

His hands clench into hot fists. His focus centers on the cuffs.

And the door flies open.

A bed pushes through, followed by the four leaders, but that's not what has Hayze's chest seizing painfully.

Tempo is lying on the gurney, a white sheet tucked up to

her chest, her lashes resting on her freckled cheeks. The same machines that are strapped and taped to Geo make sure her chest rises and falls. They glide it into position on Hayze's other side, coming to a stop an inch from the wall.

A faint, rhythmic beeping joins the same sound that Hayze has already become habituated to. Now, he's surrounded by the pulses of Geo and Tempo.

The leaders remain on the other side of the room, their faces varying shades of grim.

"That's three," Oceania says, a faint frown on her face.

"We only need one from each Element," Avalan points out.

Hayze angrily yanks on his bonds, making them creak. "You know I'm conscious, right?"

Cyclonis's gaze falls on him, his eyes narrowing. "You didn't know when to be silent in the Games, either."

"Because you made them my reality," Hayze spits back. "Just like the others who are still in there!"

Infernos crosses his arms, making his leather suit creak again. Hayze wonders if he does it for just that reason. "You're embarrassing Fire," he snaps. "Your father raised you to honor your Element, not disgrace it."

Hayze remembers Cyclonis's words from the games. *We've been watching you for a long time.*

Probably since the moment they handed over more edrian than his parents had ever seen.

"Exactly. My father raised me to honor Fire. Its passion, its power, its possibilities," Hayze snarls. "Not those who manipulate what it promises."

His father would never be okay with what's happening here.

Infernos takes a threatening step forward, but Avalan shoots a hand out to stop him. "Not yet. Not like this."

33

"What the fractal is that supposed to mean?" Hayze demands.

But Infernos steps back, flexing his arms so the leather of his suit voices the anger twisting his dark features. "Only that waking up from the Games has delayed the inevitable."

Cyclonis waves an arm, his purple robes flapping through the air as if he's clearing it of bad vibes. "Come. We must prepare for the next Game," he says.

Hayze stills as he realizes the Air leader's not in the least angry, let alone sad. He's acting as if he's looking forward to it. "Air still has two teens in the game," Hayze breathes.

Cyclonis strokes his beard as a smile plays at the edges of his mouth. "Is it really surprising that Air has been so accomplished?"

"Because Fire and Water have had their memories swapped," Infernos growls. "It was never a fair playing field."

Avalan arches a brow. "Although it's certainly made the Games entertaining," she points out.

"Entertaining?" Hayze shouts. "That's what you call the nightmare you're putting us through?"

Two of his friends are lying on either side of him, barely holding onto life. Five others are still fighting for theirs in a world that isn't even real! It doesn't get more twisted than that.

A roar builds inside Hayze. A powerhouse of rage and frustration and the furious drive for justice. He lifts his head, briefly wondering if he can become Fire itself, only to still.

The two sets of beeps are falling out of rhythm. One's slowing down...

The leaders freeze as it slows to every second beat. Then every third.

Then stops altogether.

Hayze's head snaps toward Tempo. He holds his breath as

he waits and watches, then lets it out with a whoosh when her chest rises then falls. Except that means...

Turning slowly to his left, Hayze doesn't even bother to draw in air. His chest is too tight. His lungs too frozen.

A handful of seconds is all that's needed to confirm Geo is just as motionless.

Oceania's intake of breath is faint, but inescapable. The room just became a little quieter, there's only one rhythmic beeping now puncturing the air. Nobody moves. For once, the leaders don't have anything to say.

Hayze doesn't have the same issue.

"You killed him!" he roars, fighting his bonds. "Geo's dead because of you!"

To Hayze's surprise, Avalan drops her head as if she's acknowledging the loss. Oceania reaches out to squeeze her shoulder, her gaze on Tempo, probably wondering if she'll be next.

Or *when* she'll be next.

Infernos snorts, then spins on his heel. "How long do the others need to rest before we start again?" he demands as he strides to the door.

"They're being recharged as they receive the necessary nutrition," Avalan says, turning to follow him. "It shouldn't take longer than a few hours."

Cyclonis joins them, not even glancing at Geo or Tempo, let alone Hayze. Oceania straightens as her face hardens, making her look like she's now carved from marble. She slips past Cyclonis so she's the second out the door, right behind Infernos.

"I'll send someone to collect the body," Cyclonis says as he steps through. "We'll dispose of it discreetly."

Avalan goes to follow, but Hayze refuses for that brief moment of humanity to be all that's afforded Geo.

"How far will you go?" he snarls. "When does it stop?"

Avalan turns, even walks a few steps back into the room as her gaze settles on him without flinching. "Sacrifices are inevitable."

"Conveniently, not yours," Hayze snaps back. She's not the one lying next to him, dead on a bed.

The Earth leader's dark eyes flare. She seems to still, even as her decorative feathers and flowers and furs vibrate with emotion. "You have no idea what you're talking about."

She spins on her heel and stalks to the door, her straight spine and high chin defying her short stature.

"What about Tempo?" Hayze shouts. "You have to do something! She'll die, too!"

Avalan stops at the door and turns her head, not bothering to look all the way back at him. "You've taught us much, Hayze." Her lips twitch, neither smiling nor frowning. "We've realized if you fail the Games, we don't want you to wake."

She leaves and the door shuts, her parting words as ominous as the solitary, rhythmic beeping. Tempo will eventually follow Geo. And now the leaders plan on making sure Hayze joins them. He knows too much.

"You also don't want me leaving this room," Hayze mutters. "But that's exactly what's about to happen."

He glares at the cuffs, injecting all the fury, all the desperate desire to be back by Aura's side into the need to destroy them.

It's inside you, Hayze. It always has been.

The moment the words whisper through his mind, he recognizes them. It was his father's voice he heard in the Games. His father's faith in him that reached beyond the virtual world Hayze was trapped in.

Heat fills him, feeling as if it starts in his very marrow. It expands out, spreading from cell to cell, scorching his veins, igniting him from the inside out.

The cuffs flare white hot, yet they don't burn him. The metal surrounding the thick leather turns red, then orange, then stretches and thins as it melts. It runs off as a fiery liquid just as the leather combusts.

Hayze yanks his wrists free, then his feet. With a triumphant scowl, he subdues the very fire he just created. The leather turns to ash, cradling a twisted puddle of metal in the center of each pile.

Stretching his arms, then rubbing his wrists, Hayze looks around. Geo lies to the right, his life stolen by the Games. Tempo is on the left, soon to be next.

"No more," Hayze growls.

The leaders have no idea what they've unleashed.

Spinning toward the door, he breaks into a run. He has no idea where he is. How he'll get out.

Or how the fractal he's going to get back into the Games.

But the first step is escaping this room, and that's what he's going to do.

Hayze wraps his hand around the handle, surprised but pleased to find it's unlocked. Although, he could've just melted it. Or burned the door down. He yanks it open. Nothing's stopping him from getting back to Aura—

Oceania's standing on the other side, her face grim. "You're not going anywhere, Hayze," she bites out.

"Watch me."

Hayze goes to rush forward but she raises a sleek, white gun. He jerks to a halt, and then has no choice but to walk backward as the Water leader stalks forward, forcing him into the room. She closes the door with a soft but definite click.

Oceania raises the gun, pointing it straight at his chest. "You've put me in a very difficult position, Hayze."

CHAPTER
FIVE
AURA

Once again, Aura's the first to wake. She's not surprised. It's all part of the never-ending loop she's stuck in, which at the moment seems to include being trapped in this large, white box.

Except this time, she has Pace by her side as well as Jewel. He has his hand tucked into the crook of her arm and Aura wonders if it's because in his sleep he thinks she's Tempo. Just like everyone in the Fire Quadrant had.

She remembers how tempted she'd been to stay in Tempo's life for a short while. It was comforting. Like trying on a pair of shoes that don't look like they should fit, yet somehow had felt just right. In Tempo's life, she could be with Hayze without anything or anyone getting in their way.

Hayze.

The thought of him brings her pain as if the jagged pieces of her broken heart have lodged in her chest. If she can ever find her way home, she knows she'll have to get into Aqua to look for his family. To tell them what an incredible son they raised. How much he loved them right up until the very end.

It's no wonder they did whatever they had to so they could give him the best possible life. Aura would do the same for him if only she could.

Which is impossible. Because he's dead.

She swallows, hating even the thought of the word when it's attached to Hayze.

"Are you awake?" Jewel whispers.

"Unfortunately," Aura replies, having far preferred the oblivion of sleep. She still has the fog of her dreams clouding her thoughts, and while she can't remember anything specific, she's sure they were about Hayze.

"Do you feel stronger?" Jewel asks.

Aura opens her eyes to look at her friend in confusion. "What do you mean?"

"Physically," Jewel explains, sitting up. "Have you noticed that whenever we wake up, we feel stronger?"

"That's what sleep does," murmurs Pace, his eyes still closed. "That's the whole point of it."

"Never mind." Jewel wraps her arms around her knees.

Aura sits up and realizes what Jewel means. Sleep in this strange world is like a supercharger. It's not like waking back at home in her hammock in the barge, dreary eyed and yawning.

"You're right," she says. "Just another mystery to add to the list."

But Jewel is no longer listening. She's staring straight ahead, her jaw open. Aura turns to see what has her attention.

Then her own jaw falls open.

In the wall, directly behind where Skylus and Atmos are sleeping, is a door. Above it is a sign with glowing letters that spell out the one word all of them want to see most.

"Exit," Aura reads, hardly daring to believe the promise of those four innocent letters.

Pace jolts upright. "What did you say?"

"Look." Jewel points. "It says exit."

Pace is on his feet in less than a second, marching forward.

Skylus sits up with wide eyes. "What's happening?"

This wakes Atmos, whose face is instantly filled with fright to see Pace standing over him.

"Get back!" he shouts, holding up his hands. "I didn't do anything."

"Not you, airhead," snaps Pace, his eyes on the door. "Look behind you."

Atmos turns and gasps. "Don't open it!" He scrambles to his feet and presses himself against the door.

"Why not?" Aura asks, moving forward.

"We should look for a sign," Skylus says, answering for Atmos as she stands beside him.

Pace points to the glowing letters that spell *exit* and rolls his eyes. "There's your sign."

Aura groans at his attempt at humor, but the Air couple don't seem to find it as amusing.

"We can't rush into decisions," says Skylus. "Especially ones that impact us all."

"She's right," Aura says reluctantly. "I mean, it's a bit strange to label the door with exactly what it is, isn't it? It could be a trick."

"You mean *test*," says Skylus. "Not a trick. Our leaders aren't in the business of tricking us."

Aura isn't so sure about that. She lets out a long sigh. "Whatever you want to call it, it's clear the leaders want us to go out that door. The question is why?"

"If those two got out of the way, we could find out," growls Pace.

Aura puts a hand on Pace's arm. "There could be something behind it."

"Yeah, like an exit." He tugs himself free.

"They wouldn't make it that easy," says Aura. "I agree we need to go through the door, but we need to be ready for whatever we have to face once we open it."

"You can all wait in here if you like, but I'm going out." Pace shoves Atmos to the side and reaches for Skylus. She raises her hands and a strong wind gusts into the room, forcing Pace backward until he slams into the opposite wall. Aura stumbles to catch her balance, shocked at how easily Skylus was able to summon her power and how expertly she directed it.

Pace collects himself and marches forward, his face purple with rage. "You used your powers against me!" he shouts.

"And I'll do it again if you take another step," growls Skylus, her hands still raised.

Atmos joins her, gluing himself to her side as he copies her stance.

Pace hesitates, coming to a stop as he raises his own hands. "Get out of my way or I'll throw a fireball at you."

This statement makes the Air couple laugh.

"You're more likely to set yourself ablaze if you try to do that," snarls Atmos.

Aura takes a deep breath and steps between them, not wanting anyone to use their powers against each other. Besides, Atmos has a point. Pace has been about as successful at controlling his Fire powers as Aura has been with Water. Only Air and Earth seem to be making any real progress so far.

"We're supposed to be a team," says Jewel, flicking her hand behind her back. "We already have enough to fight against without fighting each other. Please. Stop it."

A large stone slab that had been balancing on another behind them topples and crashes to the floor, sending a cloud of dust into the room.

"Was that a sign?" Pace asks, seeming to be attempting to keep the sarcasm from his voice, which is progress at least.

"Jewel did that," says Atmos, narrowing his eyes.

"I wasn't even looking at the stones!" she protests. "It wasn't me."

Aura suspects very much that it was Jewel, but she says nothing. As terrified as she is about what might be behind that door, they have to face it sooner or later. And if they can do it as a united front, they have a far better chance of succeeding. It seems Jewel must have come to the same conclusion.

Atmos looks at Skylus for direction.

"It was a sign," she says with certainty.

"Great," Pace mutters, advancing forward. "Now, will you move out of the way?"

"We'll go first," says Skylus, not budging an inch. "It's better that those of us who've reached a more advanced level with our Elemental powers are in the front."

"Let her go," Aura says quietly to Pace, trying to squash the hope there might be a swarm of flesh-eating grasshoppers to greet Skylus.

Skylus puts her hand on the white door handle and presses it down. The door swings outward and she raises her hands as she steps through, ready to blast whatever might be there with a powerful gust of wind.

Atmos moves forward beside her, with Pace hot on their heels.

"You ready?" Aura asks Jewel.

Jewel nods.

"You sure you're not too tired after shifting that stone?" Aura winks to show she's joking.

Jewel's eyes widen, then she grins. "I couldn't stand the arguing."

Aura ushers Jewel through the door, then follows,

wondering just how large the new white box they'll find themselves in is going to be.

She blinks, turning in a circle as she tries to take in their new surroundings.

They're standing in a large square room as expected, but this one has two key differences, neither of which involve grasshoppers thankfully. For a start, there's no roof. Aura glances up to see fluffy white clouds floating in the blue sky above and she draws in a breath of fresh air. Returning her focus to the room, she studies the other unexpected change. Each of the four walls has a door in it, just like the one they came through. And each one is labeled with an exit sign.

Pace groans. "Not this again."

"Not what again?" Skylus asks. "We don't know what's behind these doors."

"We kinda do." Jewel shrugs. "There will be more rooms with more doors. It will go on forever."

"Then let's get forever over with." Pace swings open the door closest to him before anyone can stop him and marches through it.

"Jewel was right," he calls back to them. "It's the same in here."

Aura chases after him, finding herself in an identical room to the one before. The other three teens follow. But before they can discuss what's happening, Pace has already gone through another door.

"She's right again," he calls as the door swings closed behind him.

"Hurry!" says Aura, worried if they don't follow, they'll never be able to find him again. "We have to stay together."

"He can't just choose doors at random," Atmos grumbles. "We need to look for signs."

"Just let him lead for now," Jewel tells them. "He'll get tired of it eventually."

"This isn't the solution," says Skylus as they follow Pace through another door, then another, then another, sometimes taking the one on the left, then the one on the right, and occasionally mixing it up by choosing the door that lies straight ahead. They pass through so many exits Aura isn't sure she'd be able to find her way back to the original room if her life depended on it. Which it very well could at some stage...

As Jewel predicted, eventually Pace comes to a stop. He turns to the rest of them and throws out his hands. "Is forever over yet? This is useless."

"That's because you're not looking for the signs," says Atmos.

"Then you choose one, genius." Pace rolls his eyes.

"I will." Atmos studies each door in turn while Pace taps his foot on the floor.

Pace is just about to open the door to their left when the exit sign above the door they just came through flickers, then turns off.

Atmos marches over to it. "This one."

"We were just in that room," Aura says. "I'm not sure doubling back is a wise idea."

"It was a sign." He puts his hand on the door handle.

"Technically, it's now the only door without a sign," Pace grumbles.

Ignoring him, Atmos opens the door and gasps, stumbling back a little.

Aura rushes forward with the rest of the teens to see what's happened, only to discover they're staring down a corridor so long it's impossible to see where it ends.

"This wasn't here before," says Jewel.

"Maybe we came through a different door," says Aura, feeling more confused than ever.

Jewel shakes her head. "We definitely came through this one."

"Why do you expect it to make sense?" Pace asks.

Aura shrugs. "I don't know. I just didn't expect...this."

"We should see what's at the end of the corridor," says Skylus. "I'm feeling a pull down it."

"Or we save our energy and stay here," says Pace.

Aura puts a hand on his arm, aware Pace is grieving. "They followed you when you wanted to explore. We need to stay together."

"Why?" he asks, stubbornly crossing his arms.

"It's our best chance of survival," she tells him.

"That didn't help Te—"

"I know," Aura cuts him off. "Or Hayze. But we're still here. We owe it to them to do our best."

Pace doesn't seem to like hearing that, but he doesn't argue.

They set off down the corridor and Aura finds her eyes continually drawn to the blue sky. It reminds her of the drawings Pace had sketched for Tempo on the ceiling of her bunker. Pace may be acting irrationally since he lost the love of his life, but he's a sweet guy underneath all that bravado. She needs to remember that.

"Are you thinking about your parents?" Jewel asks.

"Actually, no," Aura says, feeling guilty. "Why?"

Jewel shrugs. "I was just thinking how strange it is that my mom might be looking at the very same sky as us."

Aura looks up again with fresh eyes as she wonders what her parents are doing right now.

"I don't have a dad," says Jewel, answering the question

Aura never asked. "I mean, I must have one, but I don't know who he is."

Aura nods, interested, but not wanting to pry.

"But if he's out there somewhere," says Jewel. "He's looking at the same sky, too."

Aura smiles at Jewel. "That's a really beautiful thought. We could use more of those."

"What if Pace is right?" Jewel's eyes fill with moisture. "What if we're stuck in here forever?"

"We'll find our way out eventually," says Aura, keeping her footsteps moving forward. "There'll be a door or something."

Or eventually they'll fall asleep and discover some other surprise waiting for them when they wake up.

"I don't mean this corridor," says Jewel. "I mean this world. What if our entire existence is going to be like this? Waking up in strange places and trying to figure out things that make no sense."

"It won't be forever." Aura swallows, hoping this isn't a lie. "It makes no sense to keep us here indefinitely, no matter what our parents promised the leaders."

"I'll tell you what's forever," says Pace. "This corridor. When are you all going to realize there's no end to it? We should turn back."

"Everything has an end," says Atmos over his shoulder. "Apart from Eterna, of course."

Skylus spins around to add something to that and trips over her feet, tumbling heavily to the floor.

"Ouch!" She winces, grabbing at her ankle as she tries to sit up. "I think I twisted it."

Aura crouches beside Skylus, unsure how to help her. She glances down the corridor with no end, then back in the direction they just walked—which now also has no end. "Do you think you can walk?"

Skylus looks at Aura and shakes her head. "I'm not sure. I don't think so. It really hurts."

"I walked on my sprained ankle in the Scorchlands," Pace says. "Just sayin'."

"That was life or death," Atmos snaps. "It was either walk or be scorched by fire."

"This feels a little like life or death," Jewel says quietly. "We'll need food and water soon."

"I vote that we head back without her," says Pace. "If we find food, we'll bring it to her."

"No." Aura stands. "We have to stick together, no matter what."

"What if we use our powers?" says Atmos. "I can make a gust of wind to blow us down the rest of the corridor."

"And sprain all our ankles?" Aura isn't keen on the idea of being tumbled down this long space, hitting her head on the walls.

"I have another idea," says Skylus. "Someone help me up."

Aura stretches out her hands and hauls Skylus to a standing position. "What are you thinking?"

"That me tripping over was a sign," says Skylus, straightening as she takes her weight on her good leg. "Atmos is right. We need to use our Elemental powers to solve this puzzle. We've been going about it all the wrong way."

"I'm not sure Water would be helpful," says Aura, suddenly feeling anxious. "Unless you're suggesting it would be easier on your ankle to swim rather than walk."

"There's no roof," says Jewel. "If we fill the corridor with water, we could float to the top and climb out."

"But how would we get down?" Aura asks, unsure if she's even capable of such a feat. "If it's a sheer drop on the other side of these walls, it would be deadly."

"I can try breaking them down," says Jewel, knocking on a wall and frowning at the strength of it.

"Or I can burn a hole in them?" Pace suggests.

"I said I had an idea!" Skylus snaps. "Why is nobody listening to me?"

Aura holds up her palms. "Fine. What's your idea, Skylus?"

"Well." She smiles sweetly at Aura like she hadn't just almost bitten her head off. "Atmos and I have mastered being able to send blasts of wind across the land. How about we try something a little different?"

Atmos tilts his head in curiosity. "Like what?"

"Let me show you." Skylus steadies herself and pulls back her shoulders. "Stand aside, everyone."

They shuffle back as they wait, all eyes glued to Skylus, who's plastered her arms to her sides with her hands sticking out at an odd angle. She closes her eyes and pulls her face into a grimace, concentrating hard.

"I am Air!" she calls out.

Jewel slips her hand into Aura's and squeezes tightly as they watch Skylus's feet lift from the floor.

Aura's heart leaps. "What the—"

"Aura, look!" Jewel gasps. "She's flying."

SIX

HAYZE

Hayze takes a couple of more steps backward, then raises his hands another few inches, just for good measure. His gaze darts between Oceania and the weapon she has aimed at his chest.

Is he fast enough to run at her, knock her and the gun out of the way, and escape?

Maybe if he hadn't just instinctively put a little more distance between them...

His lips twist. Maybe not even then.

"You won't be getting past me," Oceania says, her voice soft, yet hard as ice. "And even if you do, I have men waiting on the other side."

Hayze clenches his jaw. "You're going to need more than that to keep me in here." To keep him away from Aura.

Oceania arches a brow. "Or you could listen to what I have to say."

"Sorry," he says, acid dripping from the one word. "I don't have time to hear your justifications for being sadistic asses."

Oceania lowers the gun as she shakes her head. "You really are single-minded."

"Compliments aren't going to get you anywhere," Hayze snaps, noting the sleek white weapon is now pointed at the floor. That's good.

Yet he's learned one thing from the Games. Nothing is as it seems.

"As I was saying," Oceania says on a sigh. "You've put me in a very difficult position."

Hayze subtly moves his center of gravity to the left. One step to the side and he'll be able to run past the Water leader. He'll bowl her over if she decides to bring that gun back up. Then he'll be out the door, dealing with whatever's on the other side.

Whatever's stopping him from getting back to Aura.

"Did you mean what you said?" Oceania asks, her eyes narrowing as she watches him.

"Yes," Hayze says immediately, even though he has no idea what statement she's referring to. "Damnatus straight I did."

Oceania subtly moves to the right, blocking the line of sight to the door even more. "Then you definitely want to hear what I have to say."

Hayze really doesn't. But he also wants out of this room, which means playing along with this. He curls his lip. "This is all *game* to you, isn't it?"

"None of this is a game," Oceania spits, taking a step forward. "It never was."

Hayze doesn't move even though the Water leader is now closer. In fact, he glances over his shoulder toward Tempo, the faint beeping signaling she's not dead. Yet. "No, it wasn't." He looks the other way at Geo. "Which makes you murderers."

"Or saviors," Oceania says, raising the gun once more. "Which do you want to be, Hayze?"

"Neither," he growls back. "I just want to be out of here."

"Which is why I came back. I have an offer to make."

For the first time, Hayze centers his entire attention on Oceania. Her bald head, her blue body suit, her shrewd eyes. "What offer?" he asks, noting the gun is pointing at him again as he registers something else.

She hasn't killed him yet.

Oceania opens her mouth just as five of the screens flicker. Flash. Then come to life.

Aura and the others appear on them, each one from a slightly different angle. But it's only one face that Hayze's gaze roams over. Studies. Absorbs.

Aura's tucked between Jewel and Pace. She stirs, her eyes flutter, and her face twists with pain. Ignoring Oceania, he walks closer to the screen most focused on Aura, listening as Jewel notes they've woken up feeling stronger.

Because their bodies have been recharged, as Avalan said.

So they can do this all again.

Then Jewel notices the door with the exit sign and a debate about whether to go through ensues. Hayze almost rolls his eyes at Atmos and Skylus's objections. He relates to Pace's need for action, even as his gut tightens at the prospect of Aura and his friends stepping through.

Hayze turns to Oceania. "What's on the other side?"

She crosses her arms, tucking the gun out of sight as she simply stares back.

"Now you're quiet?" he mutters, turning back to the screen. He squints as he's able to partially answer his question.

Another round of the Games is on the other side.

Hayze's stomach goes from tight to knots as the teens discuss using their powers and it's suggested Aura call on Water so they can rise out of it. He sees the apprehension on her face, knowing she won't want to do this. She believes she could drown them.

Pace offering to use Fire practically guarantees it.

Hayze is almost relieved when Skylus blows Pace across the room, even as he winces at the thud. There's another short discussion and the Air teens lead the way through the door.

Hayze holds his breath, then lets it out in a whoosh when he sees what the others have. They're in a maze. An endless repetition of the same room with four doors.

"They can't win," Hayze hisses, turning to Oceania. "Don't you see that?"

"I do," she says, surprising him. "That's why I'm here. The other leaders believe I volunteered to come back and finish you."

"But you haven't," Hayze observes. Despite countless chances. In fact, the gun is now hooked to a holster at Oceania's hip.

"As I said, I've come here with an offer." She levels her blue gaze. "I know how you can get back into the Elemental Games."

It takes effort to hold in the "heckus yes!" that bursts through Hayze. He crosses his arms, creating a physical band around his middle to stop the words from exploding out of him. "In exchange for what?"

"You tell them the truth," Oceania says simply.

"I was already going to do that and you know it." What is the Water leader getting out of letting him go?

Oceania's gaze shifts to Tempo, her face softening, then hardening. "The swap has put Water at a disadvantage. It's time to even out the Games."

Hayze doesn't point out it also put Fire at a disadvantage. In part, because the time for conversation is over. But mostly because he doesn't care about this in-fighting between the Quadrants. This isn't some competition. Some *game*.

This is his life. And Aura's.

And the future they've been dreaming of for as long as they could dream.

The future that was put at risk the day before they were wrenched away.

His heart stuttering, Hayze glances back at the screens, seeing that Aura and the others are now walking down an endless corridor. There's nothing else he wants more than to be there with her.

There's so much to make right.

"How do you propose to get me back into the Games?" Hayze asks, turning back to Oceania.

"I won't be helping you, myself. That's far too dangerous."

Hayze twists his lips into a smile. "Wouldn't want your life to be in danger," he says sweetly. "Not when you're a savior."

Oceania snaps a glare at him. "One day you'll understand." She straightens, drawing in a breath as if calming herself. "I won't be helping you, but there's someone in Aqua who can."

Hayze frowns, about to point out that going to her capital is clearly a trap, but he snaps his mouth shut. For once, he's going to think first, then talk. Why Aqua? And who can help him?

The answer hits him harder than the boulder he believed landed on him.

"Pace's father." His true father.

Oceania nods, her blue eyes sparking. "Yes. Tide is a trade master. He has the information you need."

Hayze blinks at the images those words conjure. Tide, also bald, also in a blue body suit, has three scars running down his left cheek. Hayze has Pace's memories. He not only knows what Tide looks like, he knows where he lives and works.

It's his only chance.

And the leaders gifted it to him without ever realizing.

He stalks past Oceania, only stopping when he reaches the door and grips the handle. "The men on the other side?" he asks, glancing back.

Oceania's lips edge up at the corners. "I lied."

"Because that's what saviors do?" Hayze mutters, not bothering to look at her as he strides to the door.

Before his heart can pump another beat, he yanks it open.

The corridor on the other side is just as white as the room he's in. Blank walls greet him, and for a second, he wonders if he's in the same maze Aura and the others are. That he's still in the Games.

But then he sees two doors a little further to the right, and two to the left. Each one has an Elemental symbol on it. Fire. Water. Air. Earth.

"You can't leave yet," Oceania says from behind him.

Hayze glares back at her. Of course there's a catch. There always is.

She smiles even as her eyes crinkle with tension. "The other leaders need to believe you overpowered me."

His stomach drops. He needs to attack the Water leader?

Even as he asks himself the question, Hayze knows the answer is yes. If he doesn't, he loses the unlikely ally he's stumbled across.

The thought makes him ill. Hurting someone in the name of getting what he wants, no matter how driven he is by love, feels a little too close to being one of the leaders. He's no murderer, and he's certainly no savior.

But what choice does he have?

His eyes flicker to the screens, seeing that Aura and the others are still walking down an endless corridor. He stills, conscious he's about to lose his one connection to her. He won't know what's happening to her in the Games.

It's another awful consequence he'll be forced to carry with him as he leaves.

Hayze turns back and steps into the room, noting the way Oceania flinches, but doesn't move away.

She draws back her shoulders, glaring at him. "One strike is all it should take," she warns.

He shakes his head, his stomach settling into a hard weight as he reaches a decision. "I'm not going to hit you."

"What?" Oceania frowns, her eyes widening as she watches him lift his hands. She glances at his open palms and he wonders if she can see they're heating. "W-what are you doing, Hayze?"

"This is what you created, Oceania," he says solemnly, his fingers twitching as energy courses through them. "This is what the Games are all about."

Unleashing his power.

Oceania goes so pale, her smooth head is almost as white as the walls. "That isn't what I meant—"

"How does it feel, great leader?" Hayze growls, drawing on the power he now knows he carries. That he always has, just like his father believed with such conviction he was willing to die for it. "How does it feel for someone else to hold your life in their hands?"

Oceania also raises her hands, but as if she's trying to ward off what's coming. "I'm trying to help," she whispers.

"No, you want Water to win these Games. To claim whatever coveted prize you're willing to kill for."

"Please—"

"I am Fire!" Hayze snarls, his heart aching at what's already been put into motion.

Oceania gasps. Takes a step back. Then cries out as she sees smoke curling around her feet. "Sweet waters," she sobs.

The smell of burning cloth and flesh is next. It hits the back of Hayze's throat just as Oceania collapses.

Just as Geo's bed bursts into raging flames.

Oceania scrambles backward over the floor, screaming at the sight she can't tear her gaze from. A roaring blaze is all that exists where Geo was once lying, the bed now nothing more than a frame of fire, the body on it charred and black.

Hayze turns away and walks through the door, not looking back. Geo won't disappear like Cyclonis said. He won't be buried deep in the soil as they do in Earth, but he will go in a blaze of glory like the people of Fire. Hayze can give him that.

Out in the corridor, he pauses at the Fire door. If he goes through it, he could go home. He could make sure his parents are still alive.

But home is hollow without Aura.

He won't go back without her.

With a quick snap of his arm, he strikes the handle. A burst of heat detonates, singing the white around it. The door pops open an inch, which is exactly how he leaves it as he continues to the Water door. The leaders need to believe he's gone back to his own pod.

It'll buy him some time.

Without hesitation, Hayze steps through the Water door, finding himself in another white room, this one smaller than the one he left. The moment the door closes, Hayze's stomach seems to lift through his body. He grips the wall beside him, overwhelmed by a sense of motion even as he's standing still. He'd say he's feeling nauseous, except he's not sure he has a stomach anymore. It's levitated just like the freaking feather in the Stormsphere.

Almost as quickly as the feeling assaults him, it stops. The wall across from him slides open, revealing it was a door all along. Hayze doesn't give himself a chance to hesitate. Whatever's on the other side is simply an obstacle to Aura. Nothing more.

Yet he still stops the moment he exits the small room that somehow moved through space. His jaw goes lax. His eyebrows hike somewhere into his hairline.

The expansive area that opens out is like nothing he's ever seen. A vast, deep-blue pool occupies the center, so calm and still it looks like he could walk on it. Walls rise up on all sides, made of opaque glass and shimmering liquid crystal. Aquatic creatures, including dolphins and jellyfish, glisten subtly when the light catches them. The sound of cascading water fills the space even though nothing is moving.

Hayze takes a step forward, blinking in wonder. Water droplets hang in the air, creating the illusion of a perpetual rainstorm. Yet when he runs his hand through one and feels nothing but air, it flickers without substance.

It's nature at its most breathtaking.

Yet it's undeniable every inch is artificial. That it's manmade.

Hayze continues to scan the beautiful, disturbing marvel, finding what he's looking for. A door. The way out.

Skirting the bottomless, unmoving pool, he strides toward it, dodging the strange water droplets even though he knows they're not real. What do the Quadrant rooms look like? What does his own, Fire, look like?

He doubts he'll ever find out. He intends on finding Aura and then going home. If the leaders try to stop them, they'll face the very Element they were so determined to unleash.

Although, that's assuming Aura forgives him...

Shoving the painful thought away, Hayze steps through, finding himself in another small, white room. He braces himself for the sensation of motion as the door closes behind him. But it doesn't come.

Instead, he's assaulted by light.

Light so white and so blinding, he's forced to raise his arm and squeeze his eyes tightly shut. Even then, the glare seems to burn through, turning his very mind white.

"Aura!" Hayze cries, terrified he never even got as far as leaving the Sect.

The blinding light is gone as quickly as it exploded through the room. Hayze squints, wondering if his eyeballs have been incinerated as he reads the two words flickering on the wall across from him.

Decontamination complete.

Decontamination? He can see that it's necessary to enter the Sect, but to leave it?

Shaking his head, he realizes some answers he doesn't care to know. Not when there's a door in front of him. One he instinctively knows is the last one before he leaves the Sect and starts his journey through Aqua.

Starts his journey back to Aura.

Hayze opens it, welcoming the sights and sounds. Beyond is a world that's familiar, yet one he's never stepped foot in.

He squares his shoulders as he takes the first step. "I'm coming, Aura."

CHAPTER
SEVEN
AURA

Skylus hovers directly above them, at the top of the high walls of the never-ending corridor. Her body is rigid, her arms still plastered by her sides with her hands poking out, the edrian in her Air tattoo catching the light and sending out glittering rays.

"I can't believe it." Aura shakes her head, her eyes glued to the girl from Air. Skylus has mastered her Elemental powers in a way the rest of them haven't been able to. This opens up endless possibilities. What else might they all be able to do? Could Aura breathe underwater? Could Pace walk through fire? Maybe Jewel could make edrian from nothing but coal.

"Can you fly, too?" Pace asks Atmos.

"No need for both of us to go up there." Atmos shakes his head firmly. "Skylus has this under control."

Aura's fairly certain she caught sight of Atmos trying to mimic Skylus when she first lifted from the floor, but she doesn't say anything. It's only natural that each of their skills will develop at different rates. Including Aura, who seems to be the slowest out of them all. And Pace really isn't in a position to be criticizing anyone. His Fire skills have been mediocre at best.

"What's up there?" Jewel calls out.

Skylus looks down without answering, and Aura holds her breath, hoping this lapse in concentration doesn't send her crashing to the floor. Skylus slowly comes back down, seeming in full control of her movements.

"Well done!" Aura claps, wishing Hayze was here to see this. Without him, everything feels muted. Her happiness doesn't feel as happy. Her excitement not quite as excited. Her motivation not nearly as motivating as it had been when he was by her side.

Jewel joins in the applause, grinning widely. Atmos, who should be the most enthusiastic of all, presses his palms together a few times in what could possibly be considered clapping to someone who's lost their hearing. Pace doesn't make any effort at all.

Skylus's feet make contact with the floor and she winces, having forgotten her ankle is sprained. She takes her weight on her good leg and rearranges her face into a smile.

"How did it feel?" Jewel asks, wide-eyed.

"Incredible." A look of pure satisfaction ripples across Skylus's features. It seems she's just as impressed with herself as they all are.

"If you keep this up, you'll be more powerful than Cyclonis," Aura laughs.

Instead of joining in the laughter, Skylus puffs out her chest. "Perhaps, I already am."

Atmos lets out a stifled gasp at this blasphemy.

"Only joking," she smiles sweetly, and Atmos lets out a sigh of relief.

"Forget the powers for a second," says Pace. "What did you see up there? What's on the other side of these walls?"

Skylus blinks, then shifts her gaze to Pace. "Nothing."

"What do you mean, nothing?" Aura asks. "There can't be nothing."

"Well, that's what there is." Skylus rolls her eyes, like telling them what she saw is a trauma. "Everything was white, apart from the sky, of course. It was quite beautiful. Tranquil. I'm sure wherever Eterna lives, it must look like that."

"Could it have been ice?" Aura asks, thinking of the icefields she grew up in. They stretch for miles. Maybe they're a whole lot closer to her home than she thought.

"It wasn't cold enough to be ice," says Skylus. "It looked more like nothingness. And by the way, this corridor goes on forever. No point walking down it, really. The end can never be reached."

Aura frowns. "That's not poss—"

"Everything's possible here," Jewel says.

Aura shrugs, conceding she has a point. "Skylus, if I fill this corridor with water and we float to the top of the walls, do you think we could climb over the edge?"

"Oh, you wouldn't want to do that," says Skylus without hesitation. "Not without the power of Air. You'd fall to your death. And it seems I'm the only one with necessary advanced powers." She glances at Atmos, who grimaces, giving Aura her first glimpse of any type of rift between these two.

"You didn't look behind us," says Pace, pointing back the way they came. "You only looked ahead."

"But we know what's behind us." Atmos lets out a frustrated sigh.

"That's right." Skylus smiles at Pace as if she's dealing with a young child. "We were just there."

"Are you worried you won't be able to turn around?" Pace lifts one brow, reminding Aura of her father who does the same thing. No matter how much she tries, her brows insist on working in tandem.

"Of course not," Skylus snaps. "Why would I be worried? I can turn in any direction I like."

"Then show us." Pace plants his hands on his hips. "Or even better, let Atmos show us."

"Pace." Aura puts a hand on his arm. "Enough, please. We're not in competition with each other. We're a te—"

Skylus shoots into the air without warning, traveling even faster this time. Aura glances at Atmos who has his arms by his side and his hands sticking out, trying so hard to follow Skylus that he's trembling. Aura subtly moves in front of Pace to block his view of the boy from Air, hoping he doesn't notice the trouble he's having.

She looks back up to see Skylus reach the top of the wall. She stops, then with her fingers wriggling at her sides, she very slowly spins around.

"She told you she could do it," says Atmos, who seems to have given up on his quest to fly for now.

"Yeah, she did," says Pace, not seeming as impressed as he should be.

When Skylus is facing the direction they came from, she stops, hovering in the air for long seconds.

"Why's she taking so long?" Jewel asks.

"There must be something back there," says Aura, her mind whirring with possibilities. Perhaps the maze of square rooms they'd come through has vanished. Or maybe it's morphed into something else. The leaders must have a large team of people working with them to be able to change things over so quickly.

Eventually, Skylus comes back down, her face as white as the landscape she'd described.

"What is it?" Atmos asks. "What did you see?"

"I could see the length of the corridor we just walked down," says Skylus, regaining her composure. "And the square rooms. But beyond them..."

"Beyond them what?" Pace hops from foot to foot. "What was there?"

"The Sect," says Skylus.

Aura's brows shoot up, proving once again they like to work in unison. She's never seen the Sect before but has heard about the tall domed tower that sits in the very center of all the capitals. Nobody's been inside apart from the leaders, and a few select trade masters. Aura would like to bet Hayze's father is in that exclusive club. The thought of him punches fresh grief into her gut and she tries to focus back on what this new information might mean.

"If you could see the Sect, we must be in one of the capitals," Jewel says, her eyes lighting up. "And if you saw white, then maybe Aura was right. We're in Aqua." She smiles at Aura like she's a genius.

"It. Was. Not. Ice." Skylus grits her teeth. "The white was just nothingness. And sitting beyond it was the tower of the Sect."

If only Hayze was here, he could confirm exactly what Aqua looks like and if it contains a stretch of ice that looks like nothingness. Aura really has no idea what's in her Quadrant's capital apart from opulent houses bursting with food and over privileged people.

"So, we need to walk back the way we came," says Pace, rubbing his palms together. "Then find our way back through the square rooms, and we should eventually emerge at the Sect."

"Why do you think anyone in the Sect will help us?" Aura asks. "Aren't they the ones who put us here in the first place?"

"Exactly why I want to talk to them." Pace cracks his knuckles, his reason for being in a hurry becoming clear. He wants to blame someone for Tempo's death. And the leaders are the obvious choice. "In fact, I can't wait to talk to them."

"Respect!" Atmos cries. "Have respect. Our great leader, Cyclonis, said our leaders have been watching us. What makes you so sure they're not watching us now? They could be listening to our every word."

"I hope they are," Pace growls, shaking his fist. "Because I have plenty more I want to say to them. Starting with why they think it was okay to kill anyone as innocent as Tempo."

Aura glances around, unable to see any possible way the leaders could be observing them. Although, she's well aware the capitals have access to technology far more advanced than she's able to imagine. Could that include invisible cameras? Or walls that appear solid on one side, yet are transparent on the other?

"Let's get moving." Aura puts her hand on Pace's elbow. "We have a long way to go."

"Are you able to walk?" Jewel asks Skylus, looking down at her sprained ankle.

"Walk?" Skylus screws up her face like Jewel had used an offensive word. "I don't need to *walk*. Have you forgotten so soon that I've mastered my Elemental powers?"

Jewel's jaw drops. "You're going to fly there?"

"Not fly," Skylus says. "I'm not an insect. I'm going to become one with my Element and move through the air. I'll get to the Sect much faster than any of you."

"But we need to stick together," says Aura, having thought they all agreed to this earlier. "You can't go ahead on your own."

A dark shadow cloaks the corridor, the result of a cloud crossing the sun.

"I'll take that as a sign," says Skylus, plastering her arms to her side. "See you at the Sect. I'll be the one inside showing our leaders what true powers look like."

"But, Skylus..." Atmos begins, giving up when her feet leave the floor and she shoots upward. She reaches the top of the walls, then goes a little higher, hovering just above them.

"Do you think she can move sideways?" Jewel asks, studying her closely. "We've only seen her go up and turn around."

"Probably not," scoffs Pace.

Skylus remains stationary as she works on this very challenge, and Aura can't help but hope her powers restrict her from flying to the Sect. She shakes her head, trying to rid herself of the unkind thought. It would be easier to remain happy for Skylus if she tried to help them rather than abandoning them the first chance she got. At least she told them which direction to head, Aura supposes. That's something.

"I am Air!" Skylus shouts, her voice echoing through the corridor as she zooms off in the direction they came.

"That answers my question," Jewel says. "Seems she really has mastered her powers."

"Come on," says Pace, marching off down the corridor.

Jewel glances at her companions as they follow. Eight are now four. Amazingly, one from each Quadrant. Nobody has a partner anymore. Although, if they can find their way through this labyrinth, Atmos may be reunited with Skylus again at the Sect.

Aura hates the envy this thought spikes deep inside her. Pace has made it clear how much he misses Tempo, but he got to spend every day of his life with her growing up. Aura only just found Hayze. Yet their connection was so deep she felt like she'd known him forever. Why couldn't they have had more time? There are so many things about him that she doesn't know. Things that she was looking forward to finding out. And now she'll never get the chance.

They walk in silence, keeping their steps fast and focused, and Aura finds herself pretending Hayze is beside her. The thought of him gives her strength. Perhaps he's still with her in some way, just not physically. He's certainly in her heart. Just as he's entwined with her soul.

Aura's bare feet ache on the hard floor, her empty stomach groans and her throat becomes parched. She says nothing as they continue on, knowing the others must be feeling the same. Nobody speaks, as if the energy to do so would tip them over the edge.

Pace is at the front of the group and is the first to break the silence. "I can see the door ahead."

"It's too soon." Jewel shakes her head. "We walked much further than that before we turned around."

"You'll see," says Pace, not seeming to have the energy to argue.

Aura agrees with Jewel that it's too soon but hopes this is one of those things that doesn't make sense. Surely, at least one of these anomalies has to work in their favor?

They continue walking and after a few seconds, Atmos clears his throat. "Pace is right."

Pace slaps his nemesis on the back. "Knew you'd come around to me eventually."

Atmos shrugs off his hand. "You didn't make the door. You were just the first to see it."

Aura doesn't care who saw it first. She's just relieved it's there.

"Come on!" Jewel runs forward. "We made it."

Aura follows, keeping her expectations hunched low. Getting through the maze of cube-shaped rooms could take even longer than this corridor if they make the wrong choice.

"Maybe we need a rest once we get inside," Jewel suggests when Pace reaches for the door handle. "To help us think more clearly."

Pace glances to the sky. "Only if it's a quick one. Skylus has a big lead on us now."

Once again, Aura wasn't aware this was a competition, but she nods, not wanting to be the weakest link in this confusing chain.

Pace swings open the door and gasps. "Food!"

They rush forward at this exclamation, finding themselves in a square room as expected, but with a round table in the center with four water bottles and plates, each with an apple and a brown rectangle.

Aura takes her bottle and plate and immediately sits down, leaning on a wall as her feet throb in relief. She drains half the bottle and has two bites of her apple before she even stops to wonder why there were four plates and not five.

"They knew Skylus had left us," says Atmos, on the same train of thought. "I told you they're watching us."

"What's this brown thing?" Jewel asks.

"I think it's called a cookie," says Pace. "Just eat it. It's amazing."

Aura puts down her apple to give it a try, closing her eyes when the sweetness of the cookie hits her.

"It's heaven," she mumbles between mouthfuls. "Hayze would love this."

"He would," says Jewel kindly.

Pace drains the last of his water. "I can't remember the last time I peed."

"Not unusual when you're dehydrated," says Aura, having noticed the same thing.

"No, I mean since I woke up in the Deadwaters." He crunches down on his apple. "Anyone else been peeing?"

Aura tries to think and realizes Pace is right. She'd been so busy running for her life, she hadn't stopped to consider something so functional.

"Nope," says Atmos.

Jewel shakes her head shyly as she wipes some apple juice from her chin.

"Weird," says Pace. "Also, kind of convenient."

This makes Aura laugh.

"Do you think the leaders are drugging us?" Jewel asks. "That's why we sleep so well and wake up refreshed. Maybe they give us a drug to stop us from peeing."

"Cyclonis would never do that," says Atmos, glancing up as he searches for a clue as to how they're being observed.

"Cyclonis would totally do that." Pace stands, leaving his plate and bottle on the floor. "Come on. That's enough rest. Finish up, everyone."

"You're not in charge," says Atmos, putting his plate on the table.

"Never said I was." Pace looks at each of the four doors, including the one they just came through and chooses one.

"Why that one?" Jewel asks.

Pace shrugs. "It's in the direction of the Sect."

"I was thinking of that one, too," says Atmos from the other side of the room.

Aura gets up and tries not to groan as her legs protest. She quickly finishes her apple and follows Pace, crashing into him when he comes to a sudden stop before even getting across the threshold.

"Wrong choice," he mumbles, stepping back so the others can see.

Aura peers around him and gasps to find it's not another square room waiting for them.

It's something far more ominous.

And she has no idea what they're supposed to do.

CHAPTER
EIGHT
HAYZE

Hayze has images of Aqua in his mind. He has memories of what it smells and sounds and feels like.

Which means stepping out of the Sect should be a simple matter of one foot in front of the other. He knows the sky is likely gray and that he'll be stepping onto a pontoon, then another, then another in a world that's more water than land. He already knows Tide's trade master post is beyond the huts and houses, nearer to the wall separating Aqua from the Dead-waters. He knows it's surrounded by stalls as people trade wares, the sellers ready to pounce on the starving and desperate holding their precious pieces of edrian.

Yet he's experiencing every sight, sound, smell for the first time. Every image and memory isn't his own. They're Pace's. Filtered through his perspective—one of someone who grew up with this as normal, someone who's never questioned it, and someone who believes he has a right to be here.

Hayze has so much more to contend with.

His own life growing up in the Scorchlands is such a stark

contrast he may as well be looking at an alien planet. Everything looks...soggy.

And he knows that Pace's ticket into Aqua was probably thanks to stolen edrian.

Hayze had struggled to hear it when Aura voiced her suspicions in the Stormsphere, back when they assumed the memories they carried were theirs.

Have you ever stopped to wonder why your parents were able to save more in a few short years than my parents were able to save in their lifetimes, given they started at the same point?

But now that he's not influenced by Pace's biases, Hayze realizes she was right. Tide and Ondine stole Tempo's parents' edrian so they could get into Aqua and give their son a chance at a better life.

Hayze shakes his head. He can process that as he's making his way to Tide's stall. He scans his surroundings, noting the thick glass pontoons reaching out in every direction, joined by glass bridges. They're all clear, revealing the ocean they're floating on, creating the sensation of walking on water. Of being as one with it without being *in* it.

Hayze steps forward confidently, intending on blending in with the sea of people milling around. He strides with purpose as he makes his way from pontoon to pontoon, over winding paths and glistening bridges. There doesn't seem to be a corner in sight, everything is smooth and curved. Hurrying, he makes his way from the Sect toward the markets that surround the gates to the Deadwaters.

He already knows what will be there. Dozens of market stalls are scattered around, built of wood and glass, holding a kaleidoscope of food and wares. Lights will be glittering everywhere, glinting and refracting like stars as people move about as if the beautiful, fantastical view is perfectly normal.

It's what Pace grew up knowing.

It's what Tempo's parents wanted for their daughter.

Hayze shakes his head, as if that'll help sort the over-whelming amount of information in his mind—two people's worth—when it starts to rain. And it's not a gentle, warm trickle, but a saturating, unforgiving deluge. He goes from dry and overwhelmed to sodden and determined.

Pace's memories may be an added layer of knowledge he has to process, but being familiar with Aqua has given him an advantage. He needs to make the most of it.

He wipes away the water on his face, even though it's already coating his skin again before he's finished. A man glances at him as he hurries past, not seeming to notice the waterfall they're now standing in. In fact, he does a double take as he goes to look away. Hayze stiffens, instinctively covering the Fire tattoo on the back of his hand, but the man keeps moving.

Hayze resists the urge to hunch his shoulders, then stops himself from wiping at the rivers running down his face again. He needs to blend in. He needs to act like Pace—as if he belongs here.

He needs to get back in the Games before the leaders find him.

Yet the more he walks, the more obvious he feels. The number of people swells as he reaches the markets, and although it means he should blend in even more, a woman flinches as he draws near. The child by her side points at Hayze. People are most definitely looking at him. When the woman rakes her eyes down his body, he realizes why—he's wearing a white outfit like Aura and the others in the Games. Everyone here is wearing the blue body suits of Aqua. The same one he woke up in on the raft, believing that's what he'd worn all his life.

He's most definitely not blending in.

"Kelp!" hollers a woman somewhere to his left. "Dried, roasted, pickled! Best prices!"

Suddenly, Hayze's glad it's bucketing rain. Visibility is now only a few feet ahead, everything beyond is a sheet of gray. Most people are just blurry shadows, which means he would be too.

Still, he needs a change of clothes before someone starts asking questions.

"Coal at the right price!" shouts a man. "Make your hard-mined edrian go that little bit further!"

The pontoon beneath Hayze's feet bobs a little as someone turns away, grumbling under their breath. "Doesn't matter the price, I can't afford it."

The aged woman shuffles past Hayze, keeping her gaze on the glass beneath her feet. Water is running over it, warping the view of the ocean below, but that's not what draws Hayze's attention. The woman has no toes. What's more, she's clutching a few, small pieces of edrian to her chest using fingerless hands. Five blackened stumps surround her palm and little else, making Hayze's stomach somersault.

"Water suits of all sizes!" another man shouts. "Stay warm! Stay dry!"

Hayze straightens, not needing Skylus and Atmos here to tell him that's a very clear sign.

Except he doesn't have any edrian...

Hayze moves closer to the voice, anyway, and a stall that's a fascinating mix of wood and glass materializes through the rain. Lights glint all over the sides and roof, twinkling in the heavy rain and illuminating the suits hanging in rows.

Hayze only needs one of them. Somehow, he has to get it without the ability to pay for it... When he sticks out like a flower in the middle of the Scorchlands.

"Keep your children warm!" shouts a coal merchant from the next stall. "Roast your kelp—"

"Suits will keep you warm for a lot longer than coal!" the suit merchant hollers. He picks up one and waves it in the dry area under his roof. "New ones with gloves! No more frostbite!"

The coal merchant scowls. "No gloves can protect you from the cold of the ice caps!" He opens his arms out to encompass the piles of coal stacked under his own roof. "Coal is heat!"

Hayze gets an idea as the two men fight for sales. He steps back so he's obscured by the people walking past as he focuses on the smallest pile of coal in the merchant's stall. "I am Fire," he whispers.

Nothing happens.

Pressing his lips together, he focuses harder. Everything in this city is either damp or wet, or somewhere in between. He pictures heat vaporizing the moisture in the coal, drying the air, warming the black pieces.

A faint curl of smoke appears.

"Get your coal here! Best prices!"

"Suits for all ages!" the suit merchant shouts even louder. "Don't depend on expensive coal!"

The coal merchant shoots him a glare. "I got the best price I could," he hisses. "Those Fire people are greedy bastards."

Defensiveness spears through Hayze. His or Aura's parents could've mined the small pile he's focused on. They would've brought it to the wall surrounding the capitals, bartering for the best deal, walking away with precious edrian they need for food and clothes. What little is left over is saved up to get into Ignis.

The curl of smoke grows, the base becoming a glowing red. Seems Hayze's emotions are linked to his powers, just like with the feather in the Stormsphere. He channels the injustice that creates these divides both within Quadrants and between them. Injustice that has people selling their children.

A flame leaps to life.

"No!" gasps the coal merchant. "How is this possible?"

He rushes forward, fanning the coal. Hayze uses the opportunity to grow the flames under the pretense the flapping hand is feeding them.

"Here!" the suit merchant shouts. He throws aside the suit he was holding and grabs a piece of cloth, wets it in the rain, then throws it to the man a few feet away.

The coal merchant catches it, quickly patting down the flames and snuffing them out.

It's all the time Hayze needs to grab the suit and disappear around the back of another stall overflowing with pots and plants he's never seen before. With quick movements, he peels off his white suit then puts on the blue one. The stretchy material molds to his body, a little tighter than he'd like, but not a bad fit. It even has gloves, meaning he can cover the Fire tattoo on his hand. He'll find a way to make it up to the stall holder later.

It means Hayze can step back out with confidence.

It means he can break into long strides as he blends in with the throng of people, his focus on navigating the connected glass pontoons. He knows exactly where he needs to go.

To see Pace's father. The one person Oceania believes can get him back into the Games.

The stalls become larger, with sparkling window-panes revealing lanterns, coal stoves, a large selection of flippers. There are more glittering lights, roofs that extend out to cover the walkways. This is the more affluent part of Aqua, where those who got lucky and found large deposits of edrian buy and sell.

Or those who stole edrian to be here.

Hayze finds Tide where he expected him to be, within a glass-walled hut with the emblem of Water engraved into the sides. He pauses as he registers what else is here. A long line of people waiting to trade with Tide.

All because Tide is known to be an honest trader. He gives people a fair price for the little edrian they have left over after feeding themselves and their families. Whether it's coal they need, or kelp, or information about the weather so they know the best time to navigate the dangerous waters around the ice caps.

Hayze frowns. How is he going to get Tide's attention without raising suspicion? He doubts starting a coal fire is going to work so well twice in a row. The thought of having to wait until the end of the day isn't a palatable one, but one Hayze may have to swallow whether he likes it or not.

The next couple in line step up to the entrance of Tide's stall and Hayze jolts with recognition. He knows them. He quickly shakes his head. Pace knows them.

It's Marina and Bayou, Tempo's parents.

Tide stiffens as he registers who's approaching him and Hayze can't help but move closer. It's the only way he'll be able to hear what's being said over the constant drum of the rain.

Bayou puts down a handful of edrian pieces on the counter and raises one eyebrow. "What's it worth?"

A muscle ticks along Tide's jaw as he places the shiny, blue grains on a scale. On the other side are two plates. He puts a few, scant pieces of coal on one, a small pile of kelp on the other. The scales even out and without saying a word, he raises his gaze to the couple.

"It's worth more than that," Bayou says indignantly.

Tide shakes his head. "It's a fair price, and what anyone else would get."

"Edrian is becoming harder and harder to find," Marina hisses, leaning forward. "And you owe us."

Tide's spine looks like it just turned to stone. "I did what I had to do."

Bayou's hands clench at his sides. "You're a thief and a liar."

Hayze glances at the long line of people waiting, some who are shifting their weight as they grow impatient. They only know Tide as an honest man. It's the same man Pace knows.

But not the one Tempo and her parents know.

Tide glares at Bayou and Marina. "You don't think I've paid the price? I lost the woman Ondine was that night." His shoulders sag, his gaze dropping to the edrian. "Not that any of it mattered. I still lost my son in the end. No amount of edrian could've stopped it."

"My baby's gone," Marina says, her voice hitching. "I prayed every night that the agreement would be forgotten."

Hayze frowns. The agreement?

Someone jostles at the entrance to the trade stall. "Hey, some of us need to get food!"

"You'd want me to give you the same level of service. Isn't that why you're here?" Tide calls out. He sweeps his hand over the coal and kelp, looking back at Bayou and Marina. "Which one?"

"You're not going to give us more, are you?" Bayou snarls, eyes narrowed.

Tide shakes his head. "I need to be fair."

Marina steps back as if she's been slapped. "If only these people knew what you're capable of..."

Bayou reaches out to snatch their edrian, then stops. His hand clenches into a fist as he draws it back. "We'll take the kelp," he growls.

Tide nods stiffly, scooping up the green straps and passing

them to him. Bayou may hate Tide for what he did to them, but he also knows he'll get the fairest trade for his edrian. That must sting.

Bayou snatches the kelp, cradling it to his chest like the precious resource it is, before wrapping an arm around Marina's shoulders. Her soft sobs follow them as they walk back out into the rain.

Hayze watches them leave, blinking as water cascades down his face and body. In a land of so much rain, do people even notice tears anymore?

A clang has him turning back to Tide's stall. The one he's closing.

"Hey!" a woman shouts. "We still have edrian to trade!"

"Closing early," Tide snaps back, pulling down the length of canvas across the front. The lights around the entrance turn off, leaving it gray and blurry like the rest of the rain-soaked surroundings.

People grumble as they turn away, disappointed and clearly not looking forward to having to trade with someone else. It's the opening Hayze needs, even as much as he doesn't like how it came about. The interaction with Tempo's parents has affected Tide as much as it did them.

Hayze circles the trading hut, seeing Tide is already at the rear through the glass walls. He meets him at the back door, wondering how he's going to say why he's here, only for the man to scowl at him.

"No more trading today."

Hayze lifts his hands in a conciliatory gesture. "I'm not here to trade," he says, even though that's not exactly true. He has something Tide wants—information on his son—and Tide has something Hayze wants.

A way back into the Games.

"Not interested," Tide snaps, closing the glass door and

walking past Hayze as if he isn't even there. "See one of the other trade masters."

Except they can't help Hayze. He leaps after Tide, who's now walking away. "Tide!"

The trade master doesn't respond, his shoulders stooped as though he's protecting himself from the rain he's grown up in.

"Don't you want to know how I know your name?" Hayze calls out.

"Everyone knows my name," Tide growls, waving a dismissive hand. "Tide the Trusted. Tide the Fair."

Hayze snaps his mouth closed before his response can slip out. *Bayou and Marina know you as Tide the Traitor.*

Instead, he focuses on why he's here.

Why this father, who's gone to extreme lengths for his son, will want to listen to him.

He reaches Tide and grabs his arm, knowing the trade master will want this piece of information. "I know where Pace is."

Tide glares at him as he wrenches his arm away. "So do I," he spits.

Then continues stalking away.

As if Hayze has nothing he wants.

CHAPTER
NINE
AURA

Aura pushes past Pace to get a better look at the room behind the door he just chose. Actually, *room* isn't the right word. It's more like a cave. The rounded stone walls have vines with heart-shaped leaves climbing across them, and the floor is completely covered in broken glass. The sharp shards sparkle brightly even though Aura can't work out where the light is coming from. The cave stretches out at one end into a passageway that's impossible to reach.

"We need to try another room," says Pace. "Unless Atmos can teach us all to fly." His sarcasm is impossible to miss.

"I'll choose the door this time," says Atmos, already walking off behind them.

Aura turns her back on the strange cave and follows behind Jewel and Pace.

Atmos stalks past the table strewn with empty bottles and plates and throws open one of the other doors, groaning loudly.

"What is it?" Jewel presses up behind him. "Oh. Right..."

Curious, Aura squeezes past to see for herself what elicited those strange reactions, only to find the second room is identical to the first—another cave filled with vines and glass.

"They can't all be like this," she says, trying to remain hopeful. "Let's try again."

Atmos stalks off and throws open the third door. He immediately steps back and rolls his eyes. "It's the same."

Disappointment lodges in Aura's gut to mingle with the grief of having Hayze torn from her side. How can all three rooms be the same? They had to have come through one of those doors the first time they made their way in here.

Jewel walks to the door that leads to the long corridor.

"We can't go back in there," says Pace. "It goes forever."

"I just want to see something," says Jewel, making a strange sound when she opens the door. She steps back and Aura shakes her head to see the corridor has now vanished, replaced by a fourth cave. Really, she has no idea why any of these things continue to surprise her. She should be well used to nothing making sense anymore.

"So, which door do we choose?" Atmos scratches his head.

"Does it matter?" Pace cocks a brow. "They're all the same."

"Let's go in this one," says Aura, returning to the first door Pace opened. "Maybe Atmos can create a breeze and clear a path in the glass?"

Atmos puffs out his chest. "I can do that."

The four of them re-enter the cave and Aura's surprised to see a wooden raft is sitting on the glass directly in front of them.

"That wasn't here before," says Jewel. "Someone put it there just now. They knew we were coming back to this cave."

"Unless a raft has appeared in all the caves," says Pace. "I bet if—"

"It doesn't matter," Aura says. "We're here now. Clearly, we're meant to figure out how to move ahead."

"And clearly, we're supposed to use Water powers to do it." Pace bends down to inspect the raft.

"I still think we try our original plan," says Aura, her stomach a ball of nerves at the thought of having to fill this cave with enough water to float the raft over the glass, without overfilling it and drowning them all. For the billionth time since she woke up, she wishes Hayze was by her side. He'd know what to do.

To her relief, Atmos steps forward and straightens his spine. "Stand clear, everyone. I'll bring the wind right down the center of the cave and carve out a path in the glass to that passageway at the back."

"Ah, yeah about that..." Pace looks up from where he's still squatting at the raft. "You might want to save your energy. The glass is glued down." He pulls on one of the larger shards, demonstrating it's firmly stuck to the floor.

Atmos's shoulders slump, seeming disappointed not to be the one to be able to save the day. But he's nowhere near as disappointed as Aura.

"Maybe Pace could melt the glass," she suggests, trying to sell everyone on any plan that doesn't involve water.

"I'd kill us all in the process," says Pace. "Glass needs about two thousand degrees to melt."

"Then, maybe Jewel could—"

"Aura!" Pace stands up. "We have a raft. It's pretty clear which of our powers we need to use."

Aura flinches and Pace's face softens. He goes to her and puts a hand on each of her arms. "I'm sorry I spoke like that. It's just that you're avoiding what you know you have to do."

"I'm afraid to use my powers," says Aura truthfully, wishing once again Hayze was the one standing before her. With him by her side, she felt like she could do anything. Pace has become a great friend but he's no match for Hayze.

Nor does he fill out his skin-tight suit in quite the same way...

"Don't be scared," says Pace. "That's not the Aura we've come to know. You can do this. And we're all right behind you."

"Thanks, Pace." Aura steps up on her toes and gives Pace a quick kiss on the cheek, making him blush. "Don't take that the wrong way."

He laughs as he brings his fingertips to his cheek. "Don't worry, I know you only have eyes for guys from Aqua."

"Can't deny that." She steps away from Pace to concentrate on the task ahead. She needs to summon just enough water to float them over the glass on the raft. To get the right level of water, she needs to turn on her powers, then somehow, turn them off.

She closes her eyes and stretches out her hands, the other three teens lining up behind her.

"I am Water!" she shouts, her voice echoing off the stone walls.

She imagines water filling the cave, concentrating hard as she tries to make it a reality. Then she opens her eyes to check if she's having any luck.

And sees...

"Smoke!" she shouts, pointing at gray tendrils weaving their way through the vines at the other end of the cave. "Pace, what's happening?"

"I didn't do anything!" He holds up his palms. "I swear it."

"Liar!" Atmos plants his hands on his hips. "You're sabotaging us!"

Pace shakes his head. "I really didn't do anything."

"Then how do you explain that?" Atmos stabs a finger in the direction of the smoke. "And you can't blame your girlfriend this time."

"I never blamed Tempo for anything," Pace growls.

"Liar again," sneers Atmos. "We all heard you arguing in the Quakelands."

Pace throws a punch, his action so fast Atmos doesn't have time to even flinch. It lands square in his nose and a loud crack rings out around the cave.

"Pace!" Aura forces herself between the two males before Atmos can retaliate.

But she needn't have worried. Atmos is in no state to fight. He drops to his knees, holding his face and whimpering as blood pours from his nose. Jewel rushes to him and puts an awkward hand on his back, trying to soothe him.

"Now *that* I did do," sneers Pace, shaking his head as if the sight of Atmos offends him.

Aura turns to Pace and glares at him. "Pace, I don't know what you've done and what you haven't done. But I do know you need to fix it. Put out that fire. And do it now before this whole place catches alight."

"Or we could just start again in another cave," says Jewel, leaving Atmos to go to the door, only to find it doesn't budge. "It's locked! We can't get out."

Aura's heart sinks to realize they're being left with no choice but to try to figure this out the hard way.

"I'm going to try again," she says, holding back a cough as the smoke filters into her lungs. "If I can get water to enter the cave, it might save us."

"And I'll try to put out the fire," says Pace. "Even though, for the record, I didn't start it."

Aura doesn't want to say that nobody else could possibly have done it. He really hadn't taken that news so well when Atmos pointed it out.

Jewel nods, returning to Atmos and helping him to his feet, doing her best to calm him down so he doesn't try to hurt Pace right when they need him most.

Aura concentrates ahead, trying her best to bring out her Water powers, while Pace stands beside her.

"I am Fire!" he calls out.

"I am Water!" she follows.

The flames flare and billow as if being fanned and Aura glances to her side, checking that Atmos isn't the saboteur in their midst. One entire side of the wall of vines is alight now and Aura coughs, trying harder than she ever has to summon her Water powers.

And finally, it starts to rain. Well, not rain exactly, but precious drops of water seep from the ceiling of the cave, running out from between the stones and falling onto the broken glass below.

"It's working!" says Jewel. "Keep doing it, Aura."

"Yeah, with no thanks to Pace," Atmos mutters.

Thankfully, Pace either doesn't hear Atmos or he chooses to ignore him, instead remaining by Aura's side concentrating on extinguishing the fire he'd accidentally sparked. A fire which is only getting worse, no matter how much effort Pace puts in.

The water droplets increase in intensity, pattering on the glass and creating tiny rivers between the shards. More water trails down the walls of the cave, and finally starts to have an impact. The flames die out, filling the space with thick smoke instead.

"Get onto the raft," says Aura, trying not to lose her focus in case the water flow stops. They still need another inch at least. "We need to get out as quickly as we can."

Atmos and Jewel climb aboard, leaving space for Pace and Aura, who clamber on the back, both working with their Element as they move.

The water level rises more quickly, gaining momentum as if something has been unleashed and Aura draws in a breath, remembering the Stormsphere and the rain she created and had been unable to stop. She drops her focus and looks to Pace, acutely aware she doesn't have Hayze here to help her.

"We should finish now," she tells him. "The fire's out and the water's coming in fast. Let's move."

They drop their hands and steady themselves as the water level gets high enough and the raft lifts from the floor.

"Everybody paddle!" Pace shouts. "Including you, Atmos!"

He grumbles something about a broken nose, but Aura can't say she blames Pace for his comment. Skylus and Atmos had been useless on the raft in the Deadwaters, preferring to look for signs and beseech Eterna for help instead.

They paddle ahead, doing their best to direct the raft to the passageway.

Jewel coughs and Aura feels her eyes sting as they get closer to the smoking vines. This isn't like traveling by raft back home where the sky is crisp, and the water is clear. Here, the water is muddy, having collected dirt and dust as it trailed through the stones, and the air is hard to breathe.

They reach the passageway and maneuver their way into it, and a shiver runs down Aura's spine. It's only a narrow space, made to feel even more so by the thick vines clinging to the walls. She can only hope there aren't any creatures hiding amongst the leaves. Especially ones with teeth or claws.

"You okay?" Pace asks from beside her. "It's not too closed in for you?"

"I'm fine," she says, even though she can feel a sheen of sweat breaking out on her forehead.

"What's happening?" Jewel asks. "We're picking up speed."

Aura sits up straight as the others do the same. Yet even without paddling, their momentum continues to build.

"We're going downhill," says Atmos, his voice nasally. "Hold on!"

The raft races ahead, forcing Aura to grip onto the edge with white knuckles to stop herself from being flung off.

The passageway twists, turns and dips as their speed continues to increase and Aura squeezes her eyes closed as her hair is blown back off her face. Wincing as stray vines whip her, she thinks of Hayze, knowing she has to hold on for him. She's thrown left, then right, her body constantly pushing back as she desperately tries to stay upright. Filling this cave with water was a terrible idea! This is just another trick set up by the leaders. And they walked straight into it just because they were given a raft. They hadn't even considered how they might use Jewel's Earth powers.

"Waterfall!" screams Atmos from the front of the raft.

Aura hopes she heard wrong. That would be—

Her stomach rises into her throat as the passageway drops away from them and the raft becomes airborne. Jewel lets out an ear-piercing scream and the four of them are flung off and sent into freefall.

"No!" Aura shouts, her hands clawing at the air and her feet kicking wildly. "No!"

This can't be happening.

Skylus will be the only one of them to reach the Sect.

And the rest of them are about to use up their...

One chance.

TEN
HAYZE

Tide continues to walk away, the rain sleeking over his bald head and running down his blue-suited body. Within a couple of steps, he's blurred and gray. A couple more and he'll be completely obscured by the rain.

Hayze leaps forward, unwilling to believe Pace's father heard him right.

"I said, I know where Pace is!"

Tide keeps walking.

Hayze's arms slice through the deluge as he throws them out wide. "I know because I was in the Games with him!"

Tide stops, becoming a statue being battered by the very Element he worships. Then he slowly turns, his face so white his trio of scars look twice as deep. "What did you say?" he croaks.

Hayze covers the distance between them, conscious this isn't a public conversation. "That I was with Pace. I was part of the Elemental Games."

Tide blinks several times. "Impossible..."

"Our memories were switched," Hayze continues. "I

believed I was Pace and had grown up in Water. He still believes he's me and has grown up in Fire."

Which means Pace and Aura both believe they're wielding the opposite Element.

While the leaders set more and more challenging *games*.

Tide shakes his head. "You're lying. I don't know how, but you are."

"Then how do I remember you and Pace building his first raft?"

"Everyone in Water builds rafts," Tide growls.

"And all the times you spent stretched out on it, gazing at the night sky with Pace, telling stories about the constellations?"

Tide draws in a sharp breath, but then shakes his head again. "Someone could've told you we did that."

"And how do I remember paddling our barge as hard as we could? How do I remember Mom trying to stop Bayou and Marina from climbing on?"

Tide is so white, he's a glowing specter in the gray rain.

"How do I know that Ondine was hurt during the scuffle and fell into the water? How do I know it took long minutes to find her body?" Hayze's chest is so tight it stings his eyes. Even though these memories aren't his, they still hurt. The echo of the agonizing moments still reverberate through his body. "How do I know that you cried the whole way into Aqua as you carried her unconscious body?"

Hayze doesn't continue, even though the images do. Pace's mother woke up, but she was never the same. Her mind had splintered, the fear of those last moments always stayed with her.

Just like they did with Pace.

All he knew was that Bayou and Marina hurt his mother. It

was that hatred Hayze inherited, along with the rest of Pace's memories and understanding of the world.

Yet his love for Aura was stronger, uniting them despite the chasm of betrayal.

Just like it will unite them despite the chasm of distance and false reality.

And their final words to each other.

Tide reaches out and grabs his hand, as if he needs to ensure Hayze is real. Or to make sure he doesn't try to run. "How?" he whispers brokenly.

"I was also chosen. I'm from the Fire Quadrant. I was there, with Pace and Tempo."

And Aura.

Falling in love with her for the second time.

"I escaped." Hayze holds Tide's gaze. "And I want to go back in."

Tide blinks again, seeming to snap to attention. "Come on," he says, not releasing Hayze's arm.

Hayze lets him lead him along the pontoons, relief just as powerful a deluge as the rain coursing over him.

I'm coming, Aura.

Stay safe long enough for me to return to your side.

Everything will be okay once they're back together. No matter what's happened.

Tide stalks through the rain, nodding as people greet him, but not stopping as they register he has someone with him. Hayze doesn't make eye contact with anyone. The less memorable he is, the better.

Tide tugs him closer. "How did you get out?"

"I died," Hayze answers, his voice low. "I wasn't supposed to make it." Like Geo didn't.

Tide glances at him, his eyes narrowed against the rain. "How did you?"

"I have a damnatus good reason to stay alive," Hayze says, his voice hardening. "The same reason I need to go back in."

Tide looks at him for a long second before focusing on taking Hayze over a bridge and onto another glass pontoon. The scenery is changing, timber huts now dotting the pontoons rather than glass-walled stalls. But Hayze already knew that, just like he knows where Tide's taking him—Pace's home. There are fewer people as they navigate the curved walkways that wind through the Quadrant, for which Hayze is glad. Not long and he can be out of sight in this world that he knows, yet doesn't belong in.

"Tide," a woman calls out warmly from where she was sitting under the porch of her hut. "You're home early. Is everything okay?"

Tide lifts a hand and waves but doesn't stop as the woman pushes to her feet, clearly expecting him to stop. "Just quickly checking in."

The woman nods, her face softening. "Good waters to you, Tide."

It's only once they reach Tide's hut, a rounded wooden structure that's bigger than most, that Hayze remembers what's inside. That he realizes why the woman didn't question Tide's early return.

The soft crying seeps through the wooden walls, undampened by the rain. Tide's shoulders hunch a little as he pushes open the door, bringing Hayze inside. The waterfall above is abruptly cut off, instantly becoming a low hum and a backdrop to the keening that fills every inch of the tidy hut.

Tide releases Hayze and walks forward to the woman sitting at a carved wooden table that's a sharp contrast to the metal one Hayze grew up eating at. Her knees are tucked up, her head resting on her arms so the remaining tufts of her hair hide her face. She's wearing the blue suit of Aqua, yet it's shredded and torn, hanging from her body like limp seaweed.

Tide kneels before her, his hand hovering over her arm. "Ondine," he says softly.

She simply curls up tighter into herself, her sobs escalating.

"We have a guest," Tide adds, taking his hand away without touching her.

She shakes her head, burying her face in her arms even deeper. "I don't care. He's...g-gone. The a-agreement..."

Tide pushes to his feet in a rush. "Was our only chance," he whispers.

"Lies!" Ondine screeches, her fingers digging into her skin. "All lies!"

Tide's face is pained as he turns away and moves to the center of the room. His wife's sobs turn to wails, making Hayze wince. He remembers the urgency to get back. The weight of responsibility Pace carries. He was often the one tasked with calming her down.

And now Ondine's lost that.

Hayze steps forward cautiously, then crouches down. "His love is still here. You'll always have that."

Ondine glances up, her haunted eyes looking over her clasped arms.

Hayze's lips twitch. "And now he has the opportunity to make this right."

Pace and Tempo carried the memories of being childhood sweethearts, Hayze and Aura's memories. The lies and secrets that defined who they are didn't exist in the Games for them.

Ondine's lip trembles as she falls silent. Her eyes flood with tears. Slowly, carefully, she nods. She doesn't ask how Hayze knows this, simply accepts his words. Possibly because they're what she needs to hear.

Possibly because she can recognize them for what they are —the truth.

With a shuddering sigh, she tucks her head back into her arms. The only sound in the cabin becomes the steady thrum of rain.

"This way," Tide says gruffly.

Hayze stands to find him pointing at the floor. He walks over, seeing a rug has been pushed back, revealing a hatch. Tide opens it, exposing a square of ocean, blue and fathomless.

"Why? Where are we going?" Hayze asks, now tense.

Tide's gaze flickers to Ondine, then quickly away. "Jump in."

Hayze looks down at the water beneath, hesitating. The belief that Tide was taking him back to the Games was an assumption.

And he's seen where they can end up...

"Hurry," Tide hisses, glancing at Ondine again.

Hayze jumps before he can give himself any more time to think. Cool water encases him in a strange feeling of being buoyed and smothered all at once. There's a splash and an explosion of bubbles as Tide jumps beside him. He breaches the surface to slide the hatch back across the floor of the cabin above them.

"This way," he says before drawing in a deep breath and diving under.

Hayze watches him power forward, moving in one direction only. Down.

Treading water, Hayze frowns. "A little more information would be nice," he mutters.

Right before drawing in a deep breath of his own and also diving down. Blinking away the sting in his eyes, Hayze focuses on two things.

Following Tide.

And the hope that each stroke is bringing him closer to Aura.

The water becomes cooler and darker, heavier. Tide doesn't alter his trajectory, slipping through the water in sinuous, easy motions. Yet Hayze can't seem to find a rhythm. The two parts of his mind are warring with each other. Pace's memories of swimming before he could walk battle his own childhood memories of fighting off a sponge bath because he didn't want that much water touching him.

It means his motions are smooth one moment, stilted the next. It means he falls behind as Tide continues his downward trajectory to what appears to be the bottom of the ocean. Focusing, Hayze spears one arm in front of the other, even as he has no idea where they're going or why.

Only that it's his only chance of ever seeing Aura again.

Within seconds, his lungs are spasming.

His chest is caving in.

Darkness is crowding his vision.

Hayze ignores it all. Stroke. Swim. Stroke. Swim. Instead of focusing on the pain, he focuses on each beat of his heart. Each one is carrying him forward in time.

One where he'll get back with Aura. Or die trying.

The rock formation that appears in the gloom is a shock. So is seeing Tide disappear between a barely visible crack in the dark stone. Hayze follows, gripping onto the slippery surface as his mind screams for him to shoot back to the surface. Back to air.

The crack turns out to be a narrow opening and he swims in without looking back. Whatever's on the other side will either save him or end him.

Blackness is all that greets him. Wet, endless blackness.

And a hand wrapping around his arm and hauling him up.

Suddenly, Hayze's head breaks the surface. Somehow,

impossibly, he can breathe! He draws in great gulps of air, breaks into a fit of coughing, then fights for more air. Tide hauls him forward until they hit rough rocks. He releases Hayze, then splashes onto the stone shelf.

Soft lighting comes on, leaving Hayze blinking and stunned.

They're in a small cave, one with large, white doors staring back at him just as blankly.

Tide climbs out of the water and walks toward them. "If you want to go back into the Games, this is the way."

Hayze also drags himself out, his body instantly feeling heavier even as it's easier to move. "You couldn't have mentioned that before we swam to the center of the Earth?" he mutters.

Tide shakes his head. "It's clear you're Fire." He wipes his tattoo over the sensor by the door. "You're all smolder and blaze."

Hayze grins. "Thanks."

"It wasn't a compliment," Tide states flatly as the doors open.

Revealing a room that's disturbingly familiar.

All white, it holds two beds, although that's where the similarities quickly end.

There are no screens on the walls. And the beds are bigger. More like a cocoon...

Hayze walks forward, trying to understand what he's seeing. The sides of each one curl up and around, faint white veins pulsing over the sides as if it's a skin. The one on his left is empty. Tempo's. Turning right, he draws in a sharp breath as he sees a face he recognizes.

A choked sound wrenches from Tide's throat as he gravitates toward it. Hayze moves closer cautiously, once more taking in what had his breath stabbing the back of his throat.

Pace lies within, his eyes closed, his face peaceful, his chest steadily expanding and deflating. It glows softly with light, encasing him in gentle white. It looks peaceful, but Hayze sees the way his friend's eyes flicker behind his lashes in rapid, jerky movements. Hayze wonders what he's experiencing.

Whether Aura's okay.

It's quickly followed by the realization she's in a pod, too, somewhere in Ignis.

"How is he?" Tide asks in a raspy voice.

"He hasn't stopped fighting," Hayze says, trying to reconcile the body in front of him with the spirited guy who was given his memories. "And once he knows he's Water, I have no doubt he's going to be an Elemental force to be reckoned with."

Tide lets out a breath that Hayze wonders has been trapped inside since the Games started. Except Tide almost looks...excited.

Another thought has Hayze stepping back, his wide eyes shooting to Tide. "You knew he was down here." He looks up at the white ceiling, picturing the glass pontoon and wooden cabin somewhere above. "He's been right below you this whole time."

Tide looks away, remaining silent as his hands clench compulsively by his sides.

"You knew what he was chosen for and you let it happen!" Hayze throws out, his voice rising.

Tide's head snaps back. "What choice did I have?" he shouts. "The agreement was binding! Irreversible! At least this way I could still be close to him. Still be here if he makes it out..."

Hayze snaps his mouth shut. Oceania sent him to Tide for a reason. In his twisted way of protecting the son he entered into some agreement with, he's created a way for Hayze to get back into the Games. He doesn't get to judge decisions he's about to take advantage of.

"How do they make it out?" he asks, his gaze falling on Pace.

"All I know is he has to reach the Sect." Tide turns blazing eyes to Hayze. "You must promise to do everything you can to make sure my son does that."

Hayze nods, glad that's a promise he can make. "Pace is my friend. I won't let him die in there."

Tide lets out a breath. He reaches out a hand to touch Pace's face, but stops, his actions echoing the ones with his wife. It paints the picture of a man, isolated by his decisions, weighed down by regret.

"Get in," he says, turning to the empty cocoon-bed. "The pods are how you connect to the G— To the simulation."

Hayze knows Tide was about to say *Games* but stopped. He's glad someone else has realized what a farce that title is. Games imply fun and enjoyment.

But the cost of losing these is dying.

Climbing in, Hayze settles down in the pod. He makes himself comfortable in the reclined position, his arms slotting into grooves as his head is cupped by softness. The whole thing encases him in warmth and light, and he hates that it's the most comfortable thing he's ever lain on.

Tide leans over, his brows scrunched low. "You would've been unconscious the first time you went in. This time, it's best if you're as relaxed as possible."

Hayze wipes the incredulous expression from his face as he nestles in a little more deeply. "Tell me it's not going to hurt, and we'll be in business."

"It doesn't," Tide says, stepping back. "You won't feel a thing."

Hayze closes his eyes, not wanting to see whether Tide's

lying. Instead, he focuses on the image of Aura in his mind. On the promise that he'd never leave her.

"Don't forget the leaders will see you the moment you're back in," Tide says. "They'll hunt you down and take you back out. I'll buy you some time, but that's all I can do."

Hayze's eyes almost snap open. That's Tide's way of calming him? Dropping a dire warning and then—

White light engulfs Hayze, snatching consciousness and reality.

He's on his way.

Back to Aura.

CHAPTER
ELEVEN

AURA

Aura braces herself for impact, unsure if she's about to connect with water or earth. Or even a pile of broken glass. Where this waterfall finishes is as big a mystery as how it got here in the first place.

The only thought that comforts her as she falls is that if she used up her *one chance* in the Stormsphere, then at least she no longer has to endure a life without Hayze.

There's a sudden pressure on her wrists and ankles as her momentum is stalled. Something grips her around the waist and she's jerked to an abrupt halt. Her breath leaves her lungs as her body burns in pain. It takes her a moment to realize what brought her to a stop.

The vines with heart-shaped leaves lining the walls of this strange cave have reached out, their tendrils wrapping around her and keeping her suspended. The waterfall behind her continues to rage as it cascades into a pool of water several feet below.

She drags in a deep breath, fighting against the constriction in her chest. Testing the strength of the vines, she quickly realizes the more she struggles, the more tightly they cling. She tries to relax against their bonds, wincing as her skin is pinched between wiry stems. The shape of the leaves crawling across her face suddenly seems ominous. It's like the vines have come to life with pumping veins and beating hearts.

"Aura!" Jewel calls out. "Up here!"

She looks up to see Jewel hanging a few feet above her, also wrapped in vines. Atmos and Pace are a little higher up again, both struggling wildly.

"Don't fight it!" Aura shouts. "It makes it worse."

"Can't be worse," Pace pants. "I can't...breathe."

They need a plan. And they need it fast. Aura's head spins as she turns over the possibilities. But it's hard to concentrate when the air is being slowly squeezed out of her. Maybe they'd have been better off to fall. At least it would have been over quickly. These vines are more of a curse than a blessing. Even someone from Air would have to agree with that.

"Atmos!" she calls. "Can you make a breeze?" She wants to feel cool air on her face, even if it has no chance of making it into her lungs.

"I don't think he can," Jewel wheezes. "He's stopped moving."

Aura looks up to see Jewel is right. Atmos is completely still, hanging in his vines, reminding Aura of the hammock she used to sleep in on her family's barge. Except that had been comfortable. This is torture!

More vines stretch out from the walls, their leaves fluttering as they inch toward the waterfall.

"Should I make a fire?" Pace suggests.

Aura grimaces, not liking that idea one bit. With the limited control Pace has demonstrated with his powers, he's likely to set the whole cave alight. Water won't be any help either. If the level of the pool below rises high enough to reach them, they'll drown.

Maybe Earth powers could be useful?

"Jewel, plants are made from carbon," says Aura, grateful she's still able to speak. "You could try manipulating them, so they let go of us."

"She can barely...breathe," says Pace, looking down at Jewel.

Aura's heart sinks at the thought of losing another friend when she's already lost so much. "You hang in there, Jewel, do you hear me? You too, Pace."

"Already doing that." Pace rocks in his vines.

Aura's surprised anyone can joke at a time like this. Then again, sometimes when things are so bad, humor is all you have left. She shifts a little, trying to take some of the pressure off her left wrist, which is twisted at an awkward angle. Except the movement only makes it worse.

"Try taking the water...out...of the vines." Pace's voice is labored and it's clear he's struggling to speak. "Like...the jellyfish."

Aura sighs, knowing it's a good plan. If only she had the skills to pull it off. Or the energy. It's hard to so much as breathe, let alone wield a power she's never been able to master. Which makes it too risky again. But finding the words to explain this to Pace are beyond her. So, instead she channels every ounce of what she has left inside her to try.

"I am Water," she croaks, imagining the moisture being sucked out of every last plant that's choking her.

Nothing happens, so she tries again, the vines only continuing to grow in strength. So, instead, Aura pretends she's on her barge with her parents in the next room. If she can fool her mind into believing she's safe, maybe she can die without her heart trying to beat its way out of her chest. Or at least buy herself enough time to come up with another plan. One that will actually work.

As more vines reach out and wind themselves around her, Aura thinks of Hayze. She imagines his handsome face. His strong chest. His powerful arms. But most of all, she pictures his dark, soulful eyes that had a way of seeing right into her soul. It's hard to believe he was ever her enemy. In fact, she refuses to believe it. He's always been with her. Just like he'll be with her forever, in whatever form that takes. Maybe Atmos and Skylus's beloved Eterna is real, and Aura and Hayze can live out eternity sitting on a fluffy white cloud?

"Aura!"

Her eyes flicker open at the sound of her name before she decides she imagined it and closes them again.

"Aura!"

This time, her eyes fly open. That wasn't just her name.

It was Hayze's voice.

Is she dead already? Surely if that were the case, she'd no longer be able to feel any pain. Fluffy white clouds aren't supposed to hurt.

"Aura! Is that you?" There's the sound of splashing, like someone is wading through water. No, not just *someone*.

"Hayze!" she calls, wriggling as much as the vines will allow her. "Here!"

"I can't reach you," he shouts from below.

She blinks, wincing as she tries harder to draw in a breath. How can it be Hayze? He used up his chance and then died again. He's gone. Yet, somehow, he's right here.

Joy filters through every one of her constricted cells.

Hayze came back to her.

He's. Right. Here.

She tries to peer out from between the leaves but there are so many of them now, it's useless.

"Aura, you need to use your Fire power to break the ties," Hayze calls up to her. "I'll catch you when you fall. Do it now while you still can."

Fire power? Has Hayze hit his head? He's talking nonsense. He must be confused and meant to say Water. Perhaps he had the same idea as Pace about removing the moisture from the vines. But if that's the case, why can't he just do it himself?

Deciding she has no choice but to give it a go, she prepares to use what little strength she has left.

"I am Water," she says again, with as much force as she can muster.

"No, Aura!" Hayze shouts. "You're *not* Water. You're Fire. You always have been. That's why you can't harness Water. You're not going to, no matter how hard you try. You're Fire."

Aura frowns, ceasing her fight against the vines as she tries to understand why Hayze is talking such rubbish. Is that even him? Or has this strange world reproduced his voice as its cruelest trick yet?

"I can't do it for you, Aura," says Hayze's voice. "I might burn you. You need to direct the flame."

"I am Water," she sobs.

"No, Aura," he pleads. "You have to trust me. Please! You're not Water. You're Fire. I'm Fire. They swapped our memories with Tempo and Pace."

Swapped memories? Now she knows this can't be the real Hayze. He'd never make up an impossible story like that. People can't just swap memories.

"Aura, I love you," the imposter continues. "And you love me. It's the way it's always been. I came back for you. I'll *always* come back for you."

She soaks in his voice, even if she knows it's not the real Hayze.

"I love you, too," she whispers as the vines wrap tighter, talking to the real Hayze, wherever he may be. *"Always."*

"None of this is real!" Hayze's voice shouts. "Aura! Jewel! Pace! Atmos! Listen to me. None of this is real. Even dying isn't. Don't let your mind believe it. You're completely safe right now, no matter how much danger you feel like you're in."

The last of the air is squeezed from Aura's lungs and her heart races to realize she's unable to draw in more.

"Fine," huffs Hayze. "I'll do it. Everyone, remember, this isn't real! Nothing can hurt you here. Hold on."

Aura's world becomes fuzzy as the roaring sound of a flame fills the cave. It's so loud it drowns out the relentless flow of the waterfall. There's the scent of smoke and, still completely wrapped in vines, Aura plunges down, landing with a splash in the pool below and sinking into its depths.

Then there are arms around her. Lifting her and pulling away vines until she can see. Breathe. And move.

She blinks up at her savior.

It's Hayze. It's really Hayze. No imitation could be this real. This warm. This gorgeous. How could she ever have doubted it?

He holds her close to his chest as she heaves for oxygen. Carrying her to the edge of the pool, he sets her down. His fingertips trail across her cheek and she leans forward, desperate to feel his lips on hers.

Except his kiss is so brief, she barely feels it at all before he turns away. Being separated from him so soon is agony and she whimpers, until she sees what he's doing.

"I am Fire!" he shouts, facing the wall of vines. A blast shoots out of his hands, the flames catching on the tendrils that had reached out to wrap around Jewel.

Aura's hand flies to her mouth as she wonders what

sorcery he used to do such a thing. It's not possible. Hayze is Water. Just like Aura.

The vines burn through and Jewel plummets, landing with a splash and sending a wave of water rushing at Aura. Hayze wades out and retrieves what looks like a bundle of leaves.

"Unwrap Jewel so I can get to the others," he pants, placing Jewel at Aura's side on the damp ground and turning straight back.

Aura finds the strength to get herself on her knees and tear at the vines, pulling them off Jewel to expose first her face, then her chest and arms. She's pale, with a bluish tinge, and Aura shakes her roughly, trying to rouse her.

There's the roar of a flame behind them and another splash, but Aura keeps her focus on her friend.

"Jewel! Wake up!" She presses her lips to Jewel's cold mouth and breathes air into her lungs. "Come on, Jewel! Breathe!"

Jewel's eyes flutter open as her spark of life returns. "Aura."

"Oh, thank goodness." Aura works on freeing Jewel from the remaining vines, stopping only when Hayze delivers another bundle of leaves.

Jewel takes over untangling her legs, while Aura gets to work on the newest arrival, quickly discovering it's Atmos. She manages to get him unwrapped and breathing just as Hayze hauls Pace out of the water and places him down. Aura hurries to help Hayze pull the vines off Pace, who's even bluer than Jewel had been.

"You have to live," Hayze growls at him. "Or at least realize you're not actually dying. Start breathing! Now!"

Aura elbows Hayze out of the way so she can breathe into Pace's mouth in the same way she did for Jewel. It works and his eyes flutter open as he gasps for air.

"He's alive!" She pulls back, her own breathing ragged.

"Thank fractal for that," Hayze sighs. Aura had never realized he cared so much about Pace. This seems like more than just a regular level of concern. Then again, Hayze is the kindest person she's ever met. It makes sense he'd want everyone to survive.

Pace looks up at them, but instead of the spark of life that had entered Jewel's eyes, it's pure terror.

"Behind you!" he gasps, pointing.

Aura and Hayze spin around to see more vines reaching out for them.

"Get back!" says Hayze, leaping in front of the terrified group. "And stay down!"

The four of them are too exhausted to argue, so do as they're told, shielding their faces with their hands.

"I am Fire!" Hayze shouts, his delusion seeming to be quite persistent.

Flames burst from his palms and shoot out at the vines, torching them before they can take anyone captive. He continues, directing the flames pouring from his hands and scorching the vines, sending their charred ashes fluttering into the pool below.

"He's not Fire," says Pace, his eyes wide and his jaw hanging open. "I'm Fire. He's Water. He's even wearing a blue suit. Explain that."

Aura shakes her head, unable to explain anything.

Jewel coughs as smoke drifts their way.

"Atmos, blow the smoke away from us," Pace says. "Jewel can't breathe."

But there's no need for Atmos to do anything. Hayze waves his hands, and the fire extinguishes as quickly as it had sparked, taking the smoke with it.

"What the flaming heck?" Pace's eyes widen even further. "How did you do that?"

Ignoring him, Hayze goes directly back to Aura and helps her to her feet. He wraps his arms around her and pulls her close.

"Are you okay?" he asks, tilting up her face so he can look into her eyes.

She nods.

And finally, he gives her a proper kiss.

It's everything she dreamed of since he left her, and a whole lot more.

His mouth is warm against her lips. His fingers desperate as they thread through her hair. His tongue searching as he reaches out, wanting more.

She moans as heat sparks between them, burning so hot she could almost believe they're both from Fire. Molding her body to his, her hands slide to his back as she yearns to explore every part of him.

She missed him. And she missed doing this with him. Which makes her determined never to be separated from him again.

Everything about him is familiar. Everything about him is just...so right.

"It's you." She pulls back to look at him, fighting the swell of emotion bubbling in her chest. "It's you. It's really you."

He shakes his head, leaning in for one more gentle kiss. "Except, it's not really me. And it's not really you."

"I don't understand." Her hands thread around his waist as she draws in his essence, no longer caring what's real and what's in her head. All that matters is this very moment where she's back in Hayze's arms.

He lets his hands slide down her arms until he's holding hers in front of her. Turning them over, he forms a cup with her palms.

"You *are* Fire, Aura," he says. "Call on it. You'll see."

"I'm not." She shakes her head, hating that he's insisting on this.

"Trust me." He raises his brows. "Call on Fire."

Aura lets out a deep sigh. It seems Hayze will need to be proven wrong before he returns to his senses.

"I am Fire," she says, staring down at her hands, not at all surprised when nothing happens.

"Again," Hayze urges. "But this time, mean it."

Resisting the urge to roll her eyes, Aura focuses on her hands and draws on her remaining energy.

"I. Am. Fire." Her voice is guttural, more like a growl, and the words unleash something deep inside her she didn't know existed.

She concentrates on her palms as the world around her melts away.

And a tiny flame appears.

"I am Fire," she says again.

And this time, she means it.

TWELVE

HAYZE

Aura slowly lifts her gaze to Hayze's, her blue eyes blinking in shock and wonder. He grins like he's never grinned before. It starts somewhere in the center of all creation, the place his connection to Aura was born, and finishes outside of him, filling the entire cave they're standing in.

"We are Fire," he whispers, words he's looked forward to saying his entire life.

They've spent their childhood and adolescence training for this moment. So many hours, days, years dedicated to searching for the powers locked within them. Hayze wishes his and Aura's parents could be here to see this moment.

Even as he wishes they were alone.

One kiss is not nearly enough after their forced separation. After the terror of not knowing if he'd be able to get back to her.

After the final words they said to each other before waking up on a raft in the middle of the Deadwaters...

Aura looks back down at the fragile flame flickering in

her palms. Hayze curls his hands around hers, nursing the undeniable truth with her. "But...how?" she whispers reverently.

He huffs out a soft laugh. "By being you. The true you." He closes his hands, encasing the flame their connection sparked, protecting it in the same way he'll protect her for as long as he lives. "The girl I've loved all my life."

Aura's brows twitch with confusion, but as she raises her eyes, she doesn't take her gaze from his. "Hayze..."

There's so much to explain. So much impossibility for her to bring into the realm of truth. A fracture she doesn't remember that needs to be healed.

Yet his gaze falls to her lips. Even as Hayze knows the leaders are watching, reacting to him sneaking back into the Games, all he can think about is kissing Aura again. He's here with her, holding her, despite the odds.

Right now, that's everything.

He leans down, his breath catching as she pushes up. The heat he never questioned but now understands on a whole new level flares to life—

"What the hell is going on?" Pace shouts, his voice exploding through the cave.

Hayze pulls back, his jaw clenched, as Aura drops down. He turns, finding Pace staring at them with his hands jammed into his hair.

"What just happened?" he demands, his voice rising even more.

Jewel crosses her arms as she turns away, her throat working. Atmos looks like a stiff breeze just went places it shouldn't. Hayze sighs, realizing there's some serious explaining to do. He glances around the cave, noting the singed vines are now hanging limply from the cave walls. He doubts very much the leaders will bring them back to life.

Right now, they'd be watching those six screens with the most focus since the Elemental Games started.

Hayze scans the rounded ceiling, the dark walls, even as he knows he'll never see the cameras recording this very moment. The technology used to create the Games is beyond his understanding. They could be tapping into their senses, recording what each one of them sees for all he knows.

He slips his hand into Aura's, knowing there's no easy way to convey this. "None of this is real."

Aura blinks back at him, the others mirroring her blank expression. Hayze can't blame them. If the tables were turned, he'd be thinking he's singed his sanity too.

"Everything is virtual reality. A simulation," he explains.

Aura's brows scrunch down as she raises a hand to rub them. Hayze notices the subtle way she shifts away from him. "A what?"

"We're plugged into a computer-generated environment that appears to be so real, we think it is," Hayze says, threads of tension tightening through his insides at the growing distance. "I wouldn't lie to you."

Atmos scowls, then crosses his arms. "Eterna wouldn't do that to us."

"The leaders would." Hayze glances around, finally registering the Air teen is alone. Seems Skylus was the next victim of the Games. "I'm sorry about Skylus, but she might not be dead."

"Of course she's not," Atmos huffs. "She's flown to the Sect."

Flown? To the Sect?

"She harnessed her powers in ways we haven't," Aura says, smiling a little. "It was pretty impressive."

"You weren't able to harness yours because you're not Water," Hayze says gently, squeezing her hand.

Aura opens her mouth, but Pace stomps over toward them.

"This ground is definitely real." He kicks a stone into the pool, looking triumphant as a splash splinters the air. "That's the water we almost drowned in."

"It looks real. It sounds real. It feels real." Hayze shakes his head. "But it's not. That's how I'm still alive. I never died."

Aura's hand jolts in his. He turns back to her, watching her closely. She's the only one he needs to believe him. But Aura doesn't look at him, instead glancing at the dark soil, the rippling water, even their clasped hands.

Pace stops in front of Hayze, breathing. "Then if I punch you, it won't hurt? If I wrap my hands around your throat, you won't choke?"

"Pace..." Aura starts, but Hayze steps in front of her, his eyes narrowing on Pace.

"You want to hit me like you did Atmos?" he growls, enjoying the flicker of satisfaction at Pace's surprise that he knows. "Because there's more to me than hot air."

"Rude," Atmos mutters, even as he takes a cautionary step back.

Hayze presses his face an inch closer to Pace's. "You want to know the real head screw? They swapped our minds, Pace, just like they did Aura and Tempo's. I'm Fire, you're Water. Your memories are mine, the ones I had were yours."

"I don't know where you've been, but it's messed with your head," Pace spits. "You're crazy!"

"Then how did I know you hit Atmos? How did I burn the vines?" Hayze steps back, his anger still smoldering, but wanting to be close to Aura again. "How did Aura conjure Fire?"

"You did it! You're the one who made the fire in Aura's palm."

Hayze narrows his eyes at Pace, a small part of him regretting fishing him out of the pool. All that was going through his mind at the time was his promise to Tide to keep his son safe. And that if something happens to Pace, the Water trade master would no longer have a reason to keep Hayze in the Games...

He certainly wasn't thinking of the way Pace held Aura in the maze.

Of how Aura put her mouth on his to help him breathe.

Or how Pace is going to be the one who's hardest to convince of the truth.

"How did I conjure Fire if I'm Water?" he growls. "And why is my tattoo the Fire symbol?" Hayze thrusts out his hand so Pace can get a better look.

Pace throws his arms out wide. "I don't know! Maybe that's the simulation! Maybe your tattoo is fake. Maybe you've harnessed two Elements!"

Hayze rolls his eyes. "That's your best explanation? We're definitely moving into the realm of make-believe now."

"You're. Not. Me," Pace grinds out, his hands clenching and unclenching.

"Heckus no," Hayze snaps. "I sure as fractal am not you. But that doesn't mean I didn't spend every moment since we woke up on the rafts with your memories of Water. Just like you have mine of Fire."

Atmos sits down in a rush, as if his knees just gave out. "This is..."

Jewel shakes her head. "Unbelievable," she finishes for him. She looks from Hayze to Aura to their surroundings. "How could any of this be a simulation? I can smell the smoke from the burned vines!"

Hayze turns back to Aura, focusing on her. It's her opinion that matters. It's her who he needs to believe him. "When you don't know what's real, you have to trust your heart." He takes her hand again. "What does it say, Aura? What is your heart telling you?"

She gazes up at him, no doubt trying to reconcile his words with their surroundings. The faint rustle of dead leaves. The scent of water and soil and smoke. The taste of ash still clinging to the air. Yet he knows their lifelong connection is also just as real.

It just needs to be *more* real.

Her fingers tighten around his. "Why are the leaders doing this?"

Relief, love, joy, then a whole lot more love courses through him. "They call this the Elemental Games. They're all about unlocking our powers."

Aura mouths the word "games," no doubt trying to process how such a childlike, light-hearted term has been used to label what they've gone through. Then she frowns. "To what end?"

"I don't know. All I know is that we—"

"Of course she believes you!" Pace cries, his hands back in his hair as he grips his head. "I grew up in the Scorchlands! I've loved Tempo all my life. I used to draw her pictures on the walls of her bunker!"

Hayze spins around, noting the uncertainty flickering across Jewel and Atmos's faces. They don't have time for Pace's stubborn denial.

Plus, the leaders are probably watching this, chuckling to themselves as Hayze tries to explain the unbelievable. And that pisses him off.

He picks up a stick and holds it out to Pace. "Fine, then. Draw me something."

"What?" He scowls, knocking it away. "We don't have time—"

"Draw something, anything," Hayze grits out through

clenched teeth as he brings it back. "Just like you did in the Scorchlands. Prove who you are, Pace."

The final words have him snatching the stick, curling his lip in annoyance even as he's unable to let the challenge slide. "Give me some room."

Hayze steps back, reaching down to find Aura's hand already waiting for his. She believed him, despite every sense telling her otherwise. He didn't think it was possible, but his love grows. Deepens. Stretches beyond the realms of anything he could've imagined.

He almost snorts. Being forced into a fake reality, then discovering the only real thing is what he feels for her will do that.

Jewel moves to stand beside Aura, Atmos also shuffling in closer to Hayze, both watching silently as Pace presses the tip of the stick to the ground. Only a few feet from the water's edge, he has a clear canvas.

A stretch of soil waiting to be graced with his masterpiece.

"I'll draw Tempo," he says resolutely, the stick twitching in his grip. "The girl I grew up loving."

For the first time, Hayze realizes neither Pace nor Tempo have ever mentioned the awful words that were exchanged the day before their eighteenth birthday. It's like they don't remember the rift that was created between two hearts that had started to beat as one.

Hayze mentally pushes the thought away. This isn't the time to wonder about it. He needs everyone to see the truth. The finer details can be revealed later.

Pace scratches in a curved line, then another mirroring it on the other side. His frown deepens as the shape clearly lacks symmetry. Hayze thinks it's supposed to be the outline of a head. Pace continues on, adding two almond eye shapes.

Several inches too high.

Huffing, Pace works even faster, flicking and twitching. He scores in deep, long lines for the features, etches short, lighter curves and waves for the hair. When he steps back, the final piece looks like a child drew one of the monkeys from the Quakelands. After it failed to escape the forest fire...

Pace scowls as he struggles to reconcile the image in his mind and the drawing in the sand.

Hayze picks up his own stick. "This is Tempo."

With bold lines, he draws the bed she's on. Then the young woman lying in it, pale and motionless. He squats down to scratch in the finer details with his fingers, wanting to capture her still hands, her lashes on her freckled cheeks, her mouth taped around the tube going down her throat.

"The machines are monitoring her," he says, drawing the fragile wire that runs to her temple. "Geo was also there, but he didn't make it."

Hayze registers Jewel's gasp as he steps to the other side, the stick already scratching new lines in the soil.

"And this is us, all hidden somewhere in our capitals."

He draws the pod Pace is in. The curved sides. The veins fanned over the side, feeding the person inside the reality they're living. An artificial womb weaving whatever the leaders want them to believe. Then Hayze draws Pace's father standing over him, stroking the three scars running down his cheek. He moves around so he can spend a few minutes capturing Tide's tension, his grief, his hope.

"And this is where we are, Aura." He sketches them lying in two pods side-by-side in Ignis as they would have been when Hayze and Aura first entered the Games. If the leaders believe that's where he is now, it might just buy him a little more time.

When Hayze finally steps back, four stunned faces are looking at him.

He lets out a breath as his gaze settles on Aura. "Like I said, none of this is real. It only exists in our minds, which are telling us it's real. And because the leaders are heartless douches," he makes sure he says that part a little louder, "they swapped the memories of Fire and Water to see if we could unlock other Elemental powers."

"What about us?" Jewel asks. "Did I get swapped with Skylus?"

Hayze shakes his head. "Earth and Air kept their memories."

Aura's eyes don't leave his as she walks around his drawings. "You drew those images in the bunker for me," she whispers, her hand settling on his chest.

He nods, placing his palm over hers. Aura wouldn't remember it, she still has Tempo's memories rather than her own, but he can see what she has remembered.

Their love.

"How do we get out?" she asks, her fingers curling in as if she's holding his heart.

"We win the Games." He reaches up with his other hand to cup her softly smiling face. "We reach the Sect."

"Then that's what we do."

Aura pushes up on her toes again, clearly intending on sealing her promise with a kiss. Hayze's eyes flutter closed, but he quickly opens them, not wanting to miss a moment of everything that is Aura. Her beauty. Her strength. Her faith.

Then stops.

"Hayze," Aura breathes as he draws her close to him, feeling like the ground has been wrenched out from under them.

Because it has.

In the space of a blink, the cave is gone, its pseudo-reality deleted.

And they're standing in a vast expanse of nothingness.

CHAPTER
THIRTEEN
AURA

A ura turns in a full circle. Everything has gone. Like…
everything. The cave. The waterfall. The vines. The small flame in the palm of her hand. Only the people remain. And thankfully, that includes Hayze.

"Where are we?" She takes in the whiteness that surrounds them. It's just like Skylus described when she flew above the maze. Not ice. Not snow. Not air. But…

Nothing.

"Our clothes," says Jewel. "They've changed."

Aura glances down to see she's wearing the red leather vest and trousers of the Fire Quadrant. Hayze is dressed the same. Jewel is in the strips of cloth from Earth and Atmos in his purple robes. And much to Pace's obvious outrage, he's dressed in a blue suit from Water.

"Look," says Jewel, pointing at Aura's hand. "Your tattoo is different."

Aura looks down to see her Water tattoo has morphed into one from Fire. Her eyes go immediately to Pace to see the opposite has happened to him.

"They're messing with us," Pace growls, rubbing at his hand like he can remove the mark that confirms what he doesn't want to believe. "They're reinforcing that ridiculous story Hayze told us. I'm not from Water. I'm Fire."

"Interesting." Hayze frowns. "So, you're prepared to believe the leaders are capable of changing our clothes, tattoos, and total environment in the blink of an eye, but not our memories?"

Pace opens his mouth to reply, then snaps it shut again.

Aura goes to him and puts a hand on his arm. "I'm struggling with it too, Pace. But think about it. It explains everything. Why we haven't mastered our powers. Why I was so drawn to Hayze. Why you and Tempo struggled sometimes to connect."

"I loved Tempo," he grinds out.

"You still do," says Hayze. "I told you. She's alive."

Pace's eyes fill with tears. "Are you sure?"

Hayze nods. "She's hooked up to machines, but she's strong."

"Yet Geo..." Pace looks down, unable to finish his words.

"I survived," says Hayze, avoiding reminding them all of what happened to Geo.

"And so will Tempo," Aura adds. "Which is why you have to make it back to her."

"But according to Hayze, she's my enemy," says Pace. "What if she wakes up and realizes she hates me?"

"She won't," says Aura, wondering why Hayze just tensed. "Tempo may not have loved you before all this, but being out here has changed everything. I mean, do you hate her?"

Pace's jaw falls. "Of course not."

"Exactly." Aura nods, hoping she's right about Tempo's feelings. But she saw the way Tempo looked at Pace. That kind of passion can't be extinguished in the same way Hayze took care of the wall of burning vines.

"Sorry to interrupt," says Jewel quietly. "But look."

She points ahead with a shaking hand, and they all turn to see the Sect has appeared in the distance. It looks different from the times Aura caught glances of it from the Traders Market in Aqua. *When Tempo caught glances of it,* she corrects herself.

"Skylus was right," says Atmos. "It's right there."

The Sect is tall and square with a domed roof. The entire structure is completely white, making its outline difficult to distinguish from the sea of nothingness that surrounds it. It has a shimmering glow, giving it the appearance of an apparition rather than a solid structure.

"Do you think Skylus has already made it there?" Jewel asks.

"She can't have," says Hayze. "The leaders said we win the Games when we make it to the Sect. If Skylus already made it, then the Games are over. She won."

"Hold on." Aura frowns. "Are you saying there can only be one winner?"

"Well..." Hayze glances up to his right as he thinks. "Cyclonis said the aim is to reach the Sect. It's how we win."

"But there could be more than one winner, right?" Aura asks, determined to believe this can't be over.

"Maybe?" Hayze tilts his head. "Maybe we can all win."

"I know we can." Aura nods, feeling now that Hayze is back she can do anything. "Let's make a pact. No more going off on our own. We'll work as a team and reach the Sect together."

She puts out her hand, palm facing down, the edrian in her Fire tattoo catching the light. Hayze immediately covers it with his own. Jewel is quick to follow, and Pace lets out a sigh as he joins in.

"Come on, Atmos," says Aura. "We need you."

He pulls back his shoulders and glances at Pace.

"We'll call it a truce," says Pace with a wink.

"Okay." Atmos steps up and adds his hand to the stack. "We're a team."

"Fire. Air. Water. Earth," says Hayze. "Together, we're stronger."

Everyone nods then pulls back their hands.

"Now what?" Pace asks, taking a few steps toward the Sect. "Atmos, do you think you can send up a breeze to push us along? That looks a little far to wa—"

Pace crashes into what can only be described as an invisible wall. He bounces back, hands flying to his face as he curses.

"What was that?" Hayze marches forward with his hands outstretched, until he too, is brought to a stop. He runs his palms across a surface none of them can see.

This has Aura curious, and she rushes forward to touch it. "It's like ice or glass, except there's no reflection."

Soon, all five of them are standing at the wall, feeling high, low and far across to see where it comes to an end.

"Maybe we can smash it." Pace balls his hands into a fist.

"You'll break your hand," says Hayze. "This is a test."

"A *game,*" Jewel corrects.

Aura nods. "One we need to figure out how to beat."

"There's an edge!" Atmos calls out from a few feet away, stepping forward past the point of the wall.

They rush over to him with their hands in front of them and follow him into what appears to be a corridor. If Aura stretches out her arms, she can touch the wall on either side of her. She's just as closed in as she was in the mines, yet she doesn't feel in the least bit panicked. It seems invisible walls are even more effective than beautiful murals painted for you by the guy you love. She flushes at the thought, overwhelmingly pleased that Hayze really had been the one to paint those images for her. It's no wonder she kept forgetting it was Pace. She knew deep in a closed off part of herself who had really done it.

If only she could tap into the rest of her memories in the same way. But it's difficult. She believes Hayze when he says she's Fire, but her entire awareness is built on her recollection of Tempo's life in Water.

Hayze puts an arm around her and one word enters her mind.

Trust.

That's what she's doing here. Trusting her instincts. And trusting Hayze. Her heart hadn't lied to her when she looked into the dark pools of his eyes in the Deadwaters, and he wouldn't either. Her brain may have screamed at her that he was her enemy, but she knew to ignore it.

"You okay?" Hayze asks, noticing her deep in thought.

She nods. "I'm just happy you're back."

"There's another bend here!" calls Atmos from the front of the group.

"And one here," says Pace on the other side of the corridor.

"It's another maze," Aura groans. "Only this time, we can't even see it."

"That doesn't mean we can't beat it," says Hayze.

Except he hasn't been with them in the other mazes. He doesn't know how frustrating it is to turn corner after corner, open door after door, and end up exactly where you started. Although, maybe that's a good thing. Looking at this with fresh eyes could be exactly what they need.

"I say we go this way," says Atmos, not moving from where he's standing.

"It's the opposite direction to where we want to go," Pace points out, not budging either.

"Mazes work like that." Atmos rolls his eyes. "If you just walked in a straight line then it would just be...a straight line."

Aura hides a smile. Atmos is going to have to try a little harder with his words if he's going to gain ground in his rivalry with Pace.

"Pace, let's try Atmos's way this time," says Aura, pleading at him with her eyes. "Next time, we'll try yours."

Pace looks at Aura for long moments with his arms firmly crossed, then nods. "Fine. It probably makes zero difference, anyway. We'll end up exactly where the leaders want us, just like we always have."

"Thank you." She smiles, knowing he did that for her.

As they follow Atmos with their hands outstretched, Aura starts to think Pace is right. They turn left and right at intervals when Atmos finds new paths to take, yet the Sect still seems as far away as when they started. Several times they walk directly into what feels like a solid wall and are forced to make a turn.

"I've been thinking," says Jewel. "Pace said we'll end up where the leaders want us to be. And when we met Cyclonis in the Stormsphere, he said we're supposed to learn to harness our powers."

"And?" snaps Atmos impatiently.

"Well, does that mean we're just going to turn in circles if we keep walking without at least trying to use our powers to solve this?" she asks.

They move forward in silence as everyone turns this over.

"She's right," says Hayze. "This approach is useless. We'll never get anywhere."

Aura stares out at the nothingness without a clue as to which power might be useful against obstacles they can't see.

"Well, I vote we keep walking," says Atmos. "I can find the way out if you just give me more time."

Pace glares at him, his feelings for the guy from Air more than clear. He flicks out his hand and a rush of water falls from above, landing directly on Atmos's head, completely soaking his purple robes.

"What was that for?" Atmos throws out his arms, his color deepening to match his robes as he wipes down his face.

Atmos may be shocked.

But Pace is completely astounded.

"I did it," he breathes. "I actually did it. I made Water."

"Told you so," quips Hayze, grinning.

Aura shoots him a look and he shrugs.

"Do it again," says Jewel. "Not on Atmos, obviously. Do it on me."

Pace grins and flicks out his hand again, sending more water rushing from above and showering Jewel. She squeals in response as her flimsy strips of cloth turn slightly transparent.

"I am Water!" shouts Pace. He throws out both fists, then splays his fingers, sending a torrent of rain down upon them.

Aura tilts up her face and drinks in some of the cool liquid, enjoying the moment a lot more than Atmos had.

Pace flicks his hand again and the rain stops as suddenly as it began.

"It all makes so much sense now." Aura shakes her head. "I could never stop the rain because I wasn't the one who started it."

"I wish Tempo was here," says Pace. "I bet she could do it even better."

"Make some more rain," Jewel giggles, and Pace sends down another spurt.

"This isn't going to help us get to the Sect," Atmos points out, still unimpressed.

Pace extends his hand to Atmos, who glares at him. "Don't even think about it."

"Fine." Pace lets his hand fall.

Atmos stalks off, muttering something about thinking they had a truce when he unexpectedly drops several feet. It takes Aura a moment to realize that's what happened given there's no floor, walls or ceiling in this world of white. Atmos crashes onto a hard surface and sprawls out groaning.

"My wrist!" he cries out, holding out his arm.

Aura moves forward beside Hayze, stepping carefully so she doesn't meet the same fate.

"He's badly hurt," says Jewel, and Aura winces to see there's a bone sticking out of his wrist.

Jewel climbs down the invisible wall and lands beside Atmos. She removes one of the strips of cloth from around her waist, revealing even more skin and quickly wraps it around Atmos's wrist, the tan-colored cloth immediately staining dark red.

Hayze lowers himself down next and turns to help Aura. She allows him to catch her, enjoying the moment of closeness before turning her attention to Atmos.

"This isn't real, Atmos," says Hayze, squatting down beside him. "Listen to me. This isn't your real body. This isn't a real injury. Right now, you're lying safely in a pod somewhere in Aeris."

Atmos groans. "If it's not real, why does it hurt so much?"

"Because your brain thinks you're injured," says Hayze.

Aura bites her lip, not understanding how any of this can be possible. If Atmos's wrist isn't really broken, had she really kissed Hayze when he returned to her? Has she *ever* kissed him?

"This is a trap," says Pace.

Aura turns, not having noticed that he'd followed them

down here.

"What do you mean?" she asks.

"It's a pit." He runs his hands along a wall as he walks. He gets to a point and makes a ninety-degree turn. "Four sides and it goes right around. Now that we're all in here, I can't even feel the top of the wall. It's like it's grown several feet."

"Great," Aura mutters.

"I think we're meant to fly out," says Pace. "Well, Atmos is. Then he can help us up."

Atmos rolls onto his back, moaning even louder now.

"Atmos," says Jewel, patting his face gently. "I think he's right. Can you try sitting up so you can use your powers?"

"I can't," he cries out. "I'm injured! And I haven't seen a sign!"

"Do you even have any powers?" Pace narrows his eyes. "I mean, I don't think I've ever seen you use them. Not without Skylus by your side, anyway. Was she doing all the work?"

"Of course, I have powers," Atmos snaps, sitting up abruptly. "Actually, now that I think about it, my arm doesn't even really hurt. I think Hayze might be onto something. Maybe this isn't real?"

"Great," mutters Pace. "Another excuse not to use your powers."

"Watch this, Water boy." Atmos raises his injured arm and holds out a clenched fist. His fingers wriggle and just as he's about to open his hand wide...

The floor drops out beneath them.

Sending all five of them plummeting.

Aura swipes at the air, her hands desperately searching for Hayze.

This is just like the waterfall, only far worse.

Back then, she'd already lost Hayze.

Now she's found him. Only to lose him all over again.

CHAPTER
FOURTEEN
HAYZE

Even as the rational part of Hayze knows he can't die, all the rest of him knows he's falling. Wind tears at his hair and clothes. His arms pinwheel as he tries to keep himself from tumbling over and over. His heart had lodged in his throat the minute he plunged into nothingness and is now choking him as it spasms out of control.

He wants to call out to Aura, to somehow grab her hand and plummet together, but the world has turned a blinding white. There's nothing but wind and falling.

"Aura—" he croaks.

Just as he lands on something hard, yet unstable.

He crumples to his hands and knees, then pushes up as quickly as he can. The ground beneath him wobbles and balancing himself takes precedence over understanding where he's landed for precious seconds.

Then shock means his surroundings register in fragmented pieces.

Endless water.

A raft that's evening out beneath his feet.

And he's alone.

"Aura!" he shouts, even as the realization that he's started the Games all over again filters in.

This all began when he woke up in the middle of the Deadwaters. A solitary, confused soul on a raft, wondering where his home in Aqua just disappeared to.

Hayze narrows his eyes as he executes a steady turn. There's a lot different this time around. He may be alone, but he knows exactly where he is. Who he is—he's actually wearing his Fire clothes. And why he's here.

To unlock his Elemental Powers.

One glance down at the only thing keeping him afloat has him admitting that Fire isn't going to be terribly helpful right now. All he can burn is his raft, and he now knows what lurks in the waters below.

He throws his head back, glaring at the endless cerulean sky. "I'll find her!" he shouts to the leaders, hard determination settling in his gut.

Hayze kneels down, dips his hands into the cool water and starts scooping. There may as well be a ticking clock hanging above him, counting down the minutes and seconds before the leaders discover him tucked in Tempo's pod in Aqua.

He needs to ensure they win the Games before that happens.

"I'll find you, Aura," he mutters under his breath.

Setting up a relentless rhythm, Hayze reminds himself this isn't draining his energy. He isn't hungry. He isn't thirsty. His body is being looked after by a high-tech womb. He doesn't slow, doesn't acknowledge the burn in his muscles.

All that exists in this pseudo-reality is his heart and mind.

And both need Aura.

He looks up periodically, registering more endless ocean. More relentless sky. It's possible the leaders have decided to put him in his very own purgatory—a world that's the antithesis of Fire. A world without Aura. But Hayze is betting they want the powers flowing through his veins more.

Either way, he's not going to stop moving.

"Hayze!"

His name fracturing the oppressive silence is the most beautiful thing he's ever heard. Sitting up, he sees her.

Aura.

Her chestnut hair catches the sunlight, her broad smile catches his breath. This time, the joy that sings through his veins makes sense. He doesn't believe he's Water, that he's hated her his entire life thanks to their parents' choices.

This is Aura.

The girl he grew up with, loved, and still does.

They paddle with single-minded determination, and the sounds of Aura coming closer only have Hayze moving faster. First, it's the sound of her raft slicing through the water. Then her excited breath.

Then, he swears he can hear her smile. A song of joy. The sweetest melody. One that echoes deep in his soul.

Their rafts bump into each other and Hayze launches onto Aura's before they can drift more than an inch apart. He draws her into his arms just as she wraps hers around his shoulders. They kiss exuberantly, happily.

Then tenderly, gratefully.

And finally, passionately and fervently. As if honoring their Element, the heat between them kindles, then detonates. Hands tighten, explorations deepen.

They pull away, panting as they smile at each other. "Near and far," Hayze murmurs, even as he knows she wouldn't remember.

"Wherever you are," Aura responds.

He caresses her cheek, her lips, his heart swelling. "We always said that after we were apart."

Aura's eyes widen as she also realizes she finished the sentence despite not having her memories. "I wish I remembered," she whispers, pressing her face into his palm.

"Your heart remembers," he assures her, ignoring the way his stomach tightens. Some things are going to be harder to remember than others. "The rest will come once we're out of this hell. Then you'll remember we used to hide in the village, drawing arrows all over the paths with charcoal so our parents could find us. That we used to find shapes and figures in the flames of the cauldron outside your home." He chuckles. "That you'd insist I wash the coal off my face after we'd been in the mines so you could kiss me without the grit."

He smiles, telling himself then will be the time to address their final words to each other. That although it felt insurmountable at the time, it will all pale in comparison to the Games.

Aura grins. "I suspect I would've kissed you, anyway."

"You never had to find out. I wasn't willing to risk it." He grins right back. "Not when your kisses are more essential than air."

They kiss again, keeping this one brief, no matter how much they don't want to. The knowledge they have to find the others is refusing to be ignored. Hayze carefully steps back onto his raft as Aura quickly ties them together.

She sits up, focused once more as she looks around. "Which way?"

"Hopefully, the others realize we need to get to the Sect." He squints up at the sun. "We have to go southwest."

They paddle until their rafts are facing the right direction. Aura's face twists. "Now I realize why being out here made me nauseous."

"More and more will make sense now that you know," Hayze says, positioning himself to get moving.

Aura joins him, and together, they get their rafts moving. He almost grins as another thing makes sense—the fact they fall into perfect, seamless rhythm.

They've barely started when a new voice reaches them.

"Hey! Aura! Hayze! Over here!"

It's Pace, standing on his raft, waving his arm frantically.

"They've already found each other!" Aura gasps as they see Jewel and Atmos bobbing on their own rafts on either side of him.

Hayze knows he shouldn't be surprised they all found each other so easily. The leaders want them together. He can't forget who's pulling the strings.

After a few minutes of paddling, their rafts bump together and Pace grins. Atmos frowns. Jewel is pale as she keeps her gaze on her hands, possibly because she's also feeling nauseous. And cold, thanks to her scanty strips of cloth doing little to protect her.

"I'd say this is déjà vu." Pace's face crumples. "But there are only five of us."

Hayze glances at the rafts, conscious there are three missing. Geo's dead. Tempo's in a coma. And Skylus has harnessed Air.

"It's not the same without Tempo," Pace mumbles.

Aura reaches out to brush his arm, compassion and understanding softening her face.

"When I first saw her, I was so conflicted. I was so happy." His gaze flickers to Hayze and Aura, at the way she moves to stand as close to him as she can. "And so angry."

"Your memories were overruled by this," Hayze says, indicating to their surroundings. No matter how real they feel, they're nothing but a simulation. "It allowed you to see Tempo in a new way. Through a lens of love, rather than inherited hate."

Pace looks away, pensive, then nods as if reaching a decision. When he looks back at Hayze and Aura, his features are set with determined lines. "We need to get back to the Sect."

"What's the point?" Atmos huffs, crossing his arms without acknowledging that one was broken less than an hour ago. "Skylus has already won."

Pace scowls at him. "You don't know that."

Atmos snorts. "If we're really in some Game, then there is definitely only one winner."

"Was there a sign that told you that?" Hayze asks as he raises an eyebrow.

Atmos's arms tighten over his chest. "We haven't seen a sign to return to the Sect, either."

"You could stay here if you like," Hayze responds, glancing at where Atmos's raft is tied to Pace's.

"The Sect is that way," Jewel says, her voice quiet as she points. "We need to reach it before night."

Hayze looks up, registering she's right, even as he remembers how this Quadrant ended. Them all fading into frozen unconsciousness, with Jewel the first to go.

"That's enough of a sign for me," he grunts, kneeling as he prepares to paddle.

Aura joins him, now looking down at the raft and the water it's floating on, then stills. Hayze is about to ask what's wrong when he freezes too. He just remembered what else they encountered in the Deadwaters.

"Eterna wants us to paddle!" Atmos screams, dropping to his knees as he frantically digs at the water.

But it's too late.

Gray fins are slicing straight toward them.

This time, Hayze knows they're dolphins. Just like he knows they're as dangerous as sharks.

"Someone make sure the rafts are bound together as tightly as possible," he calls out.

"Got it," Jewel replies, scrambling to her knees and tying Hayze and Aura's rafts to theirs.

"Pace!" Hayze shouts. They're surrounded by water. The dolphins are cleaving through it. It's the only way to stop them.

"Already on it!" he instantly replies. He lifts his hands, pointing them at the approaching threat. "I am Water!"

A giant wave rises a few feet from the raft and rushes at the dolphins. It gains momentum and size with every foot, creating a wall of shimmering blue.

One heading straight for the dolphins.

Pace drops his hands in a sharp movement and the wave crashes down on the deadly creatures with a thundering roar. If that wasn't impressive enough, Pace then smooths out any ripples that ricochet back toward the rafts, leaving them standing on calm ocean.

Which means they all see the dolphins spear through the turbulent aftermath, leaping high into the air and glistening in the sunlight.

"Atmos!" Hayze cries. "Blow them away!"

Pale and a little green looking, Atmos raises shaking hands. "I am Air!" he cries out, his voice carrying over the frothing sea.

"Another wave!" Aura shouts to Pace. "We'll hit them with both!"

Pace nods, his face tight with focus. His arms raise, his palms open out. "I am—"

He drops to his knees, screaming in agony as he kicks his legs frantically as if trying to get something off.

"The jellyfish!" Jewel gasps, freezing.

Hayze steps so one foot is on his raft and the other is on Aura's as he realizes they're facing a double threat. Spindly, sticky tentacles are crawling over the timber. Three have already wrapped around Pace's legs. Screaming in pain, he twists and kicks, trying to free himself.

Hayze grabs him under the arm as Aura does the same, dragging him closer. He stares at the venomous, gelatinous ropes of poison wrapped around Pace's legs, willing them to heat up. They shrivel and fall off.

"Atmos!" Jewel screams, her eyes so wide the white is a stark contrast to her dark skin. She's no longer staring at the rafts, but straight ahead.

Three dolphins leap into the air, their open mouths revealing the rows of jagged teeth they're not supposed to have.

"I'm trying, okay?" Atmos screeches. He throws his hands forward with a desperate jerk. "I am Air!"

The dolphins continue like arrows, opening their jaws a little wider.

"Get down!" Aura screams, dragging Hayze down with her.

He instinctively covers her as the others press themselves onto the rafts. The dolphins sail past their heads and splash into the water on the other side.

"They're coming for me!" Atmos shouts, kicking as more tentacles crawl over the rafts. The instant the first one wraps around his ankle, he curls up in a ball. "Eterna!" he whimpers. "Please, help us. Save us."

"I've got it," Aura says, already focused on the sticky lengths coiling up his legs.

Hayze maintains his attention on Pace as more jellyfish tentacles shoot up from the water, their numbers doubling, then tripling.

It won't be Eterna who saves Atmos and Pace. It will be Elemental Powers.

With a violent jerk, the rafts rock wildly, making Jewel cry out. Hayze holds onto Aura as they're shoved in the opposite direction.

"The dolphins," Aura gasps.

They're attacking the rafts!

The sound of splintering wood cracks through the moans of pain from Pace and Atmos. Hayze wraps himself around Aura. "We can't die!" he shouts.

Even though it sure as heckus feels like it.

He instinctively cries out as a tentacle slaps onto his calf, then tightens like a noose. Aura tenses in his arms, shifting her focus. A second later, the gelatinous rope becomes warm, then flakes away.

A dolphin surges forward, clamping its jaws around the edge of the raft. With a sharp crack, it snaps the wood. Water flows over the rafts as the dolphin drops back into the water, leaving behind a ragged bite mark and shattered timber.

Hayze draws Aura in tighter, focusing on the jellyfish tentacles relentlessly crawling, shooting, even piercing the cracks between the rafts. Three words are a mantra in his head.

We can't die.

We can't die.

For the first time, he wonders what would happen instead. Will they end up in the water, becoming entangled in venomous tentacles and fodder for dolphins? Because he has to admit, the pain would feel as real as the terror.

"We could try to incinerate them all," Aura says quietly, so only he can hear.

Hayze stares at her. His first instinct is to reject the idea. If they become an inferno, they may take care of the jellyfish and dolphins, but they'll also destroy the rafts. They'll all be forced to swim.

But the next thought tells him Aura's right. Another violent jerk and rush of water over the rafts only reinforces the decision. It's only a matter of time before they're fighting this below the surface.

What choice do they have?

Hayze nods and they weave their fingers, pressing their palms together. The heat is instantaneous, the energy a living being thrumming between them. He stares into Aura's eyes, conscious they've worked toward this their entire lives.

And that it could be what saves them.

Or ends them.

They say the words together. "We are F—"

"I. Am. Earth," Jewel says, her voice low and guttural.

Hayze and Aura turn to see her on all fours, staring at the water as her whole body shakes with intensity.

"What..." Aura asks, blinking.

The answer is instantaneous. The jellyfish tentacles recede. Not only that, their rippling bodies sink, disappearing into the deep blue below.

To Hayze's amazement, the dolphins slow their violent movements, then close their jaws. They surround the raft, flippers moving gently to keep them afloat.

Jewel's face softens as she reaches out. The closest dolphin pushes up before Hayze can yank Jewel back, gently bumping its snout against her palm. Jewel giggles, caresses it, then sits back on her knees.

She offers a small smile to the stunned faces around her. "I got the idea when we were in the cave and Aura said plants are made from carbon. So are animals."

Hayze blinks. Jewel has Earth Powers, which means she can control animals?

Jewel ducks her head. "If we find a way to tie the rafts to them, they can pull us to land," she offers shyly.

"Holy heckus," Aura breathes.

In the space of Jewel's three words, the dolphins have gone from deadly enemies to surprising allies. To a way to win the Games. Hayze turns toward the horizon, gazing at the faint outline of the dome. His heart is still a wild drum in his chest, even as peace settles around them. They could make it to the Sect.

Hayze turns to Aura, his grin feeling as odd as Jewel's giggle sounded less than a minute after fighting for their lives. "Holy heckus, alright. Come on—"

He stops as an impassive voice echoes through his mind. One look at the pale, stunned faces around him and he knows they heard it too.

"Level passed. Earth wins the Water Quadrant."

CHAPTER

FIFTEEN

AURA

"Where did that come from?" Aura looks straight to Hayze as if he's her compass. "There was a voice in my head."

"Earth won the Water Quadrant," he replies, using the exact words she just heard. "I heard it too."

"But..." Pace tears at his dark hair, wobbling on the damaged rafts. "But I'm Water. Jewel can't have won."

"I didn't mean to." Jewel looks down shyly, reminding Aura of Geo. "Sorry."

"Don't be sorry," Hayze reassures her. "Nobody would have won if you hadn't used your powers."

"Would we really be dead?" Atmos asks, pulling his purple robes more tightly around him. "Or now that our minds know we can't die, wouldn't we just have come straight back?"

Hayze lets out a long sigh. "I don't know. Maybe?"

"It's hard to win when I can't remember my own Quadrant." Pace crosses his arms, his competitive streak shining through. "They put Water at a big disadvantage."

Aura glances at Hayze, not pointing out she's no better off than Pace. Although, in fairness, maybe she'd feel more strongly if someone else just won the Fire Quadrant.

"So, what's next?" Atmos asks.

As soon as the words leave his lips, the blinding white world returns. This time, Aura reaches for Hayze and their fingers entwine. He squeezes her hand and the nothingness fades, revealing a wall of trees.

Aura looks down to see she's now sitting on solid ground. The ocean has vanished as if its salty depths evaporated in a blink.

"The Quakelands," says Atmos, answering his own question from both a moment ago and another lifetime.

Just like when they were last here, they're all together. And just like last time, the ground begins to rumble. Thankfully, now they're wearing their clothes from their true Quadrant rather than those strips of cloth Jewel has to endure.

"Earthquake!" Jewel gasps. "We need to get to the safe-zone. Hurry!"

"Wait!" Hayze lets go of Aura to scramble to his feet. "We beat the Water Quadrant by doing things differently. Let's not repeat our mistakes."

"We should go straight to the wall," says Aura, certain that's how they win. "We need to get there before the monkeys."

"Don't worry about the monkeys." Jewel lifts her face, a new air of confidence surrounding her. "I'll take care of them."

Pace coughs, giving Aura a strange look as if he's trying to tell her something.

"Pace," she warns. "We don't have time for secrets. What is it?"

He looks at Jewel, then back at Aura. "We can't let Earth

win two Quadrants. If Jewel takes care of the monkeys, then—"

"We're a team," says Hayze. "It doesn't matter who wins. We should be focused on getting through these so-called Games as quickly as we can with minimal injuries."

Atmos holds out his wrist that broke in the maze, demonstrating how well it's healed. "Injuries aren't really such a problem."

"It still hurt when it happened, didn't it?" Aura asks.

Atmos winces. "Yeah. A lot."

"But if each of us wins a Quadrant," Pace continues, not yet done arguing. "That would really mess with the leaders. They'll never be able to declare an overall winner. It would make us a true team."

This is actually a very good point. But before Aura can see what everyone else thinks, the rumble in the ground becomes a tremor. Trees uproot in the forest behind them, crashing to the ground and sending flocks of birds into the sky.

"Run!" Atmos cries. "It's a sign!"

Last time, Jewel had frozen in terror. But not now. She takes off in the lead, leaving them no choice but to follow. A giant tree smashes to the forest floor, missing Pace by inches. He picks up speed and soon they're all running so fast it's like they're flying. Actually, no. Skylus is the only one of them who can do that. Atmos doesn't even seem to be able to make as much as a gentle breeze.

Jewel leads them away from the path they took last time, and Aura can only assume this one will take them to the wall. Pace catches up to her, shouting something and pointing. But Jewel ignores him, continuing as if he hadn't spoken.

"Monkeys!" Atmos shouts, looking behind as he runs. "They're coming. And they're not a sign!"

Hayze takes Aura's hand and they power forward until the

five of them are clustered together as they dodge falling trees and clouds of dust.

There's a scream and the ground right in front of them cleaves open. With no time to stop, Aura tumbles down the crevasse along with the others in a mass of arms, legs, rocks and leaves. They land heavily and Aura pants hard, grateful the drop hadn't been too steep. She knows what Atmos meant when he said even though these injuries aren't real, they still hurt. Her backside is smarting and she's sure her shoulder is going to be severely bruised.

"Are you hurt?" Hayze asks, his own discomfort clear in this strained voice.

"No," she puffs. "You?"

"Never felt better." He pulls her close and presses his lips to her dusty cheek. Aura can't wait for this Game to send them to the Scorchlands so she can return his kiss.

Properly.

"Everyone here?" Jewel asks.

"Unfortunately," groans Pace.

Aura shields her eyes so she can look up. They've tumbled about twenty feet down and are sitting in the base of a fissure in the earth that looks as if it stretches for miles. At the top of the chasm are several curious furry faces staring down at them.

Aura reels back even though she's at a safe distance. Those monstrous creatures don't look anywhere nearly as cute now that she knows how vicious they can be.

"They won't climb down here, will they?" Atmos asks nervously.

"No," says Jewel. "And if they do, I'll take care of them."

Pace gets to his feet and looks around. "I've got an idea."

"What?" Aura and Hayze ask at once.

"We're supposed to use our powers, remember?" he says.

"What if I fill this area with water and we float to the top and climb out?"

"That sounds dangerous," says Hayze. "Jewel could use her powers to carve foot holes into the walls instead."

Jewel shakes her head. "The ground's too solid. It would never work."

Aura narrows her eyes, certain this is an excuse. "Are you trying to give Pace the lead role in this Quadrant so he can win?"

Jewel shrugs. "We agreed it makes sense to try to win a Quadrant each. Let Pace try."

Without waiting for an agreement, Pace stretches out his hands. "I am Water!"

Everyone who's not already standing quickly gets to their feet, preparing to swim. Out of habit, Aura is about to ask Jewel if she's okay, but decides not to. Just as Aura isn't the same person she was when they first entered these Games, neither is Jewel. She can take care of herself.

A rush of water surges toward them and Pace holds up his palms, slowing its flow so it doesn't sweep them off their feet. Despite his intense concentration, he has an unmistakable huge smile on his face, clearly enjoying having mastered his powers. It's lucky Skylus left when she did. Between Hayze, Jewel and Pace, she has some serious competition on her hands.

Pace brings the water gently toward them and it seeps into the thirsty ground, then rises to cover their feet, then ankles.

Jewel looks up at the monkeys and raises her hands. "I am Earth!"

The monkeys instantly turn and run out of sight.

Pace glances nervously at Jewel and Aura's heart skips a beat at the thought of him losing concentration and accidentally drowning them all.

"Don't worry," she tells him. "You're doing an incredible job. Keep going and you'll win this Quadrant for sure." She shoots Jewel an apologetic look, not at all certain what she said is true. Those monkeys had been deadly the last time they were here. Jewel's contribution was significant.

Jewel gives her a nod and a warm smile, showing Aura she understands.

The water level creeps up their legs and higher again until Aura feels her feet lift from the ground. Hayze lets go of her hand so she can tread water while Pace continues to work with his Element beside them.

They rise to ground level and Hayze is the first to scramble up, instantly spinning around to haul Aura out to dry land. She quickly helps Jewel while Hayze puts out his hand to Atmos. Pace practically rises out of the water like a god, the proud look on his face tinged by a hint of sadness. Aura knows it's because Tempo isn't here to see how magnificent he's become. Those two may have grown up as childhood enemies but Aura's certain if Tempo survives, they'll be far from adversaries now.

"Come on!" calls Jewel, straightening her skimpy outfit and urging them to continue. "This isn't over yet. We have to get to the wall."

Pace nods, refocusing as he runs beside her.

"Go, Atmos," says Hayze. "No time for signs."

Atmos is quick to move, although his sodden robes make his steps slower than before. Aura slips her hand into Hayze's as they run, and she wonders for the first time in the Quakelands how they might use Fire to pass this Game.

"We can't use our powers," says Hayze, reading her mind. "Remember what happened in the Scorchlands?"

Aura nods, the memory of the lava spilling into the village still clear in her mind. Let alone the way it devoured Hayze in the mines.

Except now she knows that wasn't really Hayze. And Tempo and Pace didn't cause the lava. It was Hayze trying to pull water from earth and instead drawing up fire. Which is the last thing they need right now, especially with the ground already breaking up all around them.

A giant crack carves through the terrain in front of them and they all draw to an abrupt halt, slamming into each other as the ground drops away beneath them.

Aura braces herself for impact, only to find this time she lands in water. She splutters as she ingests some. It's fresh water, not salty like in the memories of Tempo's life that she carries.

Kicking to keep herself afloat, she only has to wait a handful of seconds before the water level laps at ground level. She crawls out and heaves in some oxygen. The ground continues to shake and Aura leans into Hayze to steady herself.

"You okay?" Hayze rubs her back.

She nods, unable to speak just yet.

"Don't talk," he says. "Just breathe."

"Come on!" Pace calls, already urging them to follow. "This is fun!"

Aura isn't sure *fun* would be the word she'd use to describe this, but since learning their lives aren't really in danger, she has to admit there's a new kind of freedom to this strange reality they're trapped in.

She pulls herself together and they run on. Each time the ground swallows them up, Pace is one step ahead. This may not be his Quadrant but he's certainly in his Element.

Aura learns to hold her breath before she hits the water, her leather vest and trousers now stuck so tightly to her skin she's not sure she'll ever be able to get them off.

Eventually they reach the wall and Jewel quickly scouts around for monkeys. None of them can forget what happened last time. But it seems whatever Jewel did with her powers when they were stuck in the crevasse worked and there's not a monkey to be seen.

"Are we finished this round?" Pace puts a hand to the wall. "Is that the end of this Quadrant? Did I win?"

"There's no voice," says Aura. "We're not done yet."

Pace's shoulders slump. There's little that Water can do to get them over this high wall. He'd need to fill the entire Quadrant to be of any help.

"I think we need to get over it," says Jewel. "Then we're finished."

"Atmos, can you blow it over?" Pace asks.

"I..." Atmos bites his lip. "Umm, I can try."

"We'll burn a hole in it," says Hayze, causing Atmos to visibly sigh with relief.

"You can do that?" Pace tilts his head. "It's made from stone."

Hayze walks to the wall and picks up a sharp stick, scratching an X into the stone. "Aura, focus on this exact point."

"Oh." She nods, realizing he means for her to use her powers, too.

"Between the two of us, we should be able to make enough heat," he says, returning to her side. "Like when the lava broke down the wall in the Scorchlands."

"I'll try," says Aura, who so far hasn't done any more than create a tiny flame in the palm of her hand.

Hayze and Aura raise their hands and she stares at the mark on the wall, concentrating on bringing her powers to the surface.

"I am Fire," calls out Hayze.

Aura moves her lips in sync to the words, shouting them in

her heart rather than from her lips. She feels something unlock and she narrows her gaze.

The area surrounding the X glows brightly and Aura fixates on it even harder, trying with all her might to blast a hole through the thick stone.

Smoke billows and rises as intense heat radiates from the wall. The other three teens step back, but Hayze and Aura move forward as they continue to blast waves of energy. There's a crackling noise as more smoke pours out, and something seems to shift.

Aura gasps, letting her hands fall.

"We did it," breathes Hayze, even though it's impossible to tell just yet. "Did you feel that?"

Aura nods as a gentle breeze picks up, sweeping the smoke away.

"Impressive!" says Jewel. "It worked."

There's a large hole in the stone wall, big enough for them to squeeze through.

"I'll cool down the stones," says Pace, bringing up his hands.

"We can take away the he..." Hayze doesn't bother to finish his words. Pace is hellbent on taking over from here.

A burst of rain falls from the sky, hissing as it hits the glowing stones, sending up steam instead of smoke. Pace increases the intensity of the downfall, drenching the wall until the orange glow turns to gray. Then he turns it off as quickly as he started it, standing back proudly.

"That should do it," he says, stepping back.

"Who goes first?" Atmos asks. "It should be Hayze and Aura. They made the hole."

Pace's eyes flare in panic. "But I—"

"Level passed," echoes a voice through Aura's mind.

Everyone pauses as they wait for the next crucial words.

146

"Water wins the Earth Quadrant."

Aura lets out a breath and smiles. Pace earned that. And maybe now he can dial down that competitive streak.

Which leaves her with only one question.

Who's going to win next?

CHAPTER
SIXTEEN
HAYZE

A blink is all it takes. A flash of white.

And Hayze is standing in the windswept Stormsphere.

"For fractal's sake," he growls, registering he's alone, just like the first time. Although he knew this was coming, it doesn't mean he likes it.

Or accepts it.

He stomps around the boulder, remembering it was Aura who found him last time. He's only halfway when she barrels around. The moment their gazes connect, she leaps into his arms.

Hayze holds her tight, pressing a kiss to her temple, her cheek, her lips. Aura sighs at the first, leans into the second, and shivers as their mouths meld. It takes his breath away far more completely than any wonder in the world could.

This is all that matters. This is all that's ever mattered. Even when Aura gets her memories back, surely she'll realize that.

They pull back, clasping hands. Their fingers weave

together tightly, the feeling so familiar that Hayze's heart rate settles. He looks around, already knowing what to expect. They're high on a mountain, the Stormsphere spread out below, the sky stretching for miles above.

"Is this how it's going to be?" he calls out. A repeat in each of the four Quadrants, just to see what they're capable of. To see who will *win*. "Because it's getting monotonous!"

Aura squeezes his hand. "I'm pretty sure we don't want to be challenging them," she says. She glances up even as her brow comes down. "Even if they're being jerks."

Hayze almost grins. She's right. On both counts.

"Aura?" Jewel cries out. "Aura!"

They hurry around the boulder, finding Jewel not far away, looking frantic. Relief fills her features when she sees Aura. When her gaze rises to Hayze, the relief blends with something else. Something he can't quite place. Confusion? Frustration?

Atmos appears, stopping beside Jewel. "Did I hear you talking to Eterna?" he asks smugly as he crosses his arms in his robes, which are now completely dry.

"The moment you realize it's the leaders pulling the strings, is the moment you'll realize who's listening," Hayze responds, shaking his head.

Pace jogs up behind Atmos, looking relieved to find them. "Here we go again, huh?" he says, patting a rock beside him.

"Seems so," Hayze says dryly. "We just keep doing what we've been doing. Working as a team."

Pace nods, followed by Jewel. Atmos rolls his eyes.

"We're stronger together," Aura says. "No Element exists on its own."

Hayze's chest fills with pride. How can someone be so beautiful and wise all at once?

Pace's shoulders hunch, having the grace to flush a little. "Work together. Got it."

Hayze wonders if Pace would've agreed so readily if he hadn't won the last Game, even as he's conscious he and Aura haven't won a Quadrant yet. While he doesn't give a damnatus about winning these Games, unease still slithers through his insides. If Aura loses, what will that mean...

"Cyclonis!" Atmos gasps, his face lighting up as he stares further up the mountain.

Hayze sighs, remembering what else was waiting for them in the Stormsphere. The Air leader. He shakes his head. "He's as real as everything else out here."

Atmos scowls as he whips around to face Hayze. "He's also as real as you or me."

Hayze presses his lips together as he admits Atmos has a point. He's met Cyclonis, along with all the leaders.

"He is," he says, his voice low and tight. "He was there when I woke up. They all were. They were also there when Geo died right beside me. Cyclonis was the one who said they'll dispose of him discreetly."

"He has to be like that! He's closer to Eterna than we are," Atmos says, throwing his arms out wide. "He knows things we don't!"

Like why these Games exist in the first place.

Aura shakes her head, possibly sensing the frustration bubbling up in Hayze. "Right now, we need to keep moving." Her mouth twists bitterly. "We need to pass this Quadrant."

Atmos inflates his chest. "Exactly. And this is my Quadrant. Which means I'm going to talk to Cyclonis."

"What?" Hayze explodes. "Don't you realize we've won the past two because we didn't repeat history? We don't need to go up, we need to go down."

"To the Sect," Jewel adds quietly.

Pace crosses his arms. "To the Sect," he repeats far more firmly.

Atmos shakes his head, then turns away. "My leader is here. It's a sign. We need to talk to him. To help us understand the perfectly good reason they're doing all of this."

Hayze leaps forward and grabs his sleeve. "We're going down the mountain, not up."

"You can," Atmos snaps, snatching the material out of Hayze's grasp. "I'm going to talk to my esteemed leader."

Hayze has to stop himself from grabbing him again and trying to shake some sense into him. He doesn't have time for this. The leaders are no doubt making their way through the Quadrants looking for him.

Determined to wrench him back out of the Games.

Aura's hand presses against his arm. "We need to go with him."

The second urge to grab Atmos and this time throw him down the mountain explodes through Hayze. Aura's warm palm presses in a little harder and he looks down at her.

"Whatever you're planning, it's not a good idea," she says.

He shakes his head ruefully. "How did we not see that we're so deeply connected?" he muses, lifting her hand to kiss her knuckles.

Aura's the better half of him.

Her lips angle up in a graceful curve. "Well, we didn't exactly stay away from each other."

Pace clears his throat. "So we're going after air-for-brains?"

Hayze huffs. Once again, Aura's right. They need to stick together. That's what a team does. "Mostly so I can set his robes alight."

Pace chuckles. "I hope you're not expecting me to put them out."

Hayze grins, and their gazes connect for a moment. A strange sense of understanding passes between them. In some ways, Hayze has lived Pace's life. Just like his mind is still defined by Hayze's. It's a weird connection along with a crazy-assed invasion of privacy.

Hayze can understand Pace's drive to win the Games. His memories are those of growing up with a childhood sweetheart. And even if he can convince himself that's not real, he has no recollection of hating Tempo. Hayze knows the deep need to get back by her side.

Pace nods, as if they just agreed on something.

Either that or they're now a team.

Or that the girls who have their hearts come first.

Hayze is hoping it won't have to be a choice.

"We'd better hurry," Jewel says, striding past. "We need to catch up."

Hayze blinks even as Aura smiles proudly. Jewel is blossoming in front of their eyes.

They follow, Pace coming up the rear, moving quickly up the path they took the first time. A gust of wind buffets them and more memories assault Hayze. The run through the mountain. The great shudders that ripped through it. Cyclonis locking them out.

The storm that was powerful enough to drop a boulder on Hayze.

"We have to convince Atmos to go back down before this really picks up," Aura says, her face tightening.

Hayze wonders if she's remembering, too. "Don't forget. We can't die."

She nods even as her hand tightens around his. Aura's seen Hayze *die* twice now. First here in the Stormsphere, then in the Scorchlands. He wouldn't want to live with the images of Aura going through the same thing.

The sweet sound of the wind sculptures reaches Hayze right before Atmos's voice does. "Cyclonis! I'm so glad to see you."

They climb the final few steps to the flattened area. Cyclonis is standing in the middle this time, although just as silent and inscrutable. The silver sculptures twirl and turn with the gusts of wind, the music ebbing and flowing. Hayze instinctively looks toward the ledge where Geo stood, trying to harness Earth. His mind believed he'd died as he called rocks and boulders to him.

His body followed not long later.

Atmos bows in front of Cyclonis. "Great leader. I am here."

A powerful gust of wind billows both of their robes and angles Cyclonis's beard over his chest. "I can see that."

Hayze strides across the stone area, deciding if he's here, then he's going to make the most of it. "Is Tempo okay?" he demands.

Pace appears by his side, his hands clenched as he waits for an answer.

Atmos gasps. "You can't—"

"Your time out here is limited," Cyclonis says, his hard gaze settling on Hayze.

He lifts his chin. "Maybe it's your time that's limited."

"You will learn your place, Fire boy," Cyclonis growls as he drops his chin.

"I already have." Hayze wraps his hand around Aura's. "Seems I'm not the slow learner around here."

Atmos's second gasp is louder, sharper. "I will blow you off this ledge if you speak to my leader like that again!"

"Do it," Cyclonis says, turning to look at Atmos for the first time.

He rears back. "What?"

"You heard your esteemed leader." Another gust of wind ripples through Cyclonis's robes. "Do it. Send him off the ledge."

Hayze's pulse stutters. "Don't listen to him, Atmos."

"They're trying to divide us," Aura says, stepping in between Hayze and Atmos.

Atmos has gone pale. "I..."

"Show me what you're capable of!" Cyclonis roars. "Show me the depth of your loyalty!"

Atmos swallows, then turns to face Hayze. "For Eterna," he whispers.

Hayze steps around Aura, tucking her behind him. "Don't do this, Atmos. We're a team, remember?"

Atmos raises his hands as his face hardens. "It's not a sign, Hayze. It's an order."

Aura gasps, quickly stepping up beside Hayze again. "It's neither of those! It's a test to see what you'll do!"

Atmos's brow puckers as he focuses. "I am Air!" he shouts.

A gust of wind buffets Hayze. He draws Aura to him, knowing she won't leave his side, just like he wouldn't leave hers. He glares at Atmos, at his betrayal, his hand twitching as his side.

With this wind, fire will be hard to control. But all he needs to do is make it a little warm under the guy's feet. Break his concentration.

The cry that whips through the air comes from Cyclonis. He leaps back, glaring at the flames licking at the edges of his robes. Atmos's eyes widen as he sees them climb up, his gaze shooting to Hayze.

"I'm not doing it!" Hayze shouts, taking a step back and bringing Aura with him.

"This is what happened with the feather!" Cyclonis screams, batting at the growing flames. "Hayze didn't realize he was doing it then, either!"

Atmos's face twists with fury. "You attacked my leader!"

"I didn't!" Hayze shouts, unsure how Cyclonis caught fire but certain it wasn't him.

"Liar!" Atmos flings his hands forward. "I am Air!"

This time, there's nothing. In fact, the wind dies a little, Cyclonis's screams eclipsing the music of the wind sculptures.

"I am Air!" Atmos shouts as loud as he can.

A breeze buffets them, but it's nothing more than the rhythm of the weather.

Pace crosses his arms. "I'm pretty sure he's a dud."

Jewel appears behind Aura, wringing her hands. "Someone needs to stop this," she whimpers.

"I am not a dud!" Atmos screeches. "I am Air!"

This time, there's a powerful gust. Except it has Atmos stumbling and falling onto his hands and knees. As if he wasn't in control. Lightning cracks above, followed by booming thunder.

"I told you!" Atmos cries, just as another blast almost pushes him onto his side.

"Then save your esteemed leader," Pace sneers, bracing himself against the wind. "Blow the fire out."

Cyclonis's screams increase as he whips and whirls. The flames reach his chest, the acrid scent of burned cloth filling the air. Atmos struggles to his knees, only to be thrown onto his back. The wind seems to be targeting him.

Just like Aura said, this is a test. Both of his powers and his loyalty.

Hayze looks back at Cyclonis as he lifts his hands, prepared to put the flames out himself. He freezes before his hands have even left his side. He can't put out the flames.

Because they're not real.

Cyclonis is now standing still, glaring at Hayze. His skin isn't darkening and blistering. His hair and beard are untouched even as flames lick at every inch of his skin. With a flicker of a smile, he raises his hands.

The storm escalates. Jewel cries out as she's pushed back

and Aura quickly grabs her. A bolt of lightning cracks across the darkening sky, splitting and fracturing as it spears toward the mountain. One beam of blinding neon hits the top, another hits a boulder, exploding rock in all directions. There's barely time to duck as a third strikes a wind sculpture in an explosion of sparks.

There's a screech of metal as it topples, only to be wrenched by the wind. Jewel screams as it spears toward them, a twisting, flailing mass of deadly silver. Hayze drags Aura to the ground, who brings Jewel with them. Pace follows an instant later. Atmos never had the chance to get back up.

The sculpture whooshes over them, its music now an ear-splitting howl. It's propelled out over the edge, then up into the black sky.

Hayze gets to his feet, pushing them into the ground as the cyclone-level wind tries to take him, too. Aura joins him, clinging to Jewel. More lightning hits the stone expanse, coming closer and closer.

Hayze hauls Atmos to his feet as a deluge of rain instantly saturates them both. "This is a definite sign to get the heckus out of here!"

They should never have come up the mountain. They're supposed to be on their way to the Sect.

"Aura was right! This is Eterna testing me!" Atmos screams back, wrenching himself away. "To see whether I'll desert my leader!"

"What damnatus leader?" Hayze hurls back.

Atmos spins around, registering Cyclonis is gone. He goes still, breathing hard as he looks one way, then the other.

Hayze isn't sure what happens first. Atmos's realization that his *esteemed* leader has abandoned him. Or that he's lifting off the ground.

His panicked scream captures the shock of both. Hayze and

Pace leap forward, trying to grab him, but he's whipped away too quickly.

In a blink, he's swept away by the very element he can't seem to harness.

"You can't die!" Hayze shouts as Atmos's pale face is swallowed by gray rain.

The next bolt of lightning reveals an empty sky.

Hayze turns back to Aura as she huddles protectively around Jewel. "We need to get back down the mountain!"

Aura nods, even as the color drains from her wet face. They've done this once before and they both know how that ended.

"I can stop the rain!" Pace shouts, breaking into a run back in the direction they came.

Hayze never gets to take a step. He makes the mistake of blinking.

In the space of his eyelids coming down in an attempt to clear the water from his sight, everything changes. When they rise again, everything—the storm, the adrenaline-inducing danger, even Aura—are gone.

"Level failed," echoes a voice through his mind.

He's back down the mountain. Alone. Everything is quiet, peaceful.

No one won.

And they have to do it all over again.

CHAPTER
SEVENTEEN
AURA

"You've got to be kidding me." Aura sits up and scowls. Now she's not just stuck in a world without escape, but it's playing on repeat.

She gets up and runs toward the boulder she knows Hayze will be behind, only to find he's already rushing to her. He wraps her in his arms, and she presses herself to the broad chest she knows doesn't exist, which is even harder to believe when she can feel the beating of his heart.

"This time we do things differently," says Hayze.

"Agree." Aura leans up to kiss his soft lips. "Because I'm not doing that again."

"You're not kissing me again?" he teases, his face only an inch from hers.

She laughs. "We both know I'd last about five minutes not doing that."

"Good." He brings his mouth to hers and she does her best to forget it's not really him. She can't wait to kiss him in real life. According to Hayze, she already has—many times—

although it would be nice to be able to remember just one of those occasions.

"There they are," says Pace. "Cut it out, would you?"

Aura pulls back laughing. "Like you're one to talk. We didn't know what you looked like face-on for days after we met you."

Atmos and Jewel are standing with Pace. Jewel is looking anywhere but at Aura and Hayze, making Aura wonder if those feelings she suspected Jewel had for Hayze are still there.

"Cyclonis is here again." Atmos points up the mountain with hurt stamped across his features. His esteemed leader abandoned him. No, actually it was worse than that. He provoked him. Fooled him. And ultimately, left him to fail.

Jewel puts a hand on Atmos's arm. "We can't talk to him ag—"

"I know," he snaps, pulling away. "Let's head for the Sect."

Atmos turns his back on Cyclonis and takes a path that leads directly down the mountain. His purple robes billow in the breeze, the rich color a magnificent contrast to the glittering pinwheels that dot the terrain.

"Thank Eterna for that," mutters Pace, his tone laced with sarcasm.

They follow Atmos down the path, wanting to stay together, and knowing they need to make as much progress as they can before the leaders throw down their next challenge. Winning this Quadrant can't possibly be as simple as walking to Aeris without a single obstacle blocking their way.

"I used up my one chance," says Atmos, not seeming to be directing his comment at any one of them in particular.

"Not necessarily." Hayze lets go of Aura's hand to catch up to him.

"What do you mean?" Atmos keeps his gaze ahead as he walks. "I was sucked into the sky. I felt myself dying."

"You *felt* it," says Hayze. "But did you *believe* it?"

Aura walks a little faster, keen to hear Atmos's response.

"I'm not sure," he says after some thought.

"Your body—your *real* body—will only die if your mind believes it," says Hayze. "Theoretically, we have infinite chances as long as our minds don't buy into what's happening."

"How can you be so sure?" Atmos asks.

"I'm not." Hayze throws out his hands. "It just makes sense."

Aura clears her throat. "Let's not test that theory out though, okay?"

If Hayze is wrong and something happens to him, she could lose him again. They're on borrowed time as it is. The leaders are certain to track him down and pull him out of the Games at any moment. It's actually surprising he's still here. She thought they'd have found him in Tempo's pod in Aqua by now.

"What's that thing down there?" Jewel asks.

Aura turns to see where she's pointing, then squints ahead. There's a large patch of purple off the path to the east.

"Are they flowers?" Pace asks.

"The color's too dense," says Atmos. "It looks like something made by humans."

Hayze frowns. "Maybe it's a glitch."

"Only one way to find out." Aura steps off the path and Hayze quickly leaves Atmos's side to go to her. She can't say she's unhappy about his habit of not letting her get too far away. She'd glue herself to him if she could.

They pick their way over rocks and around boulders, heading across the uneven ground to get to the purple patch. Aura stumbles a few times, grateful for her leather shoes to protect the soles of her feet.

"Are you okay," she asks Jewel, glancing down at the Earth girl's bare feet.

Jewel smiles. "I'm used to it. I could probably have walked on the broken glass in that cave and been fine."

"Well, if you need to wear my shoes for a bit, let me know," says Aura, not wanting to be selfish.

"I'll have them," says Atmos, limping behind them. "I stepped on a sharp rock back there."

"Your feet are too big," Hayze says.

Atmos mutters something unintelligible.

"And they're too small for mine," says Hayze. "If you'd listened to us the first time we woke up here, we'd be down the bottom of the mountain by now."

"He makes a good point," says Pace.

"Nobody asked for your opinion." Atmos walks a little faster.

"I think it's fabric," says Jewel.

It takes Aura a few seconds to realize she's talking about the patch of purple.

"It could be a tent." Jewel's voice is filled with excitement, even though Aura could think of nothing worse than sleeping in a tent with Atmos and Pace bickering all night.

Jewel runs ahead, catching up to Atmos, then passing him. Pace is right on her heels.

"Let them get there first." Hayze takes Aura's hand and squeezes it. "It's nice to be alone for a moment."

Just as Aura is about to sneak in a quick kiss, there's a rumble high up the mountain. They spin around to see a cloud of dust forming as the thundering gets closer.

"Boulders!" Aura gasps as she sees several large stones tumbling toward them.

"This way!" Hayze yanks on Aura's hand, dragging her a few feet to the left. But the boulders bounce and change direction, forcing them to leap back to where they'd been standing moments ago. Again, the boulders bounce, changing their trajectory and Aura and Hayze scurry further to the right.

"It's a set up," Aura growls when the boulders follow their movements. "They want us to use our powers to stop them."

"We need Jewel," Hayze pants. "It's turning into an avalanche."

Jewel is a few yards away, staring up the mountain with her hands raised. Several of the boulders crumble, sending up clouds of dust, but more take their place as the size of the catastrophe grows.

Hayze throws out his arms and the largest of the boulders explodes in a ball of fire. He immediately flicks his hands and more rocks burst into flames.

Aura's eyes widen and she quickly gets herself into position, sending out flames of her own, her body jolting with a hit of adrenaline each time she connects with a boulder and decimates it.

Rocks crash past, missing them by only a couple of feet as Aura and Hayze keep their focus, clearing what they can and dodging what they can't.

A wall of water opens up at the top of the mountain and surges down. It sweeps the boulders off course and funnels into a raging river. Aura spins around to see Pace waving his hands with Atmos cowering beside him. Pace's face is pinched in intense concentration as the water rushes past, and Aura turns back to help Hayze take care of the remaining stray boulders coming their way.

Except there's a boulder bigger than any of the others. It bounces several feet away and heads directly for Aura.

She raises her hands, knowing she needs to use everything she has inside her to save herself from being crushed. She feels her Fire powers surge and explode out of her palms, but before she can connect with her target, she's pushed out of the way. Hayze lands on his back and raises his hands above him like he's trying to catch the mass of solid rock about to land on him.

"No!" Aura cries, getting her balance and sending out two bolts of fire.

But it's too late.

The boulder lands on Hayze, just like it had the first time they came to the Stormsphere.

There's no way anyone could survive that kind of force.

Grief tears through Aura's soul and she rushes to Hayze as the boulder bounces back up into the air and continues down the mountain. Miraculously, Hayze doesn't seem to have so much as a scratch on him, even though his eyes are closed and he's not moving.

"Hayze!" Aura throws herself on him, cradling the only guy she'll ever love. She looks down at his face in her lap and his eyes open.

"Seems my theory was correct, after all," he says with a wink.

The panic surging through Aura's veins turns to pure relief.

"You're still here," she says, leaning down to kiss his dusty cheeks.

"Actually, I'm right beside you in Ignis in a pod." He sits up and pulls her into a hug.

She wraps her arms around him, not caring if he's virtual, real or something in between. Because she can see him. Feel him. Hold him. And that's all that matters.

"Whoa," says Jewel beside them with wide eyes. "You're alive."

"Impressive." Pace shakes his head. "That thing landed right on top of you."

Aura looks around to see the surge of water has vanished

and the boulders have cleared, leaving only clouds of dust behind. Clouds that Atmos doesn't seem to have been able to clear.

"We're not finished yet, are we?" Jewel sighs. "I'm ready to move onto the Scorchlands, and that's saying something as that place was awful last time. No offense."

"None taken," Aura says honestly. It's hard to be offended by someone insulting a home you can't even remember.

"Where's Atmos?" Hayze asks, looking around. "Did he…"

"He's down there," says Jewel, pointing to the purple patch, which appears to have been magically untouched by the boulders.

"Whatever that thing is, it has to be important." Aura gets up and puts out her hands to help haul Hayze to his feet. Any excuse to hold his hand, really…

"It's definitely purple fabric," says Jewel.

They make their way further down and Aura soon sees Jewel is right. Atmos is standing beside a mass of purple fabric that he's moved to uncover a large basket. It's one of the strangest contraptions Aura's seen.

"What is that thing?" Pace asks, seeming just as confused.

"I think it's a balloon," says Jewel. "People used them to travel through the sky before the weather became too unstable for it to be safe."

"How do you know all this?" Aura asks, impressed.

Jewel shrugs. "My mom told me about them once. I've never seen one in real life though."

"Ah, and you still haven't," Hayze reminds her. "None of this is real. What happened to me just now proves how important it is to remember that."

"You're right." Jewel nods. "I keep forgetting."

"Which can be deadly," says Hayze.

Atmos sees them coming and turns to face them. "It's a

flying machine. We just need to figure out how to fill this pocket thing with air."

"Well, lucky we have someone here with Air powers," says Pace, sarcasm seeming to become his favored way of speaking. Or maybe just when addressing Atmos.

"I'm not a dud." Atmos swallows and nods. "I can do it."

"Wait," says Jewel. "It's called a balloon, not a pocket. And filling it with air won't make it fly. When balloons were used in ancient times, people would burn gas to heat the air inside. That's what lifted it off the ground."

Pace seems confused.

"Hot air rises," Jewel explains. "You're thinking about the wrong Element. We need Fire, not Air."

"But we don't have any gas to burn," says Pace.

"We don't need any." Aura steps forward. "Hayze and I can make flames to heat the air."

"That could work." Jewel's face lights up. "Fire could win this Quadrant. Which leaves only Air for next time. We can all win one each, just like we said."

Pace laughs. "Like Air has a chance of winning in Fire."

"Actually," says Hayze. "Fire can't exist without Air."

Atmos shoots Hayze a grateful smile as Aura's heart swells with just a little more love.

"We have to be careful not to burn a hole in the balloon," says Aura. "And I have no idea how we steer this thing."

Atmos plucks a pinwheel from the ground and holds it above his head. "We're in luck," he announces. "The wind is blowing toward Aeris. We could fly right over it and go straight to the Sect."

"That sounds dangerous," says Jewel. "I'm in!"

Aura laughs, not having expected that.

"Turn the balloon around," says Jewel, taking hold of the edge of the basket. "We need it to catch the breeze."

They work together to tip the large basket on its side and Atmos and Hayze hold open the throat of the balloon. The relentless wind of the Stormsphere rushes over it, catching the thin fabric.

"Pace, take over for me!" calls Hayze as it billows. "I need to work with Aura to heat the air."

Atmos doesn't seem at all pleased with his new partner but keeps silent as he holds open the balloon.

A huge gust of wind blows down the mountain and the balloon expands, dragging the basket a few feet along the ground.

"Get ready to climb in!" Pace calls, running beside the balloon with Atmos.

Hayze and Aura scramble after them as Jewel crawls inside the basket.

"We can make heat without flames," says Hayze. "We can do this! Just concentrate."

Aura nods, putting out her hands and imagining heat pouring from her fingertips. Something must work as, very slowly, the balloon starts to rise off the ground.

"Now!" Pace cries out. "Get in!"

They clamber inside the basket just as the balloon pulls it upright. It's a tight fit inside for all five of them, but they manage and hopefully it can take their weight.

Aura tries to keep her focus on the air inside the balloon, petrified she's going to set the fabric alight. She couldn't bear to have to wake up in this Quadrant and start again.

Hayze is staring intently above him and the balloon drags the basket along the ground for several feet, then miraculously lifts it off the ground.

"Woo hoo!" Jewel hollers.

Aura can't summon the same level of excitement as Jewel, but it does feel like they've made progress. Now they just need to stay alive long enough for the leaders to deem them to have passed.

The balloon picks up speed, climbing higher and the ground moves beneath them at a rate Aura's never traveled at before, not even on her family's barge back home. *Tempo's home*, she reminds herself, still finding it hard to accept these memories don't belong to her.

The wind intensifies and Aura presses herself to Hayze, not daring to break her focus on heating the air inside the balloon. To fall from this height would be lethal.

Urgh. Not lethal. Just...highly inconvenient.

How can Hayze expect them to remember they're perfectly safe when everything feels so real?

"We're going too high!" Jewel calls out, and Aura backs off on the heat she's releasing, feeling Hayze beside her do the same. But they're caught in an air current and it picks them up like a leaf on a breeze, sending them soaring across the sky at a speed. Aura's stomach climbs into her throat as her hair blows in her face.

"I can see the Sect!" Pace shouts. "Keep going!"

A voice rattles through Aura's mind. And she couldn't be happier to hear it.

"Level passed. Fire wins the Air Quadrant."

Aura waits for the world to go white so she can hurry up and get to the Fire Quadrant. Then she can wake up in the bed that's really her own and see the people who are really her parents.

Except this time, it's different.

Where there should be white, there's color. Where there should be nothing, there's...everything.

EIGHTEEN

HAYZE

Hayze is already leaping to his feet as his eyes open. He's in the Fire Quadrant. He's home!

The cement bunker that greets him has him grinning. He draws in a deep breath, pulling in the scent of the gray walls, even as he knows it's not real. It may be a simulation, but it's home. And everything is going to be different this time.

Reaching down, he picks up the dented metal box that's always sat beside his bed. Opening it, he trails his fingers over the paints inside. Images of his reunion with Aura are already forming in his mind. A mixture of the brown and red would capture her hair. The blue of her eyes has always been tricky, but he's found just the right ratio of sky blue to aqua. The art is in the details, the way the light catches the deep ocean colors, the contrast of her dark lashes. Their fingers will intertwine, fitting as if the gaps were designed for the other. She'll smile at him. He'll want to kiss her, yet be unwilling to move, so the moment stretches forever.

Aura looking at him, her soft gaze echoing his love and

tenderness and wonder, is where he wants to spend the rest of his life.

Except she'll look at him like that because she still doesn't remember...

Putting the box on the table with a soft clang, Hayze wipes his hand down his face. But the frown that just tugged everything down doesn't go away.

"You didn't trust me enough to tell me."

The same pain as that night slices through him. The betrayal on Aura's face was devastating.

And he's done it again.

Hayze spins around and strides to the door. All the same reasons are on a loop in his mind.

He was torn.

He didn't want to hurt her.

He was so freaking scared.

Yet each one undermines everything he's ever promised the girl who holds his heart.

Yanking the door open, the same room that greeted him the last time is there, and he marvels at the detail the leaders have been able to recreate in this fake reality. The coal smudges on the floor where he's drawn endless pictures and his mother patiently cleaned it off, creating another canvas in a world that doesn't have time for art. The dented can on the bottom shelf that lost its label so long ago, no one remembers what it contains. Even the faint scent of burning coal that Hayze never realized was his normal until he was wrenched away.

The leaders have been watching them closely, no doubt preparing for their eighteenth birthday.

The hatch in the floor lifts an inch, hovers, then rises the rest of the way. This time, Hayze isn't scared. In fact, he's looking forward to seeing his parents.

His mom's sooty head appears and she looks around. She blinks when she sees him, her face softening. "Ah, you're awake." She looks down the hole she's standing in. "He's awake."

"Good news," his father grunts from below.

Hayze rushes over, reaching down to grab the canary cage from her. "Let me take that."

She releases it with a grateful smile, then clambers up as he steps back, placing the cage on the table. His mom reaches down and grabs the basket of coal and hauls it out. His father follows a moment later.

"Hello, son. Great to see you on your feet again," his father says, looking at him intently.

Hayze grins. He remembers his parents being happier to see him the first time he went through this simulation, but those are the words his father said. "I'm feeling much better."

"That's good," his mother says, relief unwinding her muscles. "I didn't think you'd recover so quickly."

That's because he was never sick.

"I know you want me to get back to my training, Dad. But I have some things to take care of."

His father's brows shoot up. "No rush. It's going to take time to...adjust."

Hayze was about to move, but he stops. "I'm seriously okay. I promise," he says, although he's not certain why he's reassuring them, considering none of this is real.

His mother steps forward. "Maybe you should go back to bed, son."

Although they're the same words that were spoken to him the first time, uneasiness slides down Hayze's spine. He knew this time would be different. He intended on it being different. Was looking forward to it.

But now that he's here...

He glances up at the ceiling. "That's what you want, isn't

170

it? To make me worried." He lifts his chin. "It doesn't matter what you do, it won't change anything."

He'll find Aura. He belongs by her side.

"Who are you talking to, honey?" his mom asks, frowning.

"Sh, Sera," Hayze's father says. "Loss isn't easy."

Hayze is about to ask them where Aura is, but he swallows the words. He already knows where she is. And it's time for this mind warp to be over. "I gotta go," he says, stepping around them.

"Hayze—" his mother calls out as he opens the door.

"Let him go, Sera," his father says, his voice subdued. "You know this is going to take time for him to accept."

Hayze shuts the door behind him, the words his father spoke last time echoing through his mind.

"He'll be better once he sees Aura. Those two can't seem to spend too much time apart."

Why are his parents acting as if he's going through the stages of grief?

Outside, he strides past the first bunker, ignoring the old woman who shuffles out. He stops at the rusted, metal door two doors down. Just like last time, he opens it so fast, the flame in the cauldron not far away flickers with the whoosh of air. He strides in, stopping almost instantly.

His breath leaves his body.

His heart stutters, stammers, then plummets.

Aura's not here.

Vesta jumps up from the table she was sitting at, her cup of tea clattering. "What are you doing here?" she screeches.

Hayze rears back. Vesta's never spoken to him like that. "Where is she?" he whispers.

"Gone!" Brando roars, storming out from the room beyond. "Thanks to you!"

"W-what?" Hayze stammers.

Vesta stalks forward, jabbing a finger into his chest. "She came home two nights ago, saying you'd kept secrets. Lied to her. That she couldn't stay here anymore."

Hayze feels light-headed. "She wouldn't…"

Except he did lie to her. He did keep secrets.

And Aura was devastated when she found out.

He shakes his head, as if that will loosen the choking grip fear has on him. "Where? Where did she go?"

"Somewhere far away." Vesta shakes her head. "She has a broken heart to try to heal."

Hayze takes a stumbling step backward. Then another. Three words carousel through his mind.

This isn't real.

This isn't real.

This isn't real.

Clearly, the leaders have been watching closely enough to know that he and Aura had a terrible argument the night before their eighteenth birthday. They're trying to weave that into what can only be Hayze's worst nightmare.

He stumbles back several more steps, finding himself outside the bunker. There's a roaring in his ears even though his heart is frozen. "I have to find her," he murmurs through numb lips. "I need to explain—"

A body crashes into him, then quickly steps back. "Sorry. Oh, hello Hayze."

He registers Pyra. And the way her tone just softened and lowered.

"I was just coming to check up on you," she offers gently.

The door to Aura's house slams shut with a clang that reverberates through his marrow.

Pyra grimaces as she lifts a metal tin up to show him. "I know you're hurting. I thought painting might help."

"No."

He isn't sure what he's denying as he steps around her, but Hayze doesn't stop. He strides away from Pyra, from the worst thing that could happen to him, away from the village.

It's not real.

He makes his way toward the wall, pushing away the memories of seeing the lava burst through in its relentless drive to incinerate everything. He needs to find the others. Then they need to find Aura.

He steps through the gate, the memory of being here with Aura packing salt into the wound corroding his heart. They kissed here. It was physical proof they fell in love all over again.

Just like he lied and kept secrets all over again.

"You won't find her."

Hayze spins around, finding Rateen standing a few feet away, the gate open behind her. He narrows his eyes as he remembers she's the one who told them where to look for the others the first time they were here. And that Pace and Tempo didn't know who she was.

Just like he has no memories of ever seeing her before the Games.

"You're a messenger for the leaders," he says, realization hitting him.

Rateen inclines her head, her dark eyes glinting as if all the knowledge she holds is gold.

Hayze stalks toward her. "Where's Aura?"

Rateen lifts her hand. "Although you can't hurt me, I'd recommend you don't come any closer."

He stops, even though that's the last thing he wants to do. He needs to hear what she has to say.

"We've taken Aura out of the Games," Rateen says.

"You what?" he gasps, not expecting those words to assault his ears.

Rateen smiles. "We have Aura. The only way to free her is to leave the Games and hand yourself in."

Hayze draws in a sharp breath. He needs to think, not react, even though he's furious. And terrified.

If they have Aura...

He straightens, another realization hitting him. "You haven't found me."

If Rateen's telling the truth, they've taken Aura because he's still here. They haven't reached him in Tempo's pod.

Rateen's face tightens. "If we're forced to keep searching, it won't end well for either of you."

Hayze shakes his head, his hot palms reinforcing the next statement. "And yet, you need Fire."

The leaders have invested a lot into unleashing the power within him and Aura. They've killed for it.

Rateen lifts her chin as she takes a step backward, closer to the gate. "Your choice, Hayze. We've taken Aura out of the Games. She's under our...protection."

"I don't trust you," Hayze spits. "Lies are your truth."

"Can you afford to be wrong?" she taunts.

Hayze's hands feel like they're about to burst into flames at any moment. "I can't leave the Games on my own. You know that."

"Tell us where you are. We'll do the rest."

If he does that, he exposes Tide.

And something bigger than either of them. Something he learned about not long before he turned eighteen.

Hayze shakes his head, tortured that he's once more having to face the decision that came between him and Aura in the first place.

His love or his loyalty.

And that this time, it's going to look like he's making the same choice.

Hayze turns away from Rateen, stretching out his strides as he walks away. "Tell the leaders I'll see them in the Sect," he calls over his shoulder.

He doesn't bother to look back as he weaves his way through the black trunks of what was a forest long before anyone in the village can remember. Aura wouldn't want him to betray Tide. She wouldn't want him to turn his back on the others.

Aura would want him to believe in her, like he failed to do the first time.

He just has to hope she knows he'll come for her. That despite how this looks, he's choosing her.

Hayze hasn't got far when he hears footsteps crunching through the desiccated forest. Atmos's grumblings quickly follow, along with Pace's impatience. They all break into a jog the moment they see each other, meeting halfway.

Jewel frowns. "Where's Aura?"

Hayze swallows, feeling like he's let her down. Jewel's always stayed close to Aura. "They've pulled her out of the Games."

As punishment for his defiance.

Jewel goes pale while Atmos mutters "lucky girl" under his breath.

Pace frowns as he stares at the black soil beneath his feet. Hayze suspects he knows what he's thinking. Pace carries Hayze's memories. He knows there's a maze of mines beneath them.

That a tunnel leads directly to the wall surrounding the Sect.

He looks up, his face hard with determination. "I suggest we take the shortcut."

Hayze nods, his breath whooshing out. If Aura has been captured, then three Elements are much better than one.

He and Pace simultaneously jog to the nearest mine shaft, then step back so Jewel and Atmos can go first. Jewel clambers down the ladder without hesitating. No doubt because she's descending into the very Element she can wield, but probably because she's just as determined to get Aura back.

Atmos hesitates, then puffs his cheeks out on a huff before following Jewel.

Pace glances down, then up at Hayze. "Aura has her powers. She'll fight back."

Hayze nods, pretending his gut didn't just tighten. That's what he has to believe.

Pace's lips tip up. "She'll be back in your arms before you know it." With a quick grin, he scampers down so fast that Atmos calls out for him to get off his head.

Hayze stays where he is for a long second. Pace mustn't have all of his memories. He doesn't know Hayze and Aura fought. That a fracture opened up in what he assumed was their rock solid foundation.

Yet when Aura woke up, she would've remembered everything.

And Hayze's arms are the last place she'll want to be.

CHAPTER
NINETEEN

AURA

Aura wakes with a rush of memories flooding her mind.
She's Aura.

She's from Fire.

She's been holding Tempo's memories from Water.

And she's in love with Hayze.

Her desperate wish to recall just one of their kisses is granted and she remembers them all, from the first incredible time their lips connected until...

No!

A new memory hits her with force. Hayze betrayed her. Lied to her. Held back vital information. And when he re-entered the Games with his true memories intact, he still didn't tell her the truth.

Which means now he's betrayed her twice.

Fury throbs through her body.

How can she ever forgive him for that?

Her eyes open wide, and she gasps to see she's lying in what must be a pod. It's exactly like Hayze sketched. She's cocooned in a soft white bed with sides that curl up and around her. She reaches out to touch the glowing maze of white veins pulsing along the delicate material. Her fingertips connect and she pulls back when she discovers the surface is warm. It's a little creepy. Like being wrapped in someone else's skin.

Then she notices her hand, her Fire tattoo branding her just like it had when the Games had restarted. Just like it has all her life.

The sides of the pod unfurl to reveal four faces staring at her.

Cyclonis. Infernos. Avalan. Oceania.

"You pulled me out of the Games." Aura sits up, her fists balled at her sides. "Why?"

"We thought you'd be happy," says Infernos, his leather suit creaking as he raises a hand to his chin.

"Not without Ha..." Aura closes her mouth, reminding herself of her bruised feelings.

Infernos smiles. "I see you have your memories back."

"Don't worry." Oceania laughs. "I preferred Hayze when he thought he was from Water, too."

Ignoring the Water leader, Aura scans the large room with its white stone walls and solid door made from metal. They're clearly underground, except this is more like a prison cell than the bunker she grew up in. There's a desk with a control panel nearby and another empty pod beside hers.

"Where's Hayze?" Aura tries to swing her legs out of her pod, only for Infernos to clamp her down with a firm hand on her thigh.

"Why do you care?" he asks.

She swallows. How does she explain that even though she's angry with Hayze, it doesn't mean she wants any harm to come to him? She may have been living without her body, but she's always remained in possession of her heart.

"Where is he?" she asks again.

"Actually, we were hoping you could tell us that." Avalan adjusts a feather in her headdress. "We distinctly heard him tell you he was right here beside you, in Ignis. Was that code for something else?"

Aura thinks back to all the hurried conversations she had with Hayze after he returned to the Games. Avalan is right. He *had* said he was in Ignis. And he'd sketched himself in the pod beside Aura right here in this room. But he'd also drawn something else...

"What is it?" Oceania asks. "You remembered something."

"Nothing," Aura says quickly.

"What did you remember?" Oceania's gaze is steely. "I saw the look in your eyes."

"I'm surprised you can't read my thoughts." Aura tilts her head, relieved at least one aspect of her life has remained private. Because she'll never tell these so-called leaders what sparked that reaction in her. If they'd been paying attention, they'd remember what else Hayze sketched—Pace lying in his pod with his father standing over him. Drawn with the kind of detail only someone who'd seen the scene with their own eyes could possibly remember.

Which means Hayze is in Tempo's vacant pod.

Pace's father is a trade master. He'd know how to connect Hayze back into the Games. And Hayze had tried to buy himself some time by keeping that detail to himself. Which shouldn't be surprising. After all, Hayze is very good at keeping secrets...

"Interesting," says Oceania, her smooth head shining in the artificial light flickering from the stone ceiling. "This is the same person who attacked me and incinerated Geo's body. Why don't we see if the guy you're protecting would do the same for you?"

"Of course he would," says Aura without thinking. It seems standing up for Hayze is an automatic reflex now. But even if he failed her in real life, she can't dispute he protected her in the Games. She'd have died, just like Geo, several times over if Hayze hadn't been by her side.

"I think it's time for our NPC to give us a little help," says Avalan.

"I was just going to suggest that myself," says Oceania.

"What's an NPC?" Aura asks, fear lacing down her spine.

"Non-playable character," says Oceania, like that makes any more sense.

Avalan strides to the control desk, her headdress fluttering as she moves. She takes a seat and presses a button. A screen lights up on the wall in front of them and Avalan begins typing furiously.

"What's a—" Aura falls silent when she sees Hayze walking through the village they grew up in. The sight of him makes her heart ache with both love and pain. She never noticed before how similar the two emotions are. She both wants to hold him close and push him very far away.

Avalan continues to type.

"What's a non-playable character?" Aura asks.

Oceania steps forward. "It's someone we can use to help us manipulate the Games. Like when you and Hayze were taking too long to decide to look for the others in the Scorchlands. Our NPC gave you a little push."

"Do you mean, Rateen?" Aura asks, remembering the strange woman who'd talked to them in the village. She was the only person in the Scorchlands out of place. The one person Aura can't remember having ever met in real life.

"That's right," says Oceania. "She's quite useful. Just watch."

Aura turns back to the screen, seeing Hayze approach the

gate that leads to the Scorchlands. He spins around when he notices Rateen behind him.

Oceania marches over to Avalan. "Tell him he won't find Aura."

Avalan types quickly, her lips pursed in concentration.

"You won't find her," says Rateen.

Aura's jaw falls. The leaders are talking to Hayze directly through Rateen!

"You're a messenger for the leaders," says Hayze, making Aura smile widely. "Where's Aura?"

"I'm here!" Aura shouts, even though she knows he can't hear her. She turns to Avalan. "Please, don't do this," she begs. "Tell him I'm alright."

Avalan doesn't so much as look up from her furious typing as Hayze continues to talk to Rateen.

"We have Aura," Rateen tells him. "The only way to free her is to leave the Games and hand yourself in."

"I can't leave the Games on my own," Hayze says. "You know that."

"This isn't fair!" Aura tries again to get out of her pod, only for Infernos to increase the strength of his grip on her.

"All you have to do is tell us where you are." Rateen smiles at Hayze. "We'll do the rest."

Aura's heart thuds as she waits for his response, knowing with every cell in her body that despite what passed between them, Hayze is about to tell Rateen where he is. A part of her is screaming for him to stop, because that would mean jeopardizing Pace's dad, who must surely have helped Hayze get back into the Game. Yet without Aura, he can't possibly choose to stay. He'll want to get back to her as fast as he can.

She freezes as Hayze shakes his head.

And walks away.

Aura's heart sinks. She thought Hayze was going to do

whatever he could to ensure her safety. Not walk away like she never meant anything to him at all. Hurt stings her battered heart all over again.

Avalan presses a button and the wall goes blank. "It seems people from Fire really are quite stubborn."

Aura shakes her head, keeping her shoulders back and chin up. She will *not* let them see how upset she is. They've taken so much from her already. She's not going to give them another thing.

"Why did you pull me out of the Games?" she asks, struggling against Infernos's grip.

"We told you," he says. "When we came here and found Hayze's pod empty, we thought you could save us some time and tell us where he is."

"You need Hayze," Aura says. "The Fire Quadrant has no chance of winning the Games if you pull him out."

"We still have you." Infernos smiles. "And you've been doing so well with your powers."

"Not as well as Skylus." Cyclonis's voice beside them is filled with pride.

"Shame about Atmos," Oceania quips.

Aura shakes her head, trying to block them out as she focuses on the leader of her own Quadrant. "But I'm not in the Games," she says to Infernos. "Fire can't win if you pull us both out."

"But you can be put back in at any moment," he says.

Aura draws in a breath, thinking she finally understands. They've removed her from the Games purely to find out where Hayze is. Then she'll be put back in and forced to participate in their endless tasks as she hones her powers. The thought of it is unbearable, especially now that she knows the truth about Hayze.

"You've shown a lot of promise," says Infernos. "A lot more than Skylus, despite her strong start."

"I disagree!" Cyclonis booms, glaring at the Fire leader. "My Air girl can fly."

"According to Skylus, she's more powerful than Cyclonis himself," Oceania laughs.

Aura remembers Skylus joking about this. It's only now that she wonders if it wasn't said in jest. The leaders put them in the Games to harness powers that they themselves haven't been able to master. Which means maybe Aura isn't as helpless right now as she thought...

As the leaders argue over which Quadrant has the strongest competitor, Aura weighs up her options.

If she stays here, the leaders have full control over her. They could put her back in the Games or keep her locked in this room. Or worse, they could lock away her mind, trapping her in a reality of their making with no way to escape.

No. She refuses to be part of their sick experiment for another moment.

She's going to get herself out of here and find her way to Hayze.

Not to fall into his arms, like Aura from the Games would have.

But to release him so she, herself, can be free.

Of the Games, and of Hayze and the secrets he keeps.

"Put her back in," says Avalan, drawing Aura out of her thoughts. "It's clear she's not going to talk."

"There are only two options anyway," says Oceania, sounding bored. "He's either in Terra in Geo's pod, or he's in Aqua in Tempo's. And I can guarantee it won't be Aqua. I have my most trusted trade master in charge. I say we go straight to Terra."

"Well, he won't be there," huffs Avalan. "I also have my

most trusted trade master in charge. I say we go straight to Aqua."

Aura wishes she had more time to listen to this argument. She knew the Quadrants didn't get along at the best of times, but she hadn't quite realized the animosity between the leaders was this intense.

Before anyone has the chance to turn their attention back to Aura, she throws out her hands.

"I am Fire!" she shouts.

Flames shoot from her palms, catching on the skin of the pod and setting it alight. Fire ripples across the delicate surface, and the scent of burning flesh fills the room. Let them try putting her back in the Games now.

"No!" cries Infernos, waving his hands as if he can put out fire with desperation alone. "Not the pod!"

Aura drags in a breath and rolls out of the pod, extinguishing the flames that catch on her white suit before they have a chance to take hold. She lands in a crouch on the floor and unleashes another burst of flames directed at the other pod.

"Not that one too!" Infernos booms. "You can't do that!"

"I just did." Aura sweeps out her arms and spins in a circle, creating a ring of fire with her positioned safely in the center. The hungry flames hover around her and Aura stands, realizing she just created fire in real life. She's not in the Games. Which means her powers aren't some programming device or trick of the mind. She can actually do this!

The flames flicker as a shadow of doubt crosses her mind and she lets out a roar, fanning the ring of fire with renewed energy as she refuses to let them go.

Running for the metal door on the far wall, Aura reaches out, letting the flames die at the last moment so she can grab the handle and force it open. She steps through and turns around immediately to slam it closed. Summoning her powers again, she pours flames at the door, watching as they turn from red, to orange, then white as the intensity of the heat builds, melting the door into its frame.

Only when she's satisfied the leaders are locked inside does she extinguish the flames.

"Let us out!" Infernos shouts.

"How do you like it?" Aura cries out in response. "You're trapped, just like you trapped us inside the Games."

"Let us out this instance!" Oceania screeches.

"Why don't you use your powers to get free?" Aura shakes her head. "Oh, that's right. You don't have any."

She knows the leaders will break out of that room eventually. She just has to make sure she gets to Hayze before they do.

She looks around, finding herself in a long, dark tunnel with walls that immediately threaten to close in on her. Forcing down her fears, she draws on Tempo's memories that she still carries deep inside like they belong to her. Tempo wasn't scared of small spaces. She could run for miles through the tunnels without concern.

Aura can do that, too.

The leaders have inadvertently given her a way to cope with her fear of enclosed spaces.

Forcing one foot in front of the other, Aura turns her back on the room that held her prisoner for the longest time.

And runs.

CHAPTER
TWENTY

HAYZE

The tunnels hold more memories than Hayze knows what to do with.

So he simply focuses on leading the way through the underground maze as he holds a ball of fire in front of him. Pace is beside him, while Atmos and Jewel are a few feet behind. They're talking between themselves, but Hayze tuned out when he heard Atmos promising Jewel that Air and Earth are the perfect pair. Unlike Fire and Water, who essentially cancel each other out.

Hayze notices how Pace matches him step for step, just as confident in navigating these damp, dark tunnels as Hayze was navigating Aqua. It's odd knowing Pace has all the same images Hayze does, but with Tempo instead of Aura. And that when they're finally out of these Games, he'll have to align his real memories with what he's believed to be true.

"Thank you, Atmos," Jewel says behind them. "You're very kind."

Hayze knows Jewel's being nice just by saying something so untrue.

"Stick close to me," Atmos replies, the torch Hayze lit for him flickering as he waves it. "This fire won't go out with me here."

Except Jewel is Earth. She can control the tons of soil above them, beside them, around them. She could've probably dug these mines in a fraction of the generations it's taken the Fire people.

"He blew on that torch to get it started," Pace mutters under his breath.

Hayze doesn't comment even though he noticed that, too. He used his Fire powers to light the torch, saving the precious flint that was tucked into the shelf beside the stack of torches at the entrance to the mines. But Atmos had puffed and puffed as he helped the flames spread over the tightly wrapped cloth on the tip.

When he noticed Pace watching with raised eyebrows, he'd scowled. "What? I'm saving my powers for the Sect."

Hayze continues on, taking a right as they maintain their northeast direction. He tries to stop the memory that assails him, only to find it's too powerful. This is where Aura had her first panic attack. Deep underground, a significant distance from any chance of breathing fresh air.

He'd been terrified as he watched. She looked like she was suffocating, even as she'd breathed at a rate that made his own head swim. He'd pulled her back to the nearest ladder to the surface, relieved when the sudden affliction that gripped her in an iron fist faded away.

He'd painted the first mural the following day.

"She'll forgive you."

Hayze snaps his gaze to Pace. "What?"

"You get that pained look on your face whenever you're thinking of Aura," Pace replies, keeping his voice low. "She'll forgive you."

Hayze shakes his head, conscious Pace has no idea what he's talking about. "It's not that simple."

Pace smiles. "Tempo did."

Which is likely because Tempo also had no memory of that fateful night before their eighteenth birthday. "I'm glad for you," Hayze mumbles, meaning it in theory. He's glad Pace and Tempo were able to experience something beyond hate.

But Aura will finally have remembered by now after he kept the secret for even longer.

"Even after that awful fight," Pace adds.

Hayze almost trips over. The ball of fire hovering above his palm sputters and he has to refocus on keeping it alive. "What?" he asks, shocked once again into monosyllabic words.

Pace grins, then glances over his shoulder at Atmos and Jewel. He tucks his shoulders in as he whispers, "I know."

"You know what?" Hayze asks, knowing Pace must be careful what he says given the leaders are listening.

"Everything," says Pace. "As in, all of it."

Hayze stares straight ahead, realizing Pace is talking about the greatest secret Hayze has ever had to keep. Even from Aura.

The Elemental Alliance.

The tunnels split up ahead, one going right, the other left, the walls reinforced with extra wood and steel and whatever else Fire people can get hold of.

It's also where the first secret tunnel branches out.

Between two beams about a shoulder width apart are several planks of wood. A strengthened buttress.

And a secret entrance into a tunnel that heads straight for the Sect.

Hayze finally finds his voice as the automatic response pushes up through his tight throat. "I don't know what you're talking about."

Pace subtly inclines his head toward the intersection. "I know."

"Damnatus," Hayze mutters, accepting Pace really does know everything. And there's only one way to find out if the leaders know, too.

This time, the fireball does go out.

"Good thing I'm keeping this torch going," Atmos quips.

Frowning, Hayze brings his own torch back to life, a little tempted to nuke Atmos's. He doesn't out of respect for Jewel, but he can't help making it shrink just a little. He knows it works when he hears Atmos puff frantically.

"Definition of dud, right there," Pace says dryly.

Hayze turns to him as they stop at the tunnel intersection. "You remember..."

Pace nods, his gaze somber. "You sure had a lot for a guy to process when he first woke up."

"Why are we stopping?" Atmos demands as they approach.

"Just looking for a sign," Hayze says, his free hand roaming over the slats of timber.

In this virtual world, this should be nothing but a reinforced meeting of tunnels. It's good news if it's not, as the distance to the Sect would be significantly shorter.

But it would also mean the leaders know...

Pace steps forward. "Hopefully there's a sign behind here," he says a little too loud.

And Pace realizes it, too.

"Why would there be a sign behind some wood?" Atmos asks incredulously. He stills, angling his head. "I just felt a breeze. A definite sign we should turn right."

Pace snorts. "The only breeze is between your ears."

Hayze thinks he hears Jewel quickly muffle a giggle, but he focuses on digging his fingers into the gap between the edge of the timber and the adjoining metal beam. The wood doesn't budge, but he didn't expect it to. All the entrances to the secret tunnels are well hidden.

"Here, I'll do it," Pace says, stepping in.

"This is a total waste of time," Atmos grumbles.

Hayze draws back while Pace uses both hands to pull. The timber cracks, then a length snaps away.

All that's behind is rock and soil.

Simultaneous breaths leave Hayze and Pace.

The leaders don't know.

"Well?" Atmos asks. "What's there?"

Pace reaches in with his finger. He scratches at the dirt, then steps back. "A sign!"

Hayze brings his fireball closer, then can't help but chuckle at the small arrow etched into the dark soil.

"We need to go right," Pace announces, leading the way.

Shaking his head, Hayze follows, Atmos doing the same as he grumbles. This time, Jewel doesn't hide her giggle.

Hayze catches up to Pace, moving in close as he speaks in a whisper. "But you didn't say anything."

"Tempo and I spoke when we first woke up on the rafts. We decided trying to stay alive was our focus until we figured out what was going on." Pace smiles. "That's how I know Aura will forgive you. Tempo and I have already been through it."

Hope flashes through Hayze, far brighter and hotter than the flame in his hand.

But it banks and sputters almost instantly. Pace and Tempo talked about it. Hayze avoided bringing it up. There was little chance, but if he's being honest, he was just plain scared. He never wanted to see that look of betrayal in Aura's eyes again, the flash of ice as her feelings cooled.

He royally screwed up.

Twice.

"Come on," Hayze says, his voice rough. "We need to keep moving."

He breaks into a jog and the others join him. Their footsteps are muted by the soil and rock surrounding them, their breaths harsh. Hayze keeps his focus on navigating the tunnels, only speaking once.

"Are you okay, Jewel?" he asks, looking over his shoulder.

She nods, even though she's pale and puffed. "None of this is real, remember?"

He smiles at her, nodding back. It's nice that someone else is realizing that.

Jewel's face tightens. "Wanting to see Aura again is, though."

Turning back so they can take a right turn, Hayze's body also coils with tension. That's all he wants, too.

So he can make this right.

The tunnel angles up as they ascend, the air slowly becoming fresher, less damp and soil-scented. They reach a ladder and Hayze grabs the bottom rung.

"This takes us to the gate," he says, stepping up. "We need to stick close to each other."

He climbs, then pushes the metal covering aside, gritting his teeth as heat sears his palm. Harsh sunlight beats down as he clambers out, then scans their surroundings as the others do the same. The dusty, scorched area is empty, which he expected. His people usually go first thing in the morning to avoid the unrelenting sun. If anyone had coal to trade, they'd already have entered the markets by now, or even finished and left.

The towering gates are several yards away, embedded into the impenetrable wall that surrounds the Quadrants. Hayze looks around, still on high alert. This is the closest they've reached so far. There are guaranteed to be hurdles along the way. Will it rain ice caps? Lightning could arc up from the ground? Is there some five-legged creature that's been conceived while one of the leaders was dreaming up what next?

But there's barely a breeze to disturb the oppressive heat, let alone anything else.

"Stay close," Hayze says again, leading the way toward the gates.

"How are we getting through?" Jewel asks, frowning.

Hayze wishes he had an answer, but he doesn't. This is virtual reality, meaning there has to be a way they can use that to their advantage. He keeps walking, scanning their surroundings. The sun is harsh as it hangs high above the monstrous gates. Forged from black metal, the Fire insignia is embossed across the front, matching the tattoo on the back of his hand. At least six guards stand in front of it, keeping to the small sliver of shade created by the looming gates. Two more are stationed at the top of the wall, and Hayze knows they all carry weapons.

People become desperate in their attempts to get inside the capitals. Even knowing it could cost them their life.

There's a shout and the guards shoot to attention. Black weapons are gripped and pointed outward as they line up across the front of the gates. Above, more guards appear, more deadly guns pointing down.

"They've been expecting us," Hayze growls.

"W-what are we going to do?" Jewel asks, moving closer to Hayze.

"Show them they're right to be worried," he states flatly.

Then, he breaks into a run.

"Stop!" a guard screams. "Or we'll shoot!"

Hayze lifts his hands as he lengthens his stride. Heat explodes through his palms a split-second before a bolt of fire arcs across the distance. It hits the gates a few feet above the guards' heads, exploding in a blaze of deep red and burning yellow. They cry out and Hayze expects them to scatter.

Instead, they run at the teens as they lift their weapons.

"We can't die!" Hayze shouts, not breaking stride.

Someone appears by his side, and he's surprised to see it's Jewel. "And they can't, either."

He realizes she's right. These guards are as real as they are.

"So I can do this?" Pace shouts, appearing on Hayze's other side. He shoots out a thick bolt of ice. It slams into a guard, freezing his gun and sending him flying back into the metal gates. He slumps to the ground, unmoving.

"And I can do this," Jewel says, staring intently at another guard.

One moment, he's there. The next he's gone, his faint cry reaching up from the hole that just swallowed him.

Hayze's grin is cut off as a volley of shots punctures the scorched air. He grunts as his shoulder jerks back, a bullet shredding through it. Another hits his leg. The third feels like jagged metal as it lodges beneath his collar bone.

But Hayze doesn't slow. Three words time his unrelenting run forward.

I. Can't. Die.

"You bastards!" Pace cries, registering that Hayze has been hit.

A deluge of water comes down between the teens and the guards, obscuring them. The teens move out wider, meaning the next spray of shots sails straight past them. Hayze grits his teeth, determined to keep up with Pace and Jewel. He has no idea where Atmos is. His leg almost gives out, but he locks his knee.

I. Can't. Die.

Even though he can feel warm blood trickling down his

arm, his thigh, his chest. Even though his gait is uneven because each step pounds agony through his injured leg. Even though the thundering pulse in his ears feels like it's fading away.

"Open the curtain of water!" Hayze yells to Pace, lifting his hands.

Pace sends him a worried look even as he does it, dividing the waterfall stretched in front of them, then peeling back the thick sheets.

The guards on the other side instantly unload their weapons. Hayze weaves this time, trying to focus beyond his blood-streaked hand as he unleashes a fireball. A bullet whizzes past his head and he realizes he's the target. He's the one they want to believe will die from his wounds.

The fireball hits a guard, engulfing him in flames. Hayze winces at the agonized screams, reminding himself they're as real as the pain trying to engulf him. The guard drops, writhing in the mud.

The next rain of bullets comes from above. Hayze focuses on the guards high on the wall, his breathing harsh and labored. But before he can aim another fireball, the wall shakes beneath them as Jewel undermines the fabric of the cement. Some guards fall forward, some back, screaming as they tumble to their fake death.

"Push the gates open, Atmos!" Hayze shouts as Pace shoots another ice bolt and silences a guard.

Hayze glances back, seeing the Air guy is behind him, pale and terrified. "Hurry!" he gasps.

But Atmos shakes his head. "I...tried," he whispers so quietly Hayze almost doesn't hear him.

But he does.

And so does Pace.

"Now isn't the time to define dud!" he shouts in frustration.

Hayze tries to conjure another fireball, but he feels cold all over except for the places blood is now pouring down. Those rivers and streams are hot, as if his very essence is leaking out. He ignores it, grunting as he sends another blast at a guard trying to rise from the mud.

I. Can't. Die.

Pace holds both palms out. "Argh!" he screams as a thick jet of water hits the gates. There's a groaning as a faint crack appears between them.

Jewel is silent as she also wields her powers, frowning intensely as she stares at the gates. They buckle as if a giant's hand just gripped them.

With a scream of twisted metal, the gates crumble and fly inward under the onslaught, revealing Ignis beyond.

"We did it!" Atmos cries, finally catching up to jog beside Jewel as they all slow down.

Hayze glances at Pace. "Don't."

Pace scowls. "One little shot of ice up his ass, that's all."

"No."

"Fine," Pace huffs. "But you Fire people are real joy fizzers."

They slow to a walk and he reaches out to stop Hayze, but he shakes his hand off. "I'll stop when we get to the Sect," Hayze says, stepping around a piece of tangled metal.

When he gets to Aura.

Jewel moves in closer. "Aura's probably not in the Sect."

"But the way to end these Games is," Hayze replies. "I know it. And once we're all out, I can go find her."

The first place Aura will go is home. To try and understand how their love, something that felt so sure, was so completely undermined.

Jewel nods, then frowns as she glances down. Hayze realizes his left foot is leaving bloody prints on the cement. "I've decided I have an endless supply of the red stuff," he assures her with a wink.

Even though the pain is twisting his muscles, his gut, each and every cell. If dolphins can have teeth and monkeys can carry weapons, then he can have a never-ending well of blood.

"Come on." Hayze breaks into a jog, ignoring the way his left foot slips through his self-made lubrication.

Pace and Jewel glance at each other, but Atmos simply nods in agreement. They run through the cement streets, past the markets, past cement homes that spiral up in the shape of flames. No one stops them. In fact, beyond the markets, the streets are empty. There are faces visible in the red, glowing windows that rise high above. And although people in red leather decorated in ornate flames stand in rounded doorways, no one moves. Let alone speaks.

They simply watch as Hayze and the others run past, each one a set of eyes for the leaders. Each one watching them get closer and closer to the Sect.

To winning the Games.

It's too easy.

The words hiss through Hayze's mind, even as he's glad he doesn't have to pseudo-kill these bystanders. But it does mean the leaders have something planned.

The punchline hasn't hit yet.

The Sect looms closer and closer, a pale beacon in a world forged from cement and coal. The area ahead opens out as they reach it, a single, white door visible in the wall of the Sect.

"We made it," Jewel gasps, slowing. "I'll see my mother again."

"Tempo," Pace says, the one word laced with pain as he gazes up at the tower.

Atmos doesn't say anything as he falls back a little.

Hayze slows to a walk with the others, even as he keeps approaching the door. He can't lose momentum. Each step is one closer to Aura.

Except the door opens, forcing Hayze to finally stop.

He locks his knees as the sucker punch is dealt, and it feels like a fist of steel and stone just powered through him, connecting each of his bullet holes into one gaping wound.

Skylus steps through, her hair plaited high on her head in a crown. "You're too late," she says smugly, her robes fluttering gently as she floats forward. "I've already won the Elemental Games."

TWENTY-ONE

AURA

A ura feels like she's trapped in another maze. Only this time, it's real. The tunnels curve and twist, leaving her dazed and confused. She has to reach Hayze in Aqua before the leaders break free and get to him first. Which means she has to find her way to Ignis and talk to Hayze's parents.

Because they know things Aura doesn't.

They know things even the leaders don't.

Including the very thing that can save Hayze's life.

Holding a small flame in the palm of her hand, she turns left then right in the flickering light, drawing on her memories as Tempo so intently a few times she forgets she's from Fire, not Water. But it works to keep herself calm, and the tunnels don't seem so dark. So narrow. So terrifying.

Weaving her way, Aura eventually finds herself in the more familiar section of tunnels that lead to the Fire Quadrant's mines. She heads immediately for the intersection that changed everything that fateful night before her birthday. When she reaches the reinforced buttress of beams that divide two tunnels, she stops in her tracks, the memory of what happened here intense and painful. A breath is drawn from her lungs, and she almost loses the small flame flickering in her palm.

This is where it all happened. Where Aura found Hayze exiting a secret tunnel. She'd been shocked. And when he flat out refused to tell her where it led, she'd been devastated. A huge fight had broken out, one that felt all the more significant given they'd not had so much as a minor tiff in all the years before.

Hayze had insisted he was keeping Aura safe. That she was better off not knowing. Which led her to believe the tunnel could only lead to one place.

The Sect.

She'd heard rumors over the years of an Elemental Alliance between the Quadrants, with secret passageways and meetings designed to bring the leaders down. She'd even talked about it with Hayze, who'd shaken his head in disgust that she now wonders was directed more at the leaders than the Alliance itself. But her parents had been very clear that while the methods of the leaders may at times be harsh, they're for the greater good.

They must trust.

Except, how can Aura be expected to trust the same people who locked her inside a Game without so much as a set of rules for how to survive? How can she trust anyone when the one person who was supposed to trust her the most couldn't even tell her anything about such a large part of himself?

She studies the intersection that hides the secret tunnel, certain it can take her to Hayze. And if the leaders still don't know about it, it's a sure way she can get to him first. How ironic that the very thing that drove Aura from Hayze's side is the same thing that will bring her to him now.

She runs her fingertips down the planks of wood, tempted

to pull them back and go straight in. But she also knows she'll never find her way. She's just as likely to end up in Terra or Aeris as she is in Aqua. And she *must* get this right. Which means a small detour to get directions from Hayze's parents. They'll know which way she should go.

Tearing herself away, she jogs down the series of tunnels that stretch beneath her village. Lined with ladders that lead to the various bunkers, it's hard to believe how foreign this place had been in the Games. Running through it now is like navigating her lips across the familiar curve of Hayze's lips...

Aura shakes her head, trying to get this image out of her mind.

And runs directly into her mom. The flame in her palm extinguishes immediately with the shock.

"Aura!" Her mom takes a step back, her eyes wide and filled with disbelief before she throws her arms around Aura's neck and pulls her close. "My girl! It's you."

Aura hugs her back, tears stinging her eyes to remember how she'd failed to recognize her in the Games, thinking she was Tempo's mother. As she draws in her familiar warmth, she reminds herself the woman in the Games was nothing more than a computer-generated replica. Until now, she hadn't seen her real mother since the night before her eighteenth birthday. In fact, excluding the leaders, she hasn't seen *anyone* since then.

Including Hayze.

"Aura," her father says from beside them, and she reaches out a hand to include him in the embrace. "Why are you here?"

"Brando," her mother hisses, breaking away and dragging Aura down the tunnel. "It's not safe to talk out here."

"I can't go with you." Aura resists as her mom tries to usher her up the ladder that leads to the hatch in their small kitchen. "I need to talk to Hayze's parents. I don't have time."

"We'll talk quickly then." Her mother practically pushes her up the ladder with surprising strength, leaving Aura no choice but to comply. After being separated for so long, and living through such a nightmare with her parents in the Games, she doesn't have the heart to say no.

She gets to the top of the ladder and lifts open the hatch to her family's bunker. The first thing she notices as she steps inside are Hayze's paintings covering the walls. The last time she'd seen them, she thought Pace had drawn them for Tempo. But now they look even more breathtakingly beautiful. Because the love that Hayze has put into each stroke of paint is obvious. And it tears at her heart. How can someone who gave her so much have also held back equally as much? It makes no sense.

"Aura, why are you here?" her father asks, closing the hatch and turning to her. "Are you in danger?"

She shakes her head, even though the opposite is true. Surely, she can't be expected to be truthful when she's been fed a lifetime of lies?

"You look so pale." Her mother pulls out a chair while her father pours a cup of cold tea and sets it down on the table in front of her.

"You knew, didn't you?" Aura asks, sliding into the chair. "You knew they were going to take me away on my birthday."

Her parents glance at each other, then back at her as they sit down and link hands, seeking support in the exact way Aura had from Hayze.

"We wanted to tell you," her father whispers. "We really did. But we couldn't."

"It was part of the agreement," her mom adds, tears spilling down her cheeks. "We couldn't say a word."

Aura draws in a breath, deciding if she's spent valuable time stopping here, she should at least try to find out everything she can. Knowledge has never been more powerful since this whole nightmare began.

"Start from the beginning." Aura takes a long sip of her tea, not having realized how dry her throat is. This time, she can't ignore the sensation. Her thirst is as real as her surroundings.

"Nothing came easy to us in life," her father says.

"I know that." Aura waits for any new information they're prepared to offer.

"Not even you came easily to us," her mom says.

Aura tilts her head. "What do you mean?"

"We weren't blessed with children like other couples," her mom explains. "It was the one thing no amount of edrian could buy us. Until..."

Impatience settles in Aura's stomach along with the tea.

"Infernos came to see us," her dad says. "Long before you were born."

This has Aura sitting up straight. "He came here?"

Her parents nod. "He made us a deal," her mother continues. "He offered us a child along with enough edrian for half a ticket to Ignis. All we had to do was..." Her mom swallows, unable to get out the words.

"Give me back to them at age eighteen," Aura finishes.

"We thought we'd be able to figure out something else by then," her mother adds quickly. "Make another deal. Or find a way to get out of the one we already had. Or save enough edrian to pay Infernos back or buy your ticket to Ignis and hide you there. Anything! But it didn't work out like that."

"We couldn't save enough," her father says sadly. "No matter how much we went without."

"It wouldn't have mattered," Aura tells them. "The boy from Water's parents got enough to get him into Aqua and they still took him." She leaves out the part of the story about just how Pace's parents got it.

"We were fools," her mom says. "We thought eighteen years with you would be better than not having any at all."

Her father nods. "Foolish doesn't even touch the surface of how stupid we were. We had no idea how much we were going to love you. How eighteen thousand years still wouldn't have been enough."

"Am I even yours?" Aura asks, her voice little more than a whisper. "Or did they just give me to you?"

"You're ours," her mom says.

"We were taken to the Sect where you were created with artificial fertilization," her father explains. "We then had to return for your mom's labor to be induced so the leaders could make sure you were born healthy."

"Well, that explains why we all have the same birthday," says Aura, hardly able to believe her parents have been to the Sect.

Or that she was created with the help of science.

"You weren't conceived naturally," her mother says. "But you're one hundred percent ours."

"Are you sure about that?" Aura asks. "Because can you do this?"

She holds her mug of cold tea in one hand and hovers her other hand just below it, igniting a flame in the palm of her hand. The tea bubbles as steam rises from the top and Aura lets the flame die. Then, blowing on the tea, she takes a sip.

"Much better," she says, as she waits for her parents to close their fallen jaws and react.

"Aura!" Her father stands up, his chair crashing to the cement floor behind him. "You have Elemental powers."

"Seems they might have added something a little extra to the DNA mix," says Aura.

"But we tried training you," Aura's mom says, leaning forward.

"Seems we needed to fear for our lives during training," Aura says plainly. "You weren't scary enough."

"Oh, my sweet daughter." Her mom gets up and crosses the table to put her arms around Aura. "What did they do to you? We should have tried harder to keep you safe."

"No, Vesta," her father says, his face shining with pride. "She was safe. Look, she's here now. And more powerful than ever. Our daughter's going to save the world, just like Infernos promised."

"He promised you that?" Aura frowns as her mother pulls away.

Her father nods. "They need you for the greater good. The leaders may use extreme methods, but it's desperate times. You know the world is getting harder to live in with each day that passes."

"That's right," her mother says. "Life in the Quadrants is already hard enough to survive. Something has to change to balance that out. Infernos said that something would be you."

Aura nods, thinking she understands her parents' loyalty to the leaders. They risked everything, including their only child, to help them. Accepting the leaders are corrupt would be accepting they'd willingly set their entire lives on fire.

"I need to see Ember and Sera." Aura stands.

"But you haven't even told us why you're here," her mother says. "Are you in danger?"

"I'm fine." She reaches out to hug her mother. "But Hayze is in trouble. I need to talk to his parents."

"We missed you so much." Her father touches her on the arm, and she remembers how the virtual reality version of him had hauled her to safety before the lava could devour her. The leaders may not know everything about their lives to put into the Games, but they sure got that bit right.

"Wait," her mom says. "Go and get changed first. I don't

know what that white suit is you're wearing, but it's going to attract all sorts of attention."

"Oh." Aura looks down and sees she's wearing the same white suit she'd found herself wearing in the Games. She goes to her room and quickly changes into her red, leather pants and vest, still sitting folded on a chair just as she'd left them the night before her birthday. She focuses on the task, trying not to look at the murals on her walls. She doesn't need any reminder of all the things Hayze did for her. It's too much of a reminder of all the things he didn't.

Like trust her with the truth.

She exits her room and gives her parents another hug, making promises to try to return to them as soon as she can. Ignoring their gentle sobs, she leaves before tears of her own can fall. She still has so much to do. And she's already used up enough valuable time.

Walking quickly to Hayze's bunker, she slips inside without knocking, grateful not to have been seen. She'd half expected to come across Rateen, except she only exists in worlds that aren't real, so that shouldn't be surprising.

"Aura!" Sera gasps, wiping her hands on her trousers. "What are you doing here? Ember! Come quickly!"

Ember rushes out from one of the other rooms, looking just as surprised as his wife to find Aura standing there.

"Where's Hayze?" he asks, giving her a quick hug. "Is he alive?"

Aura nods. "It's a long story. And I don't have much time. I'm trying to get to him now, but I need your help."

"Anything," says Sera.

"Anything?" Aura lifts her brows, wishing she had Pace's ability to cock just one.

"Anything." Sera nods. "If it's for Hayze, we'll do anything at all."

"Including telling me how to get to Aqua?" she asks.

Sera glances at Ember. "You have to go through either Aeris or Terra to do that."

"Or I could use one of the secret tunnels," she says, hoping she's correctly figured things out. "Hayze is in Aqua so I really need you to tell me how to get there as quickly as possible if you ever want to see him again. I know you're in the Alliance."

Sera swallows, her face full of trepidation, then she nods, confirming Aura's suspicions at last. "We'll show you the way."

"Hayze wasn't supposed to tell you," Ember says. "It was the only thing we asked of him."

"He didn't tell me," Aura says. "I found him leaving one of the tunnels the night before our birthday."

"That was why you fought?" Sera's eyes are wide.

Aura blinks. "He refused to tell me where he'd been."

"Don't be upset with him," Ember pleads. "This is what the leaders do. They put wedges between us. They want us to be weak, so we don't undermine their strength. They don't want us to trust each other."

"Well, Hayze didn't trust me." Aura bites her lip.

"It's your parents he didn't trust," says Ember quickly. "Not because they're not good people. They're just blind to the truth. They believe what they're being told. If they found out about the Alliance, they'd go straight to Infernos."

Aura can't deny any of this is true. It's just one of the reasons she hadn't asked them about the Alliance when she saw them just now.

"That's why Hayze couldn't tell you," Ember says. "He didn't want you to be forced to keep something so big from your parents. It wouldn't be fair."

Aura draws in a breath, not wanting to hear their excuses for their son. When she gets to Hayze and sets him free of the Games, he can talk for himself.

"Tell me how to get to him," she says, cutting to the chase. "I'm running out of time."

Sera picks up a piece of coal and draws a large circle on her kitchen table. "Enter the secret tunnel and walk forward until you reach a point where it breaks into four. Keep going straight. If you turn right, you'll go to Aeris. If you turn left, you'll end up in Terra. If you take the ladder up, you'll find yourself in Ignis."

"But it's Aqua I need," says Aura.

"Which is on the other side of the Sect." Sera nods. "The fastest way there is to keep walking straight. The tunnel will take you deep down, right underneath the Sect. When you reach the center, there'll be another crossroad." She sketches this out on the table with a cross. "Keep going straight. No turns. Do you understand? Only walk straight ahead and eventually you'll end up in Aqua."

Aura nods. "And where will I emerge?"

"The Traders Market," says Ember.

"And where's Hayze?" she asks.

"Underneath the ocean," says Ember, wincing. "I hope you know how to swim."

Aura gulps. Tempo's memories had helped her navigate the tunnels. And she'd coped when the maze in the Games had filled with water. But can she swim beneath the ocean when she's nothing more than a girl from Fire?

She hopes so.

Because she's about to find out.

TWENTY-TWO

HAYZE

"No!" Pace roars, rushing toward Skylus and the door. "We can't have come this far for nothing!"

Her eyes widen in shock as she instinctively retreats. Pace uses the momentum to keep moving forward, putting his hands out as if to shove her. But Skylus shrinks back into the Sect, leaving an opening that Pace takes advantage of.

And so does Hayze.

He leaps after Pace, conscious that Jewel and Atmos are just behind. They burst into the Sect a moment after Pace does, then grind to a stop beside him. The walls of the Fire foyer are constructed from dark, obsidian-like materials with veins of glowing, molten lava running through them. It's a sharp contrast to the Water entrance that Hayze passed through last time. A pillar rises up in the center, black and intricate, a large flame roaring from the top. Skylus is in front of it, hovering several feet above them, the torch-like sconces lining the walls flickering with real flames, casting eerie shadows all around her. The air is heavy with the scent of smoldering embers.

"We've reached the Sect!" Pace screams as he does a slow turn. "Just like we're supposed to."

Skylus's light laughter rains down on them. "I already told you, you're too late. There is only one winner." She sweeps her arms out wide so her purple robes flow around her like fluttering petals. "And it was me."

Jewel whimpers, then buries her hands in her face. "I'll never see my mother again."

Atmos's shoulders slump as he says nothing. If he wasn't able to harness his Elemental powers, then it's not like he expected to win, anyway.

Hayze glares at Skylus, unsure how to feel. He never wanted to win the Games. Skylus can have the title and whatever comes with it. He's here to be free of them. To find Aura and try to undo the hurt he caused before any of this started.

"Like heckus you've won!" Pace screams, lifting his hands and pointing his palms at Skylus. "The Games aren't over yet!"

Hayze leaps forward but Pace unleashes several glittering ice shards straight at Skylus. They sing through the air, but she simply twists and twirls in a flutter of purple. The shards sail past, melting before they reach the monolith behind her. The water hisses and fizzes as it hits the obsidian floor, evaporating into nothing.

"You shall see why I am the winner!" Skylus cries out.

She jerks her arms and the fires in the sconces flare in response, blasting heat through the room.

"She's feeding the flames!" Atmos gasps.

Hayze throws his hands out, already working on dampening them. Pace shoots balls of water at the closest ones, extinguishing them.

"We have to stop her!" Pace shouts. He focuses on the next sconces, preparing to soak them, but a targeted gust shoves him back. Stumbling, he leans into the wind, his hair whipping his forehead.

"Stop, Skylus!" Hayze orders. "We were never meant to turn against each other!"

Skylus's robes are now still, even as she blasts Pace. Even as she feeds the monstrous fire high above her on the central pillar. "That's why you lost, Hayze," she tells him, her gaze hard. "You weren't willing to consider how big this could be."

She whips in a tight circle, sending out a blast of wind that sends them all back. Hayze grunts as he hits the obsidian wall, then hisses at the heat searing him through his leather vest. He strains as he peels himself away, fighting the powerful flow of air trying to trap him. Jewel's screams are his motivation. They slice through the single-minded wind like a razor, more painful than the burn against his back.

Hayze wrenches himself away from the wall, only to be plastered against it, front first. He cries out as his cheek hits the burning obsidian surface, a vein of lava pulsing right next to his eye. Cutting off the cry, he shoves away, reminding himself the pain isn't real.

Keeping himself braced and ignoring the sickly scent of his burning palms, he makes his way to Jewel. She's writhing against the wall, the straps of her Earth clothes doing little to protect her. Hayze peels her away, putting his hand, then arm between her shoulders and the lava-laced wall. Pain scalds through his skin, eating away at the muscle below.

"Pace!"

A deluge of water pours down a moment later, soothing the burns that are getting harder and harder to believe aren't real. Turning into the wind, Hayze roars as he unleashes a fireball. It flares bright as it shoots toward Skylus, and she quickly deflects it with another burst of air. But the fast maneuvering does what Hayze hoped it would—it breaks her concentration.

Jewel falls from the wall and Hayze yanks himself away, his stomach lurching at the red, mangled mess that is his forearm.

"The power's gone to her head," Atmos screeches, breaking into a crazed run. He yanks open the door, clearly intent on escaping in a world where there's no escape.

"I don't think so!" Skylus laughs.

A sharp burst of wind slams the door shut, trapping him.

And everyone else.

"I've got this," Jewel snarls. She glares at the monolith behind Skylus and Hayze realizes she's going to topple it. The obsidian column and the eternal flame it carries will fall right on Skylus.

The column shudders, then stills.

Jewel's brow lowers as she tightens her focus, her whole body straining with it. "It's...strong," she gasps, a bead of sweat running down the side of her face.

"You can do it," Hayze urges her. He looks from one sconce to the other, extinguishing them. It'll make the room darker and cooler.

Another burst of wind hits them, once more pushing them toward the walls. "Hurry!" Pace cries, shooting blasts of water at Skylus. They're blown into harmless droplets within seconds.

A rumble rips through the monolith and elation soars through Hayze. "Yes, Jewel!"

A cry rips out of her as she throws her hands forward. As if she's hurling everything she has at the obsidian column.

Nothing happens.

"I can't!" Jewel gasps, looking shocked. "It won't break!"

"What do you mean, it won't break?" Atmos screeches. "You're Earth!"

"You don't get to judge, dud boy!" Pace shouts, fighting to raise his hands so he can use his powers again.

Jewel doesn't have the opportunity to answer. She's thrown back against the wall, screaming as her skin sizzles.

"I am Air!" Skylus cries.

"Skylus!" Hayze shouts. "You need to stop! This isn't—"

The sconces that were extinguished burst back to life, far bigger and brighter than before.

"Get your emotions under control, Hayze!" Pace screams, pushing into the wind as he tries to stay away from the wall threaded with lava.

"It wasn't me!" Hayze clenches his hands as uncertainty flashes through him. He thought he was past this. That he could control his Element.

"I am Fire!" Skylus shouts triumphantly.

The ground below them rumbles, more veins of lava crackling along the floor like lightning.

"I am Earth!"

Jagged ice sculptures shoot up from the cracks, making Hayze leap back before he's impaled.

"I am Water!"

"What's going on?" Pace gasps,

This time, Skylus's laughter is maniacal. "I've mastered *all* of the Elements!" she crows. "I win the Elemental Games!"

Hayze can't move. He doesn't breathe. His heart is stuck in suspended animation.

Skylus just wielded all four Elements. How can that be?

Hayze doesn't get a chance to answer the impossible question. Atmos is blown back so hard, he slumps down the wall, unconscious. Pace cries out and Hayze spins to see a serpent of water winding its way around his friend's legs. With each pass, the shimmering water blends with the coil below, forming a bubble. Pace thrashes, his arms and legs flailing as he desperately tries to break free, but the water simply splits and reforms as it continues up.

Jewel lets out a choked gasp. She goes to run only to find she can't move her feet. Crying out, she wrenches at her legs, but they don't move. She shoots upright as her eyes open wide, focused on Hayze. With a strangled gasp, she twists at the waist. Her legs don't move, as if the bottom half of her body is immobile. As if she's turning to stone.

"You can't die!" Hayze tells them desperately, torn between who to run to first.

"But the alternative is to be trapped by their own Element," Skylus cackles from above. "How long before they choose death, Hayze?"

"Hay—" Pace's panicked cry is cut off as water engulfs his head. His expression turns terrified as he stares through the clear, sparkling fluid, his mouth working open and closed.

Jewel's whimper is cut off a moment later. Her entire body stills, her eyes unblinking as a single tear seeps out and tracks down her marble cheek.

"No!" Hayze shouts, unsure what he's denying. Watching his friends be tortured alive, or the fact that one person has done this to them.

Skylus laughs again. "This isn't a choice, Hayze. It's inevitability."

"No!" he shouts again, stalking forward. "This isn't real!"

A burst of flames explode at his feet, climbing up his legs as furiously as the heat. Hayze ignores it, not bothering to try and extinguish them. A different realization is detonating through him.

The flames can't hurt him.

Because none of this is what it seems. It never was.

"We never reached the Sect, did we?" he demands, still walking as the flames engulf his chest. "You're not Skylus, you're a simulation. All of this is fake!"

Skylus's eyes flare.

Her body jerks.

And she disappears.

Hayze stops, astounded even though he knows he shouldn't be. He called the leaders' bluff.

And he was right.

Spinning around, he throws the next words out, wanting his friends to hear them as they're freed. "No one can harness all four Elements!"

Except they never hear them.

The Fire room is gone. Pace, Jewel, and Atmos are gone.

Everything is gone.

Hayze does a slow turn, willing his mind to catch up with his surroundings. He's in a white expanse of nothingness. Growling in frustration, Hayze stalks forward, gasping when he crashes into an invisible wall.

"Get some new material," he spits out for the leaders' benefit.

Slapping his hands on the cool surface, he heats his palms. The burst of fire is big, billowing out in an explosion of blazing orange. The flames lick up and around, as if he's encased by a bubble.

"It's no use," says a voice behind him. "The walls are impenetrable."

Hayze spins around, unsure how to feel as he registers Skylus a yard away, sitting cross-legged and smiling.

"You're not real," he spits, finding the invisible wall on this side and planting his hands on it again.

"Of course, I am," Skylus says, rolling her eyes. She stands, opening her arms. "I'm most definitely real."

"None of this is real," Hayze grinds out. He sends out a blast of flames. "It's all virtual." The next burst is even bigger, hotter, hungrily spreading over the surface. "A simulation."

The invisible barrier remains. There are no scorch marks. No signs of melting or cracking or weakness.

Skylus blinks. "And you think I'm crazy for believing in Eterna?" she asks incredulously, convincing him that she is indeed the real Skylus.

"How do we get out of here?" Hayze demands, noting the endless white. Even when he does, he has eternal nothingness to traverse.

But he'll do it.

To get back to Aura.

Skylus laughs, the sound unerringly the same as just a few moments ago, when her existence was duplicated into the Games. "Why would we want to leave?" She places a hand on her own invisible wall, smiling. "We're here because we won."

Hayze stills, registering the way Skylus's gaze falls to the floor. He looks down, seeing a large square insignia etched over the floor, one side stretching from him to Skylus. There's a circle within it, lines criss-crossing through the center, creating an intricate, interconnected pattern. Four, smaller circles rest along each side. The one beneath Hayze has the Fire symbol. The one beneath Skylus is Air. Water and Earth are empty.

Skylus beams. "I beat Atmos. You beat Aura."

Hayze's knees go weak. "I can't have..."

And what about Pace and Jewel? They're both the only ones remaining from their Quadrant.

"I don't know what you did," Skylus says with a shrug, practically reading his mind. "But it's more than just being better than your partner. It would've involved thinking for yourself. That's what I did when I left you all behind." Skylus's smile grows. "Those are the ones Eterna chooses."

Hayze collapses onto the floor as his knees give out. He stares dumbly at the Fire symbol he's inadvertently claimed.

He never wanted to win the Games.

All he wanted to do was get back to Aura.

Yet every choice he's made has taken him further away from her.

And now he's trapped in a cell. His powers are useless.

By winning, he's lost everything.

CHAPTER
TWENTY-THREE
AURA

Aura re-enters the mines with a small flame burning in the palm of her hand, trying to ignore the sick feeling in her stomach.

"I am Tempo," she whispers, trying to convince her brain she's not afraid of the tight space. "I am Tempo."

The flame flickers and she realizes that might not be such a wise plan. If she thinks she's from Water, how can she wield Fire?

She closes her eyes and remembers all the courageous things she did in the Games. She battled deadly Elements. Fought off mutant creatures. She ran. She climbed. She fell. She cried. She screamed.

And here she is.

Alive.

And kicking.

"I am Aura." She grits her teeth and walks deep under the earth. She has to get to Hayze before the leaders reach him and do who knows what to him. She doesn't trust them for a second.

Trust.

She thinks about this word as she heads for the intersection where she'll find the secret tunnel. Does she trust Hayze? She thought she did. And what Ember said about Hayze keeping secrets so she wasn't forced to lie to her parents made a little sense. Although, it also sounded like an excuse.

The only way to know for sure what Hayze really thinks is to get him out of the Games. Which means continuing to put one foot in front of the other.

She reaches the entrance to the secret tunnel and looks around to make sure nobody's followed her. Counting the beams that act as supports between the two regular tunnels, she tugs on the fifth one across. It moves, and she lets her flame extinguish while she works in the darkness, wriggling it out of place. Then, turning sideways, she squeezes through the small gap and eases the beam back in its spot.

Puffing from exertion, she turns and holds out her hand, reigniting her flame and squinting as she peers ahead. The tunnel looks similar to the others she just passed through, except smaller. Which makes sense given it had to be dug out in secret, but this was the last thing she wanted.

"I am Aura," she says through gritted teeth, trying to remember what it feels like to be filled with courage. She walks quickly, wanting to get this part of the journey over as soon as possible. Her throat is dry, and she touches the water canteen strapped around her waist that Sera had given her. She needs to be a lot thirstier than this before she'll take a sip. And she only just had that tea her dad made her.

She walks for what must be at least an hour before she reaches a crossroad. It's just like Sera described with a ladder that goes up to a hatch.

An arrow has been etched into the rockface beside it along with the Fire symbol.

Ignis.

It's strange to think the capital of the Fire Quadrant is right above her head. The very place her family couldn't afford to take her, no matter how hard they worked. And the lucky ones who live there have no idea there's an Alliance scurrying about like mice beneath them.

The tunnel to the right has another arrow pointing to Aeris, and the one on her left points to Terra. They both look far more tempting than the one that stretches straight ahead. Because that one angles down in a sharp slope that will take Aura even deeper beneath the earth.

With a few tentative steps forward, she wishes she asked Ember and Sera how much longer it would take to reach Aqua using the tunnels to Aeris or Terra, rather than going underneath the Sect. Anything else would be preferable.

A sweat breaks out on her forehead, and she relents, taking a long sip of water. She can't afford to have a panic attack now. That would force her up the ladder to Ignis and she has no idea what that would mean. She might give away the existence of the Alliance and their tunnel network and ruin everything.

Whatever *everything* is.

Steeling herself, Aura closes the cap on her water bottle and marches ahead with her hand held out in front of her. Her flame flickers and she concentrates harder, finding the distraction useful to keep herself calm.

The tunnel levels out and she keeps her pace constant, hoping she doesn't meet an Alliance member coming the other way. It's with huge relief when she eventually reaches the crossroad under the very center of the Sect. This time, she doesn't pause, too afraid of the places her brain will go if she allows it to compute what's towering above her head. And how much it must all weigh...

Ignoring the paths on either side, she runs forward past the symbol etched in the wall for Aqua. She keeps her shoulders hunched, glad she's not any taller or broader.

Her body wars with her as she moves. Half of her wants to turn around and run back to her parents and her home. And the other half wants to run to Hayze. She may be furious with him, but she can't deny she's as drawn to him as the moths that flitter around her family's cauldron at night. And just like the moths with their fragile wings, Aura knows she's in danger of getting burned.

The tunnel slopes up beneath her and she reaches the end faster than she expects. The narrow space opens out into a small chamber with a rack of blue suits beside a ladder. There's a box of water bottles and a pile of torches with some flint. Feeling foolish for being so conservative with her own water, Aura quickly drinks what remains in her bottle. Needing her hands free, she lights a torch with her fingertips to conserve the flint. She changes into a blue suit, leaving her leathers from Fire hanging on one of the hooks, noticing there are also some scraps of cloth from the Earth Quadrant and a purple robe from Air. Just how many rebels from the Alliance are wandering around the capital cities unseen?

Hayze's parents had been correct in their assumption that Aura's parents wouldn't approve. The way her father had talked about the leaders needing to do what was best for the greater good had been proof enough of that. As well as the stars he had in his eyes for Infernos. It reminded Aura of the way Atmos looked when he talked to Cyclonis.

But Aura would have understood if Hayze told her. *Wouldn't she?*

She smooths down her suit as she tries to convince herself of this, knowing she's really not sure. When she found Hayze coming out of the secret tunnel, her entire world crashed down on her, and it wasn't just the fact he'd hidden things from her.

It was adjusting to the fact he was part of the enemy side before she knew who the real enemy was.

Pushing these thoughts away, she puts out the torch and climbs the ladder, pressing on the hatch at the top. It cracks open and she peers out, seeing a set of very large bare feet. One of the feet lifts up and stomps on the hatch, slamming it closed.

Aura steadies herself on the ladder, realizing she must have arrived at a bad time. But when exactly is a good time to sneak into a foreign Quadrant and break someone out of a virtual reality pod they're being kept in against their will?

She slows her breathing and presses her ear to the hatch, listening to the sounds above her.

"How much coal do I get for this?" a man asks.

"This much," another more familiar voice replies.

Aura frowns, trying to place the voice, quickly deciding it must be someone from Tempo's memories. She's far more likely to know someone here than Aura, even if Tempo only visited Aqua on her brief trips to the Traders Market.

"It's a fair offer. Take it or leave it," the voice commands.

Pace's father.

The two words echo into Aura's mind almost without her thinking them. That's who the man is. Tide. A feeling of betrayal filters through Aura's core. The same feeling that Tempo experienced as a result of this man her entire life. This is the person who stole from Tempo's family so his son could have a better future. A son whose life turned out to take an identical path as the girl he stole from.

Aura reminds herself he's the same man who helped Hayze get back into the Games so he could go to her. Hopefully a man who's also about to help her, given he seems to be part of the Elemental Alliance. Why else would the tunnel lead here?

"Closing early!" Tide shouts and there's the sound of

canvas being pulled across his shop amidst the grumblings of his waiting customers retreating.

A few minutes later, the hatch flies open and a furious face hovers above Aura.

"You didn't do the knock," Tide growls.

"What knock?" she asks.

Tide narrows his eyes, then sighs. "Not another one."

"Another what?" Aura climbs out of the hatch, forcing Tide to step back to allow her clearance.

"You're the girl from Fire, aren't you?" says Tide. "You look just like the boy."

Aura frowns, unsure what he means. She shares many things with Hayze but her appearance isn't one of them.

"I don't mean literally." Tide rolls his eyes, his bald head shining with sweat. "It's the look in your eyes. Like you're out of your depth."

"I need you to take me to him." She straightens her spine, doing her best to look more confident.

"Both pods are taken." He folds his arms across his broad chest. "Sorry."

"I don't want to go back in," she says. "I want to get Hayze out."

"Not going to happen." Tide shakes his head. "Your boyfriend promised to look out for my son. I need him in there."

"Pace is quite capable of looking after himself," says Aura.

Something that almost resembles humanity crosses Tide's harsh face. "Has my son mastered his powers?"

"Your son is amazing," says Aura. "He can make a monsoon with his fingertips. He can create a tidal wave out of thin air. And he can take it all away again, leaving not so much as a drop behind."

Tide's eyes widen, and he nods.

"And he's fallen in love," Aura adds, working hard to get Tide in exactly the position she needs him. "With Tempo."

Tide reels back. "No."

"Yes." Aura nods. "If you take me to him, you can pull him from the Games and ask him about it yourself."

"He thinks he's from Fire," says Tide. "When he regains his memories, he won't feel that way about...*her*."

"I wouldn't be so sure," says Aura. "My feelings have changed quite dramatically since I got my memories back."

Tide waits for her to elaborate, but she doesn't.

"The Games have a way of changing things," she says. "Which is what you must surely want after selling your only child to the leaders."

Tide's face turns purple, making him seem like he should be from Air, not Water.

"I did not sell my child!" he booms.

"You did," says Aura, keeping her voice level. "As did my parents. You traded our lives for a pile of edrian. Then again, as a trade master, you should know all about making deals."

Another look crosses Tide's face, only this time it's riddled with shame. Exactly the feeling Aura was trying to evoke.

"You can make this right," she says quickly before she loses him altogether. "Take me to Pace. We need to get him out of the Games so we can put a stop to all of this. Hayze, too. It ends now."

Tide draws in a slow breath as he turns this over. "How did you get out?"

"The leaders discovered Hayze missing from his pod," she says. "So, they took me out instead."

"And they let you just walk away?" Tide's lips part.

She smiles. "Not exactly. I used my Fire powers, then locked them in the room with the pods."

Tide's jaw falls wide open. "You did what?"

"You heard me," she says. "Which is why we must move quickly. Before they get out."

"You mean...they're still in there?" Tide looks at Aura with a whole new level of respect.

"I sealed the door shut." She nods. "Still think I'm out of my depth?"

"I don't think it." Tide takes a step toward the glass wall at the back of his trading hut. "I know it."

She follows him out the door, blinking in the heavy rain that's falling.

"Hasn't stopped since Pace left," Tide mutters, glaring at the dark clouds. "Come on then."

He leads her along the glass pontoons and Aura looks around in fascination at the glittering lights and sparkling water. Everything here is so much more vivid than it had been in Tempo's memories. Besides, as a resident of the Deadwaters, Tempo never got to walk beyond the market stalls and see any of this opulence up close. The wealth and excess being splashed around here, quite literally, is immense. How can so many have so much when even more have even less?

"Are you taking me to the pods?" Aura asks, realizing he never told her where they're going.

Tide nods. "There are three ways to get there. The regular tunnels that the leaders use, although they're useless now, mainly because I caved them in to buy your boyfriend some time. Then there's another more discrete entrance via a tunnel the Alliance uses, except that would take more time than you currently have."

"And the third way?" Aura prompts, remembering Ember telling her she'd be required to swim.

"You'll see," Tide grunts.

They cross a curved bridge made entirely from glass and pass some timber huts with lanterns swinging from their doorways. Nobody pays Aura the slightest bit of attention, thanks to her blue suit. If they stopped her, they might notice the Fire tattoo on her hand or the fascination in her eyes at the novelty of walking around this glistening fairyland she's only heard about in stories.

Tide opens the door to a large round hut and ushers Aura through. It's only when she sees a woman pacing the room that Aura realizes he's taken her to his home. The woman has wild, graying hair and deep wrinkles around her eyes, the sort that can only be earned through years of grief.

"Pace!" she gasps, despite Aura looking nothing like her son. "Is that you?"

Aura steps forward with conflicting feelings. This woman was party to the theft from Tempo's parents. A betrayal that Aura has felt firsthand. Yet, it's clear what that decision has cost her. There's nothing Aura can do to change what happened or make this woman feel any worse.

"You have a wonderful son," Aura says. "Kind. Brave. Smart. And he loves you very much."

Pace's mother's eyes fill with tears and she nods. "I want him back."

Aura nods. "That what I'm trying to—"

"Ondine," Tide says, going to his wife and putting a hand on each of her arms. "It's time for Project Eterna. Do you know what you have to do?"

Aura tilts her head. "What's Project Eterna?"

But neither Tide nor Ondine answer, too busy staring into each other's eyes.

"Ondine," Tide repeats. "Do you understand?"

Ondine nods solemnly.

Aura frowns. "What's—"

"Come on," Tide snaps, pulling back a rug and revealing another hatch. "This way."

Aura looks down and sees the ocean through the hole. Ember and Sera had warned her of this. She knew she was going to have to swim to get to Hayze. She just hadn't known it was going to be quite this terrifying.

"The Fire boy did it," says Tide as he lowers himself into the water. "And he survived. You can do it, too."

Aura nods as Tide plunges into the ocean.

"I don't like the water," Pace's mother whispers, which is an odd thing for a woman from the Water Quadrant to say. Perhaps if she knew her beloved son was down there that might change her thinking.

Aura follows Tide into the cold water and pulls in a deep breath, unaware of how long it will need to sustain her. Seeing movement ahead, she dives down, kicking her legs and pulling herself through the water with her cupped hands.

Her lungs scream at her for oxygen, yet she continues down with a new appreciation of what Hayze went through to get back to her. She can do the same for him. She just needs to keep swimming.

She continues forward, her muscles complaining more and more with each stroke. Each kick. Each desperate blink of her eyes.

"You can do this," she tells herself, over and over. If she fails, everything that came before this moment has been for nothing. It's never been more important to keep moving.

Tide reaches a rock formation in front of her and turns back to face her.

Aura tries to swim to him, except her body trembles as she reaches the limit of her capabilities and she finds herself unable to propel herself forward.

Tide expertly swims back to her and extends his large hand, grabbing the back of her suit and forcing her through a crack in the rocks. Her body goes limp and she concentrates on not allowing water into her lungs, having given up entirely on trying to swim. She's hauled upward by Tide and finally, blissfully, she breaks through the surface.

Coughing and heaving, she draws in precious air as Tide drags her over to a stone shelf and places her down.

"You're an even worse swimmer than the boy," he mutters. "And he was terrible."

Aura tries to steady her breathing, still unable to speak as she notices a set of white doors that Tide is making his way to.

"I told you that you were out of your depth." Tide lets out a strange sound that could possibly be him laughing at his own joke. "And don't expect me to carry you."

Pulling herself together, Aura gets to her feet and scurries over. Tide swipes his tattoo on a sensor and the doors slide open.

Aura gasps as she sees two pods with their sides curled up, white veins pulsing across their delicate skins. It's exactly like the room where she trapped the leaders in Ignis. She runs to one of the pods to find Pace lying inside with his eyes moving frantically behind his closed eyelids. Leaving him, she races over to the other pod.

And there he is.

Dressed in a blue suit from Water, Hayze is as handsome as he's ever been. His skin is pale and his hair is mussed, and Aura has to stop herself from reaching out to fix it.

This is the first time she's laid eyes on the real Hayze since this nightmare began, and she aches with longing to hold him close. But it's also the first time she's seen him since he betrayed her, revealing how little he really trusts her. It's a feeling that leaves her equally as longing to shake him.

Tide marches over to the control panel and starts typing on a keyboard.

"Stand back," he instructs.

Aura tears herself away from Hayze's pod and takes a few steps back. This must be Project Eterna. Tide was telling his wife that he was about to bring back their son.

"They're waking up now," Tide says, typing more furiously than before.

The sides of the pods unfurl, and Hayze turns his face, locking his gaze directly on Aura.

Her eyes fill with tears she refuses to shed as she studies him with a thousand questions desperate to fight their way out.

"You remember," Hayze says, grief of his own rippling across his face.

She nods. "I remember it all."

TWENTY-FOUR

HAYZE

Hayze leaps out of the pod, conscious his future is far more tenuous than it ever was in the Games. Death will be nothing compared to a life without Aura.

She's frozen as she looks at him, yet he can sense the way her heart is in a chokehold. He can see it in the pale, tense lines of her face. In the way her chest barely moves. In the shimmering, endless pools of pain that are her eyes.

She remembers.

"And yet you came for me," Hayze whispers.

Aura's face twists, yet the wrenching pain still doesn't draw out the tears glistening in her eyes. "I couldn't leave you behind."

Hayze takes a step forward, hoping it's a sign that forgiveness is possible.

Aura takes one back.

He stops, his heart a throbbing mass of agony in his chest. "How did you get out?"

"The leaders," she says, then clears her voice. "They went

looking for you and when you weren't there, they took me." She shrugs. "I sealed them in the room to buy us some time."

His strong, amazing girl. "Aura..." Except she's not his anymore.

"You lied to me," she whispers. "Twice."

The first time he kept his knowledge and his parents' involvement in the Alliance a secret. Then he failed to tell her *again* once he returned to the Games.

"I..." He stops, conscious that what he says now matters. That it could make the difference between holding her again and this soul-shredding pain—a future of breathing the same air as Aura, yet never having her.

"You didn't trust me," Aura whispers.

"I didn't want you to have to make the same choice I did— you or my family."

She shakes her head. "You chose them."

His parents. The Alliance.

"I tried to choose all of you." He shakes his head. "And I was wrong."

Aura's bottom lip trembles. "And when Rateen told you I was in danger, you chose the Alliance again."

Hayze closes his eyes. A shuddering breath rattles through him as he realizes Aura saw him walking away from Rateen as if she didn't matter. "Would you have wanted me to turn my back on the others in the Games?" he asks, opening his eyes.

Aura shakes her head.

"Would you have wanted me to risk Tide?" Aura's eyes flicker to Pace's father, then back to Hayze. "The leaders would've found out he's the one who helped me get back into the Games. To get back to you, Aura."

A tear forms, welling along her lashes, but she dashes it away. "How can I trust you again, Hayze?" There's a rasp to her voice, an edge roughened by betrayal.

Trust was the foundation of their relationship, first as friends, then as so much more. They knew they'd always be there for each other. That there was one person they could depend on in a world where nothing is certain.

And Hayze took that away from the one person he'd never want to hurt.

"I made a mistake. And then, because I'm clearly not a fast learner, I made it again." He takes a small step toward her, not allowing himself to hope when Aura doesn't retreat. "I think my consciousness knew that. It's why I chose you each and every time in the Games, even when I thought I hated you."

Aura's lashes flicker.

A tear swells again, shimmers, then spills over and down her cheek.

How Hayze wishes he could be the one to wipe it away. That he wasn't the one who put it there.

"And I know it doesn't seem like it, but I chose you when I walked away from Rateen. I believed that even if the leaders were telling the truth, you'd be strong enough to come back to me. Just like I did you."

Just like he should've trusted she'd be strong enough to carry the same burden he was given.

Another tear tracks down Aura's other cheek. "I..."

"You bastard!"

Pace's scream has them both spinning around. He launches out of his pod, standing in front of his father with his hands clenched and trembling.

"How could you?" Pace shouts.

Tide reaches out to his son. "I had no choice, Pace."

Pace leaps back, furiously pointing at the pod. "Unlike the other parents who made the deal, you sent me in there knowing exactly what I was about to be put through."

Tide flinches. "It was the only way to unlock your Elemental powers."

"I could've died!"

"They told me that wasn't possible." Tide opens out his palms, wanting his son to understand. "That's the whole idea of the Elemental Games. It's a place for you to discover your powers safely."

"Tell that to Geo," Hayze says quietly, remembering the still form he woke up beside. Geo died minutes later.

"And Tempo!" Pace yells. "She might not survive this either!"

Tide scowls. "Whether she dies or not is of no consequence to you."

"Her life means *everything* to me!"

Tide rears back, horrified. "You can't mean that."

"You knowingly sent me in there," Pace snaps. "You don't get to say what it looks like now that I'm out."

"None of us knew what it would look like when we came out," Hayze interjects, almost wincing at his own words. There was no way he could know that the day after his argument with Aura, they'd be yanked from everything they know and their memories stolen. "But now the three of us are out, we need to discuss what to do next."

Pace turns to look at Hayze, then his eyes widen. "I remember..." he whispers.

Hayze nods, conscious of the overwhelm that he would be going through right now. Pace's own memories, his *true* memories, now have to replace everything he's known since he started the Games.

Pace staggers back a step. "Tempo..."

"She'll hate you," Tide growls, glaring at his son. "When she remembers who you are and where you come from."

Pace's eyes widen. "Because her family hates us." They widen even more. "You stole from them."

Aura steps forward and clasps his hand. "There's a lot to discuss." Hayze grits his teeth to see her touching Pace with such familiarity. His jaw clamps even tighter when he sees some of the tension fade from Pace's body. "But we need to do it later."

Yet Hayze doesn't move. Even though he's feeling jealous. Possessive. He doesn't get to call Aura his. Not anymore. He can only hope that one day he'll have that honor again.

Pace lets out a long breath. "You're right. Now that we're out, we need to save the others." He glares at his father. "And save Tempo."

Tide presses his lips together in a hard, flat line. "Which you have a chance of doing now that you have your Elemental powers."

Pace stiffens, then looks away.

"There's a way to end the Games." Tide turns his focus to Hayze. "The main control room is in the Sect."

Hayze straightens, liking the sound of that. "Where in the Sect?"

"Right in the very center," he replies.

"And what do we have to do to end the Games?" Aura asks.

Hayze doesn't move, wondering if she noticed the way they're already working like two halves of a machine. They're two cogs that have seamlessly slipped back into rhythm with each other, despite the separation.

Tide opens his mouth to respond but a faint beeping rises from the control panel along the side wall. His head snaps toward it, then toward the closed door. "They're here."

Hayze moves without thinking, instinctively stepping closer to Aura. "The leaders?"

Tide rushes to the control panel, pressing a button so the beeping stops. "There's no way of telling, but we can't risk it."

Hayze yanks up his hands, preparing to defend Aura. She steps beside him, her hands also raised, and sweet pride rises through him, making his throat tight. He should've known she was strong enough to face anything.

Including the four leaders who are about to step through the door.

Pace appears on Hayze's other side, but Tide grabs his upper arm. Pace shakes him off, glaring at his father. "Isn't this what you wanted? To see my powers in action?"

"You don't think they'll be prepared this time?" Tide hisses. "They've spent years planning this, ensuring they can control what they create."

Hayze blinks, most definitely not liking the sound of that. "What do you mean?"

But Tide spins around and stalks to the back wall. It consists of five panels held in place by white beams. Four of the panels are identical, but the one in the center is narrower because the wall wasn't long enough for five full lengths.

Hayze draws in a sharp breath. Surely not...

Tide stops in front of it. He pushes his fingers in between the beam on his left and the panel and pushes. There's a pop and a scrape, and the panel swings in, revealing a secret tunnel.

"Hurry!" he hisses as he turns to the others.

Hayze has to stop himself from taking Aura's hand as they rush to the tunnel now waiting for them. Aura enters first, then Hayze, then Pace.

Tide stands in the doorway, his bald head and suited body outlined by the light spilling from the pod room. "Keep right. We haven't made it to the Sect, but we're close."

Hayze draws in a sharp breath. Tide is far more than he

realized. He's one of the parents desperate enough to sell their own child. He's a trade master. And Tide is also part of the Alliance.

His gaze falls on his son, softening in a way that Hayze knows Pace remembers. It's the same face that lay beside him on the pontoon as they gazed at the stars. The same face that cared for Ondine during her most hysterical moments. "I was always going to get you out, son. Once you had your powers." Tide glances over his shoulder, his eyes widening.

Pace steps forward, but Tide shoves him back. "Dad—"

The door slams in his face, plunging them into darkness. "What the hell?" Pace demands, the sound of scrabbling suggesting he's trying to find a way to open the door again.

"Tide!" a voice roars.

Hayze, Aura and Pace freeze as Oceania's voice carries through the thick door, muffled but unmistakable.

"What have you done?"

CHAPTER
TWENTY-FIVE
AURA

"We need to go." Aura tugs on Pace's arm.

"I can't leave my father," Pace whispers.

"It's what he wants," Hayze points out, a small flame burning in his palm and lighting up his annoyingly handsome face.

Pace holds up his hand, pressing his ear to the door and listening hard.

"Give him a moment," Aura whispers, understanding Pace's need for closure. Especially after having to deal with Tempo being torn away from him without warning in the maze. It's not easy to let go when you've already lost so much.

Hayze nods his agreement, even though the shuffling of his feet gives away his impatience to leave. He wants to get them to safety. He wants to get *Aura* to safety. Which is almost as annoying as his face. Staying mad with him is proving to be as impossible as it was not to fall in love with him for the second time when she thought he was her enemy.

"Where are they?" Infernos booms, his voice echoing through the secret door. "What have you done with them?"

"The pods were empty when I arrived," says Tide, his voice surprisingly level. "I was too late. They'd already gone."

"They?" Avalan's voice is shrill. "So, you admit you had the Fire boy here?"

Aura holds her breath as she waits for Tide's answer. Admitting Hayze was there would put Tide in grave danger. But telling them he wasn't would jeopardize the others, sending the leaders to search the pods in Earth and Air.

"He was here," Tide says coolly. "I assumed there was trouble with his pod, and you placed him here. I cared for him as per the protocol."

"We wouldn't place him here without issuing further instruction," hisses Oceania. "You should have reported it."

"My mistake," says Tide, stopping short of an apology. "Won't happen again."

"No, it won't," sneers Oceania. "I'm revoking your duties as trade master, effective immediately."

"He can't be trusted," growls Cyclonis, the other leaders mumbling their agreement.

"Send him back to the Deadwaters," says Avalan.

Pace looks across at Aura, his face filled with worry. Tide's entire life has been built around his position in Aqua. He risked everything to get there.

"No!" Tide shouts, all hints of steely control in his voice having vanished. "My wife. She needs me."

Aura puts a hand on Pace's back, both to comfort him and to make sure he's not about to burst back into the room. His mother's his soft spot. Aura knows that from when Hayze thought he was Pace. He not only loves her. He feels responsible for what happened to her.

"Your dad knows how to take care of things," Aura whispers. "Come on, Pace. We need to go."

"I can't," Pace whimpers.

"You must." Aura takes his hand and squeezes it. "Come on. It's what your dad wants. Don't let all his sacrifices be for nothing."

"But where will we go?" Pace asks.

"To the Sect," says Aura, doing her best to keep her voice low. "You heard what your dad said. If we get to the Sect, we can end the Games. And besides, that's where Tempo is."

Just as she can feel Pace about to give in and go with them, there's the sound of a scuffle on the other side of the thin door.

"You'll never get my son!" Tide shouts before letting out an agonized moan. "He's more powerful than you'll ever be!"

"He's telling you to go," Hayze says, leaning in closer. "He's talking to you."

Pace studies Hayze with his brow furrowed. Aura recognizes his confused expression from when she was woken from the pod herself. Pace is trying to sort out the muddle of memories swirling in his mind as he separates his own life out from Hayze's. It's not easy given everything else he's being forced to think about. Including leaving his father behind.

"He loves you," says Hayze. "It's time to show him you love him, too."

His words seem to work. Aura smiles at Hayze, realizing he understands Pace better than anyone, having lived inside his head. He knew exactly what he needed to say. Pace allows Aura to pull on his hand, leading him a few steps away from the door.

"Are you okay?" Hayze asks Aura, glancing at the narrow space they've entered.

"I'm fine. Honestly." She nods and they move down the tunnel.

Hayze takes the lead and Aura pushes Pace in front of her, afraid if he's not between them he might change his mind and run back to his father.

Like the other secret tunnels Aura went through to get to Aqua, this one is low and narrow, forcing them to run with their shoulders hunched. The air is heavy and hard to breathe with the strong scent of damp earth. With every step they take, the roof gets lower and soon they're forced onto their hands and knees as they crawl forward. Darkness descends as Hayze puts out his flame, needing to use his hands to move. It seems the Alliance didn't have time to dig out this tunnel properly, which makes sense given its purpose was purely as an escape route from the pod room. It's a tunnel that was hoped would never need to be used.

They crawl with agonizing slowness that reinforces why Tide had insisted on swimming down to Pace and Hayze. Even though it had almost cost Aura her life, they'd never have made it in time if they'd taken this route. As it was, they'd only just beaten the leaders to the room. Tide had been well aware that every minute counted. And he'd been right.

Aura crashes into Pace in the darkness when he comes to an abrupt halt, face planting him in the butt.

"You only had to ask," Pace quips, a sign of his personality returning. "But sorry, I'm taken."

"What a pity." Aura smiles as she rubs her nose. "Why have we stopped?"

"Because Hayze did," he says.

Hayze reignites his flame to study the solid wall of stone ahead of them. "We're at a dead end."

"It can't be." Aura leans to the side, trying to peer around Pace to get a better look, keeping well clear of his butt. "This must be an entrance to the Alliance's tunnels."

Pace nods his agreement as he sits back on his heels. "Try pushing on that rock. See if anything moves."

Aura lights a flame to give Hayze the use of his hands as he pushes on a large rock in the center of the wall. It moves slightly and he tries harder, managing to wedge it out of place. Aura concentrates on her flame, trying not to think about the consequences if they're wrong and the entire tunnel caves in.

Hayze leans through the gap he's created and peers through. He pulls back and turns to them.

"Yep," he says. "Another tunnel. Let's go."

He squeezes through, only just managing to fit. Pace follows and when it's Aura's turn, she can't go fast enough, not wanting to be left alone in such a small space.

Hayze helps her through on the other side then carefully reaches back and replaces the rock. Thankfully, the tunnel they're now in is tall enough for them to stand. Despite the roof being only inches above Aura's head, it feels positively cavernous as she stretches out her back. She's never been so grateful to be standing upright. Her muscles ache and she can only imagine how Hayze and Pace must be feeling, having only just been woken from their pods then put through that.

"You okay?" Hayze asks.

"Stop asking me that." She shakes her head. "I'll let you know if I'm not."

He grimaces and she sees the pain in his eyes. Not from the torturous crawl they just endured but her words. He wants her forgiveness. Perhaps *needs* it. The problem is she's not ready to give it yet.

They walk ahead and the tunnel quickly begins to feel familiar, the ground dipping down, taking them deeper into the earth.

"I've been here before," says Aura. "This is the same tunnel I came through to find your father. It leads right underneath the Sect."

"Is there a way up?" Hayze asks.

"Not that I could see." Aura remembers seeing the symbols for each of the four Quadrants, but nothing indicating there was any way to go up to the Sect. "But we'll figure something out."

"Is it too much to hope for another secret tunnel?" Pace asks. "They've been quite handy so far."

Aura laughs. "I think we may have used up our quota of secret tunnels for now."

"I suppose it's too risky to have a tunnel to the Sect," says Hayze, deep in thought. "If the leaders found it, they'd find everything else and the entire Alliance would be torn apart."

"Good point." Aura rubs her palms on her blue suit, her skin scratched and stinging.

"Let's keep moving," says Hayze.

They continue on with Hayze in the lead and Aura in the rear, their steps slowing when they hear voices ahead.

"Who do you think it is?" Hayze whispers, extinguishing his flame as he turns to them.

"The Alliance?" Pace suggests, not sounding at all certain. "Hopefully not the leaders."

They walk forward quietly, ears straining to hear what's being said. A soft glow lies ahead and people are talking, along with the unmistakable sound of shovels slicing through the earth.

"They're digging their way up," says Hayze.

Aura presses up behind Pace, catching a glimpse of the scene ahead.

"It's the intersection," she whispers, seeing the four tunnels with their symbols etched into the stone for each of the Quadrants. There's a group of people in the very center with ladders, picks and buckets, working to dig their way through the ceiling. They're wearing clothes from all four Quadrants. Before the Games, Aura had never seen anyone from rival lands cooperating like this.

Pace lets out an enormous sneeze and the tunnel falls silent.

"Who's there?" A broad-shouldered man in a Water suit marches toward them with a torch in his hand.

"I'm so sorry," Pace whimpers with his hand over his mouth. "I don't know where that came from."

"Well, bless you," Hayze grumbles, clearly unimpressed as he rolls his eyes.

"We're part of the Alliance," Pace calls out to the approaching man. "We come in peace."

The man reaches them and holds out his torch to inspect them.

"You're Tide's son," he says, staring at Pace like he's a ghost.

Pace nods. "I told you. We're part of the Alliance."

"And who are these two?" The man turns his attention to Hayze and Aura.

"I'm Hayze, Sera and Ember's son of the Fire Quadrant," Hayze says, holding up his hands. "And this is my friend, Aura. We mean you no harm. In fact, we'd like to help."

The man studies Hayze, then Aura. Seeming to be reassured, he shifts his attention back to the group of workers.

"They're clear," he announces.

The people get back to scraping dirt and stone from the ceiling of the tunnel, collecting it in their buckets and carrying it away.

"What are they doing?" Pace asks the man.

"Didn't you hear?" The man narrows his gaze. "It's Project Eterna."

Aura gasps, remembering Tide's words to his wife when they passed through their hut. "It was a code," she says. "I heard Tide tell Ondine."

"That's right." The man nods. "She raised the alarm. She knew exactly what she had to do."

"Hold on." Pace seems more worried than ever to hear his mother's name. "She raised the alarm for what?"

The man turns his attention back to Pace. "Your father knew this would come one day. It's time to break into the Sect."

CHAPTER
TWENTY-SIX

HAYZE

P roject Eterna.

Hayze has only ever heard the words said in hushed, furtive tones. His parents told him the ultimate goal for the Alliance as they hunched their shoulders and eyes darted around. As if they weren't sure they'd see it in their lifetime. The words felt about as real as Eterna herself.

Yet here he is.

And Project Eterna has commenced.

Hayze goes to move closer to Aura, instinctively wanting to protect her as if just thinking the words have willed a war, then stops himself when he senses her tense. She knew he'd move in. And braced herself for it.

Hiding his wince, he focuses back on the man across from them, opening his mouth to speak, but Pace beats him to it.

"Break into the Sect?" he asks as if the man just suggested Air is the greatest Element of all. "And then what?"

"We overthrow the leaders," the man says, like it's simple. "The time for division is over."

Excitement surges through Hayze. He's never heard truer

words. Sure, almost impossible ones, but still exactly what needs to happen.

Aura's brows contract. "But..."

It's Hayze's turn to tense, and he's most definitely bracing himself. Aura's parents believe the leaders are working in everyone's best interest. Mutiny is the last thing they'd want.

Is that what Aura wants, too?

"Waverly!" a woman calls out from the end of the tunnel. "We've hit stone!"

To Hayze's surprise, the man grins. He turns back to the group digging upward. "Great news!" He glances back at Hayze and the others. "The Sect rests on stone. We're getting close."

Aura draws in a sharp breath, and for the first time in as long as he can remember, Hayze isn't sure what it means. He rubs at the ache in the center of his chest, even as he knows it's not going away. There's a crack in his heart, one that's waiting to see if it will be healed by the only person who can.

Or whether it's just the start of it splintering, shattering, then never being whole again.

Waverly assesses the three teens. "Hope you're feeling strong. Getting through is going to take some serious muscle power."

The sound of metal bars hitting rock carries down the tunnel as the rebels begin to chip at the last barrier between them and the Sect. Each clang rams home the realization Hayze is expected to help.

And if he does, Aura will think he's choosing the Alliance again.

"Water is the Element you need," Pace says, his eyes narrowed as he stares at the hole in the top of the tunnel, probably conscious Tempo is on the other side of the expanse of stone. "I'll blast jets into the cracks, then freeze them."

The ice will expand, fracturing the rock. They could get through the stone within hours.

Waverly's eyes light up. "You have your powers?"

Pace's mouth twists. "That's what the Games were for," he says, bitterness lacing his words. He's the only one whose parent sent him into them, knowing what was coming.

Waverly's hand tightens around the torch. "We've all paid a great price to be here. Including Tide."

Pace's gaze snaps to his. "Some more than others," he mutters through tight lips.

Waverly inclines his head. "All so that the chosen ones can end this suffering."

Pace blinks, probably trying to reconcile the very same thing Hayze is—being 'chosen' with having a heart that hopes and hurts, just like anyone else.

Waverly turns to Hayze, his eyes flickering to Aura. "So, if you two are Fire, what can you do to help?"

Aura stills.

So does Hayze.

If she helps, she betrays her parents and everything they believe in.

If he helps, he betrays Aura and everything they've forged together over a lifetime of love.

Hayze has to resist rubbing the center of his chest again. The Games have wrenched them apart. Undermined their foundation as surely as the Alliance has with the Sect.

Waverly frowns. "It wasn't a trick question. You're either part of the Alliance, or you're not."

Schnit.

Aura isn't part of the Alliance. It's why Hayze didn't mention her parents' names when introducing her. She turns slightly, her blue eyes slowly trekking up his chest, his throat, unerringly finding his eyes like she has so many

246

times before. A single question shimmers in the pools of pain.

She's waiting to see what he'll do.

Who he'll choose.

And he's already made his decision.

"Hayze?"

"Hayze!"

He spins around as the two achingly familiar voices echo through the tunnel. "Mom? Dad!"

His parents break into a run, tears running down his mother's coal-stained cheeks, a huge grin splitting his father's. Hayze launches forward, meeting them a few feet away. They crash together, collapsing into a tight hug that squeezes his heart just as completely as his lungs.

His father pulls back, clasping Hayze's face. "It's good to see you, son."

Although Hayze has already seen them twice in the Games, this time it's real. This time, the truth is free.

"Look, Dad," he says, taking a step back.

It barely takes a thought and a flame leaps to life in his palm. Hayze focuses a little more and it grows. He lets out a breath and it shrinks. He twists his hand over and the fire curls over his skin almost playfully, flickering merrily as it now sits on the back of his hand.

"Oh, Ember," his mother whispers, her own hands now clasped at her chest.

Hayze's father looks from the flame to Hayze, back to the flame as Hayze passes it to the other palm. When his father's eyes return to Hayze's face, they're glistening. "Hayze..."

He grins as he clenches a fist and snuffs out the ball of flame. "You were right all along, Dad."

All those hours and days and years of training weren't for nothing.

247

The same hours and days and years where Hayze was terrified he was letting his parents down were most definitely for nothing.

Now, pride is shining in his father's eyes. It glistens in the tears on his mother's face. It has Hayze's chest inflating even as his throat tightens.

"Aura, too," he says, grinning again. "She's harnessed her powers."

To Hayze's surprise, his father frowns. "That's a concern."

Pace clears his throat and Hayze's parents look past him, registering the Water teen walking toward them.

And Aura beside him, her chin raised a notch.

Hayze's mother gasps as she draws back. "She's here?" she whispers.

"I followed your instructions and got to Hayze," Aura says.

"And then you told your parents about the Alliance." Ember's eyes glare.

Aura holds up her hands. "I didn't tell them anything. I swear."

"Then how else did they find out?" Sera asks.

"She wouldn't do that!" Hayze reaches out a reassuring hand. "She's not the enemy, Mom."

Unless Aura chooses—

Hayze cuts off the thought before it can fully form. There is no reality where Aura could be his enemy. Even the most fantastical virtual reality couldn't create such a cruel scenario. He knows that because the leaders already tried that and failed spectacularly.

His father scowls, his body expanding as he draws in a breath. "But Brando and Vespa are the enemy."

Aura tenses. "They want the same thing you do. To save others."

Hayze's mother jolts as if she's been slapped. "Your parents are betrayers of the Alliance!"

Pace stops beside Aura, scowling. "What do you mean, betrayers?"

"It's why we're here," Hayze's father says, his voice low and heavy. "Brando and Vespa have gone to tell Infernos about the Alliance."

His mother points an accusing finger at Aura. "How do we know she's not on their side?"

Shock rams through Hayze. They've been betrayed. By the parents of the girl he loves.

"No!" Pace says, the word exploding out of him. "We're so close!"

Aura shakes her head. "They wouldn't—"

"I overheard them talking in the tunnels," Hayze's mother hisses. "We came straight here to warn the others. An attack is imminent."

Hayze's father crosses his arms. "You still think they're trying to save people?" he asks Aura. "They're guaranteeing a war. Bloodshed is inevitable."

She frowns. "So is attacking the Sect."

Hayze's mother sucks in a sharp breath. "Of course you'd say that."

"After everything we've been through..." Pace shakes his head, looking at Aura as if she just attacked him personally. "How can you think they're right?"

Hayze angrily steps in front of Aura, blocking her from Pace and his parents. "She's been through just as much as anyone," he growls. "This isn't easy on any of us."

The Games haven't just uncovered their powers.

They're demanding they take sides in a battle that will decide the future of humanity.

Hayze's mother's eyes widen. "Hayze?" she asks, her voice hiking. "You're protecting her?"

He doesn't answer, hoping the unsaid words are clear on his face.

He will *always* protect Aura.

His father's brows slam down at the same time as the edges of his mouth. "Son, the Alliance needs you. It needs Fire." He glances at the rebels still chipping away at the stone, the clang, clang, clang counting out the seconds. "This is what you've been working toward your whole life."

Hayze stills as the weight of his decision closes in around him.

Clang.

Clang.

Clang.

It's time to choose.

Pace spins on his heel and stalks away. "I'm going to help them dig," he says, his voice as hard as the stone he intends on fracturing. "Aura's parents will be too late. We'll be inside the Sect by daybreak."

Which means Pace will be by Tempo's side as the sun rises.

Where will Hayze be?

His father stares at him, his gaze growing heavier by the second. His mother watches him, tears once more shimmering along her lashes. But this time they threaten to spill over as worry and betrayal fill her eyes. Hayze realizes at that moment that they also made a choice when they signed the agreement. That deciding to have a child they would inevitably lose to the leaders sparked an idea. He was raised to take down the leaders. To stop this from ever happening again.

Except he also grew up loving Aura.

A hand presses softly into his back and he turns around to

find her looking up at him, her face pale yet calm. "I...can't, Hayze."

He goes still as he gazes at her. Can't what?

"And you don't have to decide." She takes a step back. "I don't want you to."

She spins on her heel and breaks into a run, past his parents and into the darkness of the tunnel. And he already knows where she's going. Hayze may not know where her loyalty lies, but Aura's still the girl he grew up loving. He has no doubt she's going to look for her parents, to either stop them...or help them.

Hayze takes a step forward, only for his father's palm to slam into his chest.

"She's made her choice, son. You need to make yours."

Clang.

Clang.

Clang.

Pace's voice carries down the tunnel. "Stand back. Let's speed things up."

There's a rush of water. The faint crackling of water freezing. Then a monstrous boom as several feet of rock split, the tremors rippling through the soil and stone like thunder. A cheer rises from the rebels, followed by another blast of water. Pace is going again.

He won't stop until the rock is broken and crumbling, opening up a way into the Sect.

To Tempo.

Hayze already suspects the legacy of Water is going to affect Pace and Tempo's relationship as deeply as Fire has scorched Hayze and Aura's. But he can't think about that now. Not when his father and mother are waiting.

Not when he's made his choice.

CHAPTER
TWENTY-SEVEN

AURA

Aura has to get to her parents before they reach Infernos. They don't understand. They never have. And it's all Aura's fault. She should've tried harder to explain things when she returned home to their bunker. Instead of asking questions about her birth, she should've been answering their questions about the Alliance. She should've told them everything. She should've got them on the same side.

She exits the rebel tunnels, connecting through to the main network used by the people of the Fire Quadrant. If she hurries, hopefully she can catch up to her parents before they arrive in Ignis. At least it's unlikely they'll find Infernos there given he's busy searching for Hayze. Or punishing Tide...

Pushing that uncomfortable thought from her mind, Aura runs ahead, her footsteps echoing through the dark tunnels behind her. These tight spaces still make her chest cave in on itself as breathing becomes something she has to consciously think about rather than happening on its own. But she knows she can do it in the same way she knows she can make fire with her bare hands. Both skills were a gift of the Games. Which is

252

why she can't hold a grudge against her parents for the decisions they made before she was born. In fact, she'd never have been born at all if they hadn't taken the leaders up on their agreement.

She turns a corner and continues on, noticing she can no longer hear the echo of her footsteps. Which means it wasn't an echo.

Someone's behind her.

Pressing herself against the earthen wall, she extinguishes the flame in her palm, catching her breath as she waits to see who's about to come around the corner. It could be an innocent person from the Fire Quadrant making their way to their latest blast site to mine for edrian. Or it could be one of the leaders.

Or...

She pants, restoring her breath to its usual rhythm as she realizes who it will be.

"Hayze," she whispers as a shadow moves around the corner.

She thought he made his choice. That he decided to stay with his parents and help them blast through to the Sect. Yet, somehow, she'd known he was going to follow her here just like he'd follow her to the end of the Earth.

"Aura," he says quietly, his voice breaking with emotion. "You knew it was me."

She nods in the darkness.

"Did you follow because you still don't trust me?" she asks. "You think I'm going to help my parents?"

He steps up so close to her that she can feel the warmth of his breath on her cheek. "I trust you, Aura."

She blinks, trying to see his face in the shadows. "Then why are you here?"

"Because you're here," he says.

A bubble of emotion rises to her throat, and she leans forward, pressing her lips to his. So many parts of her still want to push him away rather than bring him close. But here in the darkness, none of those parts seems to count. Here, she can pretend everything's like it used to be.

Aura and Hayze.

Connected by their Quadrant.

Brought together by fate.

Joined by their hearts.

She kisses him gently at first, then he spears his fingers into her hair, letting out a moan as he presses her back against the wall and deepens the kiss. She trails her hands down his torso, remembering how much she'd wanted to explore his body in the Games when the truth is she already knows every line and curve of his muscular frame.

He runs his tongue across her bottom lip and Aura feels herself splinter into three.

Her mind stings from betrayal.

Her heart swells with love.

And her body...yearns.

She pulls back from him, panting hard. "Hayze, we can't. My parents...I have to find them."

"Do you forgive me?" he asks, hope lacing through his voice.

"I want to." This is the most honest answer she can give him. Because she *does* want to. More than anything.

"That's a start." He runs his fingertips down her arm, slipping his hand into hers and squeezing. "Come on, then."

"Okay," she says.

Hayze ignites a flame in his free hand and the soft glow lights up his face. She's glad she couldn't see it a few moments ago or she'd have forgiven him on the spot, having spent her entire life tumbling into the depths of his dark eyes.

They walk forward in silence, keeping their footsteps fast and light. Aura's mom moves notoriously slowly, which could be their only hope. Aura can imagine her dad urging her along, willing her steps to go faster.

"They're not bad people," Aura says.

"I know," Hayze says from behind her. "They think they're doing what's right."

"Exactly." Aura lets relief slide through her to realize Hayze can see the truth.

"But taking people against their will to fight it isn't the answer," he adds. "Geo should have had a choice."

"I know," she says quietly. "Geo gave his life for a cause he didn't know he was fighting. Nothing can make that okay."

"So, you're on our side?" he asks.

She sighs, pushing down her disappointment. Can't he see that this is exactly the problem? He doesn't trust her. Not really. Because if he did, he'd know she's desperate to get to her parents so she can bring them to the Alliance's side, not to help them with this dangerous quest they've set out on.

"Sorry," he says, sensing her frustration. "There's just so much at stake."

"There is." She grimaces, aware this includes both their hearts.

The ladder that leads to the Scorchlands appears ahead and Aura's flame flickers as she remembers the last time she'd seen it, even if it was during the Games. This was where she thought she lost Hayze forever, making it the worst moment of both her real and virtual lives. She averts her eyes as they pass the fan where Aura's blindfold was dragged in, choking her as the sea of lava approached.

Hayze had saved her.

Again.

Just like he's trying to save her now.

Except, this time, she doesn't need it.

These are her parents. And she can fix the mess they've gotten themselves into.

She reaches the ladder and scales it without waiting for Hayze, her need to get out of this enclosed space surpassing everything else. It's with enormous relief that when she emerges, she discovers it's night. Hayze is still wearing the white suit from the pod and Aura's in the blue suit she'd put on before entering Aqua. They're going to stand out in Ignis, making darkness their best friend right now.

Hayze exits the tunnel behind her and she puts out a hand to help him up. Or maybe it's just an excuse to feel his skin against hers once more. The warmth of his palm sends a tingle up her arm, giving her the strength she needs to find her parents.

Maybe she does need his help just a little bit...

"We might be too late," Hayze whispers. "I hoped we'd find them in the mines."

Aura doesn't mention that maybe they would have if they hadn't stopped for that kiss, mainly because she doesn't regret it one bit. She needed that kiss almost as much as she needed oxygen in her deprived lungs.

Linking hands, they walk in the darkness, heading for the wall that surrounds Ignis. As the shadow of the high structure looms in the distance, the sound of hushed voices filters through the night.

They deviate off the path, crouching low as they walk. Finding a burned bush with spindly branches reaching out like clawed hands, they squat down and strain their ears, hardly daring to believe their luck.

"We need them," says Infernos. "The gift you gave us will save countless lives."

"Our daughter wasn't a gift," Aura's father replies.

Aura's heart both rises and sinks to hear his familiar voice. They've found them! But her parents are in far more danger than they realize. Infernos isn't the loving leader they've always assumed him to be.

"Aura *is* a gift," Infernos insists. "And a powerful one at that. I'm very proud of her, as I know you are."

Aura rolls her eyes in the darkness. Infernos has nothing to be proud of. He might have created her, but her parents were the ones to raise her. They made her who she is.

"We love our daughter," Aura's mother says. "More than anything. You don't understand how hard this has been on us."

"I do," Infernos reassures. "But let me remind you that all of this is for the greater good. We need your daughter's powers. It's the only way. The storms have been getting worse. And the quakes. And tsunamis and floods. And that's not even mentioning the fires. We have nothing here left to burn. Even the capitals are no longer safe."

Aura fights a feeling of overwhelming sadness. This situation is far more complex than she realized. Both sides have a point. The human race is in grave danger of extinction if they can't figure out how to tame the Elements and forge a safe existence. But the leaders have it all wrong. They need to work together, not live in divided Quadrants like enemies. They need to convince people to fight for what's right, not trick them into risking their lives to save each other. What's the point in surviving if you lose what makes you human in the first place?

"You're right, Infernos," Aura's mother says, her awe for her leader clear in the revered tone of her voice.

"Which is why we came to you," Aura's father says. "There's something you need to know."

Aura winces, feeling Hayze tense beside her. This is it. The moment where the leaders learn about the Alliance and everything Hayze and his family have been fighting for.

Hayze gets to his feet and Aura tugs on his hand, willing him to get back down. If Infernos turns around, he'll see Hayze's shadow and all hell will break loose. Hayze lets out a quiet whimper, torn between Aura and what he believes is right.

"There's an Alliance," Aura's mother says.

Hayze sinks to his knees, accepting he's already too late.

"A group of rebels," Aura's father adds. "They're working against the leaders to bring you all down."

"How do you know this?" Infernos snaps. "Give me your source."

"We can't," says Aura's mother. "And besides, it doesn't matter. What we tell you is true. They're trying to break into the Sect right now. You must stop them!"

Infernos lets out a cackle, seeming completely undisturbed. "The Sect is impenetrable. They'll never get in."

"They're blasting their way up from underneath," Aura's father says. "Our source tells us they're close."

"Who is this source?" Infernos booms, his amusement turning to anger.

Aura listens harder, wanting the answer to this question just as much as Infernos. It seems the Alliance has a mole. And it's someone from the Fire Quadrant.

"Tell me," says Infernos. "As your leader, I demand it."

"Pyra," Aura's father squeaks. "A girl from our village. She wanted to go to you herself, but she was too afraid."

Hayze vibrates with anger to hear that the girl he thought was his friend is the source of this betrayal. He was teaching Pyra to paint as she helped to mix his paints, and all this time it seems what she was really doing was listening into his family's conversations and reporting them back to Aura's parents.

"Tell her to come to me," says Infernos, his voice sweetening. "I'll reward her greatly for any more information she can provide."

"Yes, Infernos," Aura's mother says.

"Is there anything else you need us to do?" Aura's father asks. "Do you need us to hinder the Alliance? Perhaps we can pretend to join them and slow down their efforts."

Infernos laughs again. "No. Let them dig. This is a perfect way to dispose of them all. If they're coming up from underneath the Sect, they'll soon reach the sea of lava that lies below it. Mother Nature is far closer to the Quadrants than anyone realizes. Once they break through the final layer of rock, their foolish Alliance will come to an end very quickly."

Horror floods Aura as she remembers the agonized screams of the people in the Games as they were consumed by lava.

It's happening again.

Only this time it's far worse.

Because not only are Hayze's parents down there, but so is Pace.

And this time, it's real.

CHAPTER
TWENTY-EIGHT

HAYZE

Hayze spins on his heel and runs. Silently. Swiftly. Desperately.

He reaches the hole to the tunnel, not surprised to find Aura right behind him. There's one thing they can agree on— sides don't matter right now. Lives do.

He scrambles down the ladder, pausing long enough to make sure Aura lands safely by his side. Wordlessly, their hands brush each other's in the dark. It's all hope needs to unfurl in his chest as they break into a frantic run. They just need to get there in time...

Yet as they weave through the main tunnels, Hayze holding up a small flame with his spare hand, the tiny kernel of hope struggles to thrive in the harshness of reality.

Mother Nature is far closer to the Sect than any of them realized.

Pace is using his powers to break through the rock, clueless there's a sea of lava on the other side.

And Hayze's parents are there with him.

They reach the hidden entrance to the secret tunnel and

slip through, their hands once more coming together on the other side. The image of Hayze's parents being engulfed by lava as they stood by the wall plays through his mind with every thump of his feet on the earthen floor. The leaders knew his father believed in Hayze and were trying to use it against him.

Hayze has to make sure that nightmare doesn't become reality.

"They...think they're doing...the right thing," Aura gasps through panting breaths.

Hayze nods sharply in acknowledgement. Isn't that what they're all trying to do—the right thing? Even as the question filters through his mind, another thought follows.

Aura's parents betrayed his parents. Infernos won't stop until the Alliance is exterminated.

A second question is hot on its heels.

If Aura's parents are responsible for the death of his own, will he be so understanding?

Hayze's hand twitches, and for the first time he's not sure if he wants to touch her again or pull away. He now understands Tempo's animosity toward Pace. His parents did what they believed was right. And Tempo and her parents paid the price with a lifetime of poverty and struggle. Death hovered over them each and every day.

If they ever do reach Tempo, if she wakes, will she be able to forgive Pace for that?

"Hayze," Aura gasps. "I—"

Whatever she was going to say is cut off as they turn a corner and the rebels come into view. Pace is standing beneath the opening reaching up to the Sect, his hands stretched up. Jagged stones and boulders are littered around him and the rebels are working to move them away, including Hayze's parents.

Even from a distance, their grins are apparent.

"Pace!" Hayze roars. "Stop!"

Pace turns around, frowning as his gaze flickers to Aura and his hands lower to his side. "I knew you'd choose her side!"

Despite the accusation, Hayze lets out a breath. They got here in time. Pace hasn't dealt the final blow that will—

The crack that shoots through the tunnel has Hayze instinctively stepping closer to Aura, even knowing she may not like it. The rumble of the walls has him screaming one word.

"No!"

"Yes!" shouts Waverly, stepping in front of Pace as he looks up. "I can see light!"

The roar of victory from the rebels is drowned out by a thunderous shudder. The walls groan. The roof heaves. The sound of grinding and popping has Hayze launching forward.

A waterfall of lava pours from the hole, thick and viscous and iridescent crimson. Pace leaps back but Waverly isn't quick enough. The acrid, molten river engulfs him, instantly turning him black. His agonized screams go from high pitched to garbled to nothing but an echo as his body burns and melts.

They're too late.

Hayze breaks into a sprint, his parents' terrified faces engulfing his vision. "Run!"

"Get out of there, Pace!" Aura screams.

He's already running, his face pale in the dark tunnel, a curtain of glowing red behind him.

"Everyone, get out!" Hayze shouts, waving his arm frantically. "Get out of the tunnels!"

Screams bounce off the walls as the rebels move as one. Behind them, the lava pours through the hole at a greater and greater rate, as if a dam has burst. A woman trips on the rubble and falls. Her cry is cut off as her head hits the sharp edge of a boulder. She sprawls on the uneven ground, lifeless. The quick death is a blessing as her body is devoured as easily as the jagged boulder beside her.

"This way!" Aura calls out.

Hayze doesn't look back, glad she's stayed behind to keep people focused and give directions. The scent of panic is almost as strong as the sulfur. He reaches his parents at the rear as they usher everyone forward, making sure no one is left behind. They're both red-faced and coughing as the rising lava crawls over stones and laps at the sides of the tunnel.

Suddenly, thunder rumbles along the roof, making Hayze instinctively duck as it shoots past him as if it's following the rebels. His mother stops to look up, her eyes expanding as she stills.

Fractures are spreading through the rock and dirt like lightning. Except these veins are red and won't be fading.

The lava is spreading over the tunnel, looking for a weak spot so it can pour down in more than one place. If it finds one ahead, it could trap the rebels.

"Sera!" Hayze's father screams. He grabs his wife, jerking her out of her terrified stupor, but it's too late.

A chunk of rock falls and hits her on the side of the head. Dark blood rushes down her face as she blinks, dazed.

"Mom!" Hayze leaps forward. He and his father slip under an arm each and break into a run, trying to carry her to safety. Her feet shuffle and trip as her head lolls.

A quick glance over his shoulder tells Hayze those seconds were all the river of lava needed. The more that pools, the faster it moves. It's only feet away.

"Pace!" Hayze screams. "Slow it down!"

Pace turns toward the approaching lava and extends his hands. He shoots out a thick blast of water, trying to cool the red river of rage. Hissing fills the tunnel as the lava cools and slows. It gives Hayze and his father the time they need to get his mother away.

And it also fills the air with sulfurous steam.

"Pace!" Hayze shouts, coughing and looking around in panic. They need to keep moving, but all he can see and breathe is yellow-tinted mist. Images of the woman who tripped and hit her head fill his mind. She was devoured by lava seconds later.

"On it!"

The droplets freeze and Hayze sees something he's only ever painted for Aura—snow. Tiny, frozen flakes tumble down, melting long before they reach the ground.

The air clears and Hayze sees two things.

The lava is coated with a thick crust of black that's already fracturing with veins, just like the ceiling.

And Aura hasn't run ahead with the others.

She ensures the last of the rebels have disappeared down the tunnel before turning and running back. "If we can cool it down, we can buy them some time."

Hopefully long enough for the fighters of the Alliance to get out of the tunnels.

Except Hayze can't do that and carry his mother. He needs to focus.

His mother slips her arm from his shoulder as if she just read his mind. "I can run," she says weakly. "Really, I can."

Hayze turns to his father, certainty settling in his gut in sharp shards. "Get her to safety."

"But..." His father scowls. "We both will."

Hayze shakes his head. Aura's right. This is going to need the two of them if anyone is going to survive this. "This is what all that training was for, Dad."

His father nods, even as the color drains from behind his coal streaks.

Hayze steps back. "Get everyone out of the tunnels." He turns to Pace. "Go with them, just in case."

If the lava breaks through, if Hayze and Aura fail, Pace is the Alliance's only chance of survival.

Pace hesitates but purses his lips. "Okay. But I'm coming back so we can kick Sect ass."

Hayze almost grins. "Excellent plan."

His mother reaches up with surprising strength and squeezes his arm. His father clasps his head as he communicates two words with nothing but an intense stare.

Don't die.

And then Hayze's parents and Pace are gone.

Aura reaches out to brush his hand. "You should go with them."

Hayze turns to her, frowning. "Isn't that my line?" It's taken every ounce of self-control not to tell Aura to get to safety.

It's only that he knows this is the only way to show he believes in her. That he knows she needs to fight this as much as he does. That ultimately, he loves Aura more than the one thing he sure could use right now—peace of mind.

And now she's trying to send him away?

Aura steps in closer as the sound of crackling peppers the air. The lava is about to break through any second. "You don't have to stay. It's my mom and dad who betrayed the Alliance."

Hayze shakes his head. "We learned in the Games we aren't our parents' choices."

They rose above that and fell in love for the second time in their lives.

It's all the reminder Hayze needs. He loves Aura. He always will. No matter what.

She caresses his cheek. "Then it's time to make our own."

Hayze lifts his hand and Aura presses her palms to his. Their fingers interlace, their hands form a tight bond.

"We are Fire!"

Heat explodes where their palms connect, flaring out. The instant explosion blasts the lava back, splashing molten rock on the walls.

"We need to draw the heat out of it," Aura says, her face tense with focus.

Their fingers tighten, turning white as they grip hard. They simultaneously pull in a breath, sucking in ash and sulfur and determination. The heat is drawn to them like a magnet. The lava flares bright, flames licking over its surface.

"More," Hayze rasps.

They have to suck thousands of degrees of heat out of the body of molten rock coming at them.

Aura closes her eyes and Hayze does the same, focusing his entire being on the place their palms connect. He calls for the heat. The fire. The flames. He beckons them to come.

It hits them with a blast that rocks their bodies. A burn starts deep within his muscles, then burrows deeper. And hotter.

"Hayze!"

He snaps his eyes open, then his mouth follows suit as he registers what Aura's seeing. They *are* Fire. They're surrounded by it. Engulfed by it.

At one with it.

Red and orange and yellow dance around them, licking over their suits and skin, curling around their torsos, lifting strands of Aura's hair and entwining with them. They're a living torch, blasting the tunnel with light.

Stealing the heat from the lava and combusting the very air.

"Aura, look," Hayze says as he glances at the lava.

It has a thick crust on it, the surface black and rippled. And unbroken.

They're slowing its spread!

"It's working," she gasps.

They move closer, tightening the human pyre they've become and flare it hotter. Higher. Bigger.

The lava stops, the crust crackling as it thickens. Victory dances around Hayze as intensely as the flames.

The next crack is louder. Closer.

And above them.

Hayze and Aura look up. His pulse combusts as he registers the veins of lava above them. The ones that are growing, fracturing, splitting. He grabs Aura and leaps out of the way just in time as the ceiling cleaves open and a second river of lava pours down.

"We called it to us!" Hayze cries, spinning around as a second roar fills the tunnel.

More lava is pouring from the first hole, the one they naively hoped would take them to the Sect.

Hayze and Aura jump away from the new threat, only to stop as the fresh lava pours over the hardened crust, melting it. Within seconds, it will form a river twice the size and twice as fast.

"There's too much!" Aura cries.

And they're surrounded by it.

They underestimated what they're up against. Lava is Fire and Earth. By drawing the heat to themselves, Hayze and Aura drew the molten earth to them. And with Geo dead and Jewel still trapped in the Games, they only have half the equation. They can't manipulate the lava itself.

They can't stop it.

Hayze's gaze finds Aura's. They stare at each other, realizing this is where their choices got them.

About to be devoured by the very Element they thought they could harness.

"We'll go down fighting," Aura whispers fiercely, turning away from the lava encroaching from both sides. "We'll go down in a blaze of glory."

The fighting spirit flashing in her blue eyes has Hayze bringing their hands in close and tucking them in between them. It has his heart flaring with love.

And an idea bursting to life.

"Let it come," he tells her, hope flashing as bright as the flames they're keeping alive.

Aura's eyes flare wide. "What?"

"We need to heat the lava." They'll burn the freaking equation.

Her brow flutters with confusion before clearing. Realization dawns across her beautiful face. "We'll fight Fire with Fire."

Hayze nods, knowing she'd understand.

This time, when they press their palms tightly together, when their fingers intertwine with every shred of their strength, they do two things.

They call the heat to them. They draw the lava closer.

And then multiply the burn that engulfs them.

The impact is instantaneous.

The flames around them go from red to blue to nothing more but ripples of air. The temperature rockets so high, Hayze's very lungs are burning.

So. Much. Heat.

It's as if his whole body is on fire. His veins are alive with it. His marrow is smoldering with it. Hayze has never felt anything more exhilarating.

Or terrifying.

Their clasped hands rise, their arms vibrating with the power coursing through them. A roar erupts from Hayze, Aura's echoing cry weaving through it. The lava pours faster as it grows hotter. It thins as it heats, becoming liquid rock that's all the colors of the sun.

Strands shoot toward them as if Hayze and Aura are now the center of this self-made universe. A supernova the river of fire is undeniably drawn to. The thick threads never reach them, hitting the cocoon of invisible heat that now encases Hayze and Aura. Instead, the ribbons of lava curl around them, rising higher and higher.

Within seconds, a whirlpool of gold and amber and bronze surrounds them. It coils faster and faster until all Hayze can see and feel is Fire. As it rises above their heads, then their extended hands, the threads thin, unravel, and vaporize.

The lava comes faster and faster. Hayze and Aura burn hotter and hotter. The powerful cyclone roars, tearing at their clothes and hair. The sulfur stings their eyes. They *become* Fire.

Until there's nothing left.

The last ribbon of lava swirls around them, lifting into the air, splitting into fine threads, then disappearing.

Hayze and Aura's hands slowly descend as their panting breaths mingle. They blink. Their chests shudder. Then they smile.

They did it.

The tunnel is empty. Now black, it only holds the two of them, the air still stained with sulfur.

Aura leans forward, resting her head on Hayze's chest. His arms wrap around her, awed at what they just accomplished. That he's here, gifted with the ability to hold her.

Aura turns her head, then stills. "Hayze, look."

He follows her line of sight, also losing the ability to move.

There's a reason he can see the beautiful, amazing girl he's holding. The one whose spirit burns as hot as his.

A beam of light spears down at the end of the tunnel, creating a pool of white on the ground. They rush over and look up, now bathed in the glow pouring down.

And above them is a clear line of sight to the Sect.

CHAPTER
TWENTY-NINE

AURA

Aura pokes her head out of the top of the tunnel. Hayze is directly below her, ready to catch her if she should slip from one of the footholds they blasted into the rockface to get up to the Sect.

She blinks in the harsh artificial light, taking in the empty room. It's not as grandiose as she imagined, but thankfully the leaders don't appear to be here to greet them. Things could have been far worse.

"It's safe," Aura calls down to Hayze, keeping her voice low. She heaves herself out of the tunnel and spins around on the shiny white tiles to help Hayze up. Drawing in a deep breath of clean air, she feels good to be out of the mines, even if they're in enemy territory now.

Hayze gets immediately to his feet and stalks around the room looking for any danger, his breath steadying when he returns to Aura.

She steps up to kiss him, then remembers that's not who they are anymore and quickly withdraws.

"You kissed me in the tunnel," he reminds her.

"We're not in the tunnel now." She bites down on her lip, knowing her logic is flawed.

He nods, as annoyingly patient as always, prepared to give her whatever time she needs.

"What do you think's behind the door?" she asks, pointing at the far wall.

He glances across at it, frowning. "It looks like the door I went through last time I was in the Sect. When it closed behind me, it felt like I was moving. When it opened again, I was in a whole different place."

"Weird." Aura walks to the door, needing some distance from Hayze to collect her thoughts. It's impossible to think about anything except kissing him when he's so close.

"We need to go in there," Hayze says, coming up behind her. "And find that button Tide told us about."

Aura nods, thinking about Jewel, Atmos and Skylus still trapped in the Games. It's time to end this.

Hayze reaches out and touches the door. A blinding white light fills the room. Aura covers her eyes blacking out for a split second, then drags in a deep breath, determined to regain her senses.

"What was that?" she asks, rubbing at her eyes as the light dissipates.

"I don't know," says Hayze, blinking rapidly. "But that happened last time too."

The door slides open, revealing a tiny room. Aura finds her hand slipping into Hayze's as they step inside, acutely aware this could be a trap. The door closes and there's the sensation of movement. Aura holds on tightly to Hayze as her stomach lurches.

The world shudders as the room regains its balance and the doors slide open. This time, they're looking at a room completely different to the one they just left. The walls are about two dozen feet in length, covered in buttons from the floor right up to the ceiling. The wall across from them has purple buttons, the one to the left has green, and the one to their right has blue. They step inside and spin around to see the door closing as it disappears into a wall covered in red buttons.

"What the schnitness is this?" Hayze scans the room. "We came up through the center of the Sect, so this must be the room Tide told us about. He didn't say which button we had to press, did he?"

Aura shakes her head as she follows him further into the room. "We could try pressing all of them in turn?"

"Are you serious?" Hayze's brows shoot up. "That would take hours. And who knows what impact they have."

Aura's shoulders slump. "We don't even know if any of them will end the Games."

"Get back!" Hayze shouts, grabbing Aura and dragging her toward the green wall as the door in the red wall reappears and slides open.

A woman wearing long black robes steps through and Aura blinks as she realizes the impossibility of who it is.

"Rateen," Hayze breathes.

"But you're an NPC," says Aura.

"A what?" Hayze asks, reminding Aura there's still so much she hasn't told him.

"A non-playable character," Aura explains. "She was a device the leaders used in the Games to manipulate things. She's not real."

"Maybe I'm not real." Rateen's wrinkled lips pull back as she laughs. "Or maybe you're not. Who knows."

"They must have based her on a real person," Aura says to Hayze. "That's who this is."

"Welcome to the Sect." Rateen extends her arms. "I've been waiting for you."

"Who are you?" Hayze asks.

"Apparently I'm an NPC," she replies with a smile.

"The real you," says Hayze. "What's your role in the Sect? And tell us the truth this time."

"I'm nobody important." Rateen waves her hand. "I'm but a humble servant."

"In that case, tell us which button to press." Aura steps forward, putting a hand on Rateen's bony arm, which is very much real flesh and blood. "You've helped us before. Help us again. We need to end the Games. Our friends are trapped in there."

"Are you sure you want to do that?" Rateen blinks at Aura with an intense sharpness behind her cloudy eyes.

"Of course, we do." Aura takes a step back to Hayze, who pins himself to her side.

He sneers at Rateen. "The Games are just as evil as the scumbags behind it."

"The Games are challenging," says Rateen. "Brutal even. But they're far kinder than the alternative of not having them."

Hayze turns purple with rage. "You can't m—"

"No!" Aura puts a hand on Hayze's back. "Let her finish. I want to hear why taking eight people against their will and putting them through a series of deadly tests is a kinder option than leaving them alone to live in peace."

Rateen shoots Aura a smile. "Ah, the naivety of youth."

"Why am I naive?" Aura asks. "Tell me."

"Anyone who thinks they can live in peace out there is a fool." Rateen extends her index finger and points to the red wall. "After global warming, the environment was already an impossible challenge. But it's getting worse. More storms. More disasters."

Aura's heard this a thousand times from her parents, and more recently from Infernos. It's the reason her parents made their agreement with the leaders in the first place. They weren't just worried Aura wouldn't survive the quickly worsening environment. They were worried nobody would.

"And how does stealing us from our families help with that?" Hayze asks. "Every single one of us would have helped our leader if only they'd asked. There was no need to make an agreement."

"If our parents didn't make the agreement, we wouldn't have been born at all," says Aura quietly, realizing this is another thing she hasn't had time to fill Hayze in on. "We weren't born like ordinary babies. The leaders created us in the Sect."

Hayze reels back. "Well, just because they made us, doesn't mean they own us."

"They gave us our powers," Aura points out.

"That's right," says Rateen, pleased that someone is finally agreeing with what she has to say. "And then they kept watch over you to see if you'd harness your powers. And not one of you did. That's why the Games are necessary. If just one of you had shown even the slightest potential, the leaders would have called them off. But we couldn't wait any longer. It was either send you into the Games or sit back and watch the entire world be torn apart by natural disasters until there was nothing left."

"Geo died," says Hayze. "And Tempo still might."

Rateen nods. "Which is a tragedy. But they would both have died at the hands of Mother Nature if we did nothing. Along with everyone they've ever known. Is that really a better option?"

Aura finds herself nodding as she turns to Hayze. "You saw how strong we were when we fought the lava. Maybe the world really does need us?"

"That doesn't mean the others should stay trapped in the Games," says Hayze. "They can help in real life, just like we are."

"Atmos hasn't harnessed his powers," Rateen says sharply. "We can't end the Games until he does. If you go back in, you could help him."

"Never!" Hayze booms. "Besides, Skylus has her Air powers. She's strong enough for both of them."

"We need a winner from each Quadrant." Rateen rubs her chin. "And we also need a spare. Just in case."

"In case we die," Hayze sneers.

"We *all* die one day," says Rateen.

The hidden door slides open again and this time, Pace comes running in.

Aura's heart leaps at the sight of her friend. "Pace!"

He draws to an abrupt halt at the sight of Rateen, then looks to Aura for an explanation.

"This is Rateen," she says.

"She's a humble servant, apparently," Hayze adds.

Rateen nods her agreement. "That's right."

"Where's Tempo?" Pace asks, seeming to have decided an old woman poses no threat.

"We haven't found her yet." Aura puts a hand on his arm. "But we will."

"As soon as we end the Games, we'll search for her," Hayze adds.

"I told you the world's ending!" Rateen booms. "We can't end the Games. We need them to save humanity. Even your girlfriend is starting to see that what I'm saying makes sense. Why can't you?"

Hayze glares at Rateen. "If you're not going to help us, I suggest you get out of our way."

"Never," sneers Rateen. "I'll die in this room before I help you."

Hayze steps up to the old woman, his face riddled with conflict. Aura knows he could never raise a hand to someone like her. Which might be the very reason she was chosen to greet them.

"I didn't pick you as the problem child," says Rateen, fury staining her gaze as she glares at Hayze. "The leaders were prepared to let you be victorious in your Element over Aura. But I think they got it wrong. *You* are the spare, not Aura."

Rateen jams her hand into the long pocket of her robe and pulls out a dagger.

"No!" Aura screams as Rateen raises the dagger with lightning speed.

But Hayze is just as fast. His hand flies up, gripping Rateen's wrist tightly before she can strike him.

"I don't think so," he says. "Now drop it."

Aura takes a step toward them. Hayze could use his powers against Rateen and finish this at any moment. Maybe he should. But Ember and Sera raised him better than that. Striking an old woman isn't in his handbook.

"I said drop it," Hayze repeats, his grip on Rateen so tight her hand is turning purple. Anyone else would have let go by now. But not Rateen who's holding on with impossible strength.

"Let it go, Rateen," says Aura, coming up beside her. "There's no need for this. I heard what you had to say about the Games and I get it. It's the same thing my parents always said to me. Sometimes we have to make sacrifices for the greater good. I can make Hayze see that. Now please, just drop the weapon so we can talk. Nobody needs to get hurt."

"Watch out!" cries Pace as Rateen reaches into her other pocket with her free hand. There's the flash of another blade and a frenzy of movement as bodies fly through the air, landing with a crash on the hard floor.

Aura gasps to see Rateen is on top of Hayze, pinning him down with her knees and holding a dagger at his throat. Somehow, he's lying on his back with his hands underneath him, unable to move or use his powers without scorching himself first. He struggles but the more he tries, the firmer Rateen holds him down.

"Get off him," Aura pleads, finding it hard to believe how easily Rateen overpowered someone twice her size and strength. "Let me talk to him. He'll understand what you said. How can he not when it makes such perfect sense? We wouldn't even be alive if it weren't for the leaders. They never meant to hurt us, just like I know you're not meaning to hurt Hayze now."

"If I get off him," Rateen says. "You'll end the Games."

"That's not what I want," says Aura. "Not anymore. We need Atmos to stay in there to harness his powers, then we all need to work together. Including Hayze. That's why you have to let him go."

"He won't listen to me," says Rateen. "Nor will he help me."

"She's right," snarls Hayze. "I'll die in this room before I help her."

Rateen laughs to hear her same words from earlier being thrown back at her. "Then so you must die."

"What?" cries Aura. "No!"

Rateen begins to drag her dagger across Hayze's throat. A single drop of blood falls to the shiny white floor and Aura's hands automatically shoot out, her need to protect Hayze overwhelming every other thought.

A hot ball of fire blasts from her palms.

Rateen's long black robe catches alight, and Hayze throws

her off him, sending her skidding across the room to the red wall.

Pace blasts out a stream of water, soaking Hayze and any spark that might have decided to leap onto him.

"Pace!" Aura shouts, panic clawing at her insides as the flames hiss and grow as they spread across Rateen's robes, consuming the old woman inside them. "Put her out!"

"But she..." Pace looks from Rateen to Hayze, who gives him a firm nod.

"Put her out," he says.

Pace immediately douses Rateen in water, turning the flames to smoke.

But his hesitation has come at a cost.

He's too late.

Rateen screams, struggling to sit up as steam rises from her charred body. Losing her fight, she slumps against the red wall, her head falling back.

She moans in agony.

Then goes very still.

Very silent.

And unmistakably, very dead.

Aura's hands flutter to her mouth and she lets out an agonized whimper.

"What have I done?" she sobs, wringing her hands. This wasn't in her handbook either. She just killed an old lady.

"You had no choice," says Pace. "She was going to kill Hayze."

Aura turns to Hayze, knowing as much as she hates what she just did, she'd do it time and again if it means keeping him alive and breathing.

But Hayze isn't looking at Aura. Nor is he looking at Rateen. His eyes are glued to the wall behind her.

Aura gasps to see that every single one of the red buttons is glowing brightly.

"The back of her skull is pressing one of them," says Pace, his eyes wide. "It lit up the wall."

"You're right. Let's see if we can light up the others." Hayze goes immediately to the purple wall and studies it. His fingertips hover over the button directly in front of him.

"Don't!" Aura runs to him. "We don't know what these buttons do. You can't know which one is the right one to press."

"Maybe it doesn't matter which one," he says. "Rateen can't possibly have randomly pressed exactly the right one."

Aura winces, unsure if slumping against a wall in your death counts as pressing a button.

"Do it," says Pace, standing on Hayze's other side.

"Don't do it, Hayze," Aura begs. "We need to talk about this first."

"Sorry, Aura." Hayze jabs at the wall without hesitation and presses the closest button, holding it firmly down.

And...nothing happens.

The room doesn't explode. The buttons don't light up. There are no sirens or secret panels or noxious gasses seeping under the walls.

"It's the wrong button," says Pace. "This is a puzzle, just like the maze."

"Then we have to solve it." Hayze withdraws his finger and scans the wall.

Aura steps away from him, feeling betrayed once more as Hayze and Pace begin pressing buttons at random, holding them down and waiting for an inkling of a response. Her eyes are drawn to Rateen's charred remains as guilt continues to clutch her by the throat. Her parents would have done exactly what Rateen just did. Would she have killed them too? Would Hayze? Is sacrificing a few to save many, a crime worthy of death? Because Rateen died protecting the Games, yet somehow, she inadvertently unlocked the first part of the puzzle that will put an end to them.

And that's when Aura thinks she realizes how this all works.

"Hayze is right," she says without thinking. "It doesn't matter which button you press first."

"What did you say?" Hayze turns to her.

Aura's hand flies to her lips. "Nothing."

"You said it doesn't matter which button you press *first*." Hayze goes to Aura and gives her a hug that she doesn't return. "You're a genius! No, scrap that. You're a freaking genius. A frenius!"

"I don't get it." Pace runs a hand through his dark hair.

"You know," says Hayze. "Freaking plus genius equals fr—"

"Not that," says Pace. "The button thing. I don't get it."

Hayze returns to the purple wall. "You begin the puzzle by pressing any button at random on any one of the walls. Then you press the corresponding button on the other walls." He squats down at the purple wall at roughly the same position Rateen is slumped at the red wall. He jabs at the buttons and it doesn't take long until he finds the right one and the entire wall glows purple.

"You did it!" Pace pats Hayze roughly on his back.

Hayze removes his finger, only for the lights to extinguish along with his smile.

"You have to hold it down." Pace runs to the blue wall as Hayze lights up the purple buttons again. Pace works quickly, trying out the same section of buttons until he gets the right one and a blue glow filters into the room.

Only the green wall remains unlit.

Pace and Hayze both turn their gazes to Aura, and a new realization slides through her.

This room has been set up so that four people must agree to end the Games at once. No doubt it was expected those four people would be the leaders. But the leaders aren't here. And there's only one person who can press the final button and light up the green wall.

Aura.

"Please." Hayze pleads at her with the same eyes that just betrayed her. "We need you to do this."

A sick feeling winds through her gut as she hears her parents shouting at her not to do it. Pressing that button will make all their sacrifices and suffering for nothing. The Games are just one part of something a whole lot bigger than themselves.

"Taking people against their will is wrong," says Hayze. "Humans are better than that. That's why we're worth saving. And we can still do it. But let's do it a better way. The *right* way."

Aura walks slowly to the green wall, knowing everything comes down to what she does next. She crouches down, counting out the buttons until she finds the right one and stares at it.

"Do it, Aura," Pace shouts. "My finger's getting tired over here."

"No," says Hayze.

Aura turns to him, confused.

"It's up to you, Aura," says Hayze. "Obviously, we want you to, but..."

"I'm an individual who can make up my own mind," she finishes, turning back to the button. Her parents made up their mind when they forged their agreement with the leaders. Aura and Hayze made their own decision when they left the Games. Rateen made a choice when she tried to kill Hayze.

Aura extends her shaking hand with her finger outstretched, the enormity of the moment weighing heavily on her. She remembers all the good things she experienced in the Games. Making friends. Falling in love. Gaining confidence in herself. And harnessing her powers. The Games made her who she is today.

Then she remembers all the bad things.

The pain.

The confusion.

The terror.

The death.

Aura drags in a deep breath, feeling the weight of her parents sitting on one of her shoulders, and Hayze on the other.

She presses the button.

And chaos erupts.

THE END

Ready for the next book in Elemental Games?

Check out Elemental Wars now!

http://mybook.to/ElementalWars

BOOK THREE - ELEMENTAL WARS

ELEMENTAL GAMES

Elemental powers. Deadly games. No escape.

Hayze and Aura have broken free. Only to discover they're nowhere close to being in control of their fate.

The time has come for them to take down those responsible for the chaos that's been raining down upon them. But with each Elemental power they learn to harness, Mother Nature steps up her war. And life in the Quadrants is getting even more difficult as the divide between the capitals widens.

Hayze and Aura desperately cling to the only thing that feels real—their love. But how can you love in a world drenched in deceit? How can you trust in a Game you're destined to lose?

And how can you hold on when everything around you is falling apart?

An intoxicating thrill ride packed with twists, romance and nail-biting action! Lovers of Maze Runner and Hunger Games will devour Elemental Wars. One-click your copy now.

Grab your copy now!
http://mybook.to/ElementalWars

WANT TO STAY IN TOUCH?

If you'd like to be the first for to hear all the news from Tamar and Heidi, be sure to sign up to our newsletter. Subscribers receive bonus content, early cover reveals and sneaky snippets of upcoming books. We'd love you to join us!

SIGN UP HERE:

https://sendfox.com/tamarandheidi

About the Authors

Tamar Sloan hasn't decided whether she's a psychologist who loves writing, or a writer with a lifelong fascination with psychology. She must have been someone pretty awesome in a previous life (past life regression indicated a Care Bear), because she gets to do both. When not reading, writing or working with teens, Tamar can be found with her husband and two children enjoying country life in their small slice of the Australian bush.

Heidi Catherine loves the way her books give her the opportunity to escape into worlds vastly different to her own life in the burbs. While she quite enjoys killing her characters (especially the awful ones), she promises she's far better behaved in real life. Other than writing and reading, Heidi's current obsessions include watching far too much reality TV with the excuse that it's research for her books.

MORE SERIES TO FALL IN LOVE WITH...

ALSO BY TAMAR SLOAN AND HEIDI CATHERINE

The Thaw Chronicles

The Sovereign Code

ALSO BY TAMAR SLOAN

Keepers of the Grail

Keepers of the Light

Keepers of the Chalice

Keepers of Excalibur

Zodiac Guardians

Descendants of the Gods

Prime Prophecy

ALSO BY HEIDI CATHERINE

The Kingdoms of Evernow

The Soulweaver

The Woman Who Didn't (written as HC Michaels)

The Girl Who Never (written as HC Michaels)

Made in United States
Troutdale, OR
03/28/2024

18801027R00181